Blood in the Bluegrass

Virginia Slachman

Taylor and Seale Publishing, LLC. Daytona Beach, Florida 32118

for Lauren

Acknowledgements

I'd like to give special thanks to Barry Irwin, founder and CEO of Team Valor International, who was a catalyst in bringing this book to fruition. I thank him not only for breeding my beautiful Thoroughbred, Corredor dela Isla, but also for his public stand to outlaw drugs on the racetrack and his many years of service to this wonderful breed. And to Staci Hancock, of the Water Hay Oats Alliance (WHOA), for working so tirelessly on behalf of drug-free horse racing.

I'm also grateful to Duncan Taylor of Taylor Made Farm as well as to John Hall, Cesar Terrazas, and Steve Avery who were incredibly generous with their time and expertise, aiding this manuscript greatly. My thanks to Jeff Ramsey of Ramsey Farm, as well, for giving me a glimpse into the world of Kitten's Joy and sharing his time, expertise, and innovative rehab facility with me. Thoroughbred trainer Ignacio Correas of IC Racing deserves thanks, too, for letting me hang out early mornings (5 a.m.!) at Keeneland Racetrack with him and his crew; their stories and example provided valuable insight for the book. Jen Roytz, Executive Director, Retired Racehorse Project, also deserves my thanks for her valuable input from years of experience with the breed and the world of racing. Editor Elaine Parker of Thoroughbred Research Services in Lexington was instrumental in assuring the accuracy of the text; her expertise in editing and research proved invaluable. As well, Jimmy Pollard, Henry County, KY, coroner and consultant for the Kentucky Coroner's Association, deserves thanks for his uniformly congenial and informative input. Thanks goes also to my wonderful agent,

Amanda Mecke, without whom this book would not be what it is today. Veterinarians who deserve thanks include Dr. Kevin Keegan of the Missouri University Veterinary Health Center and Dr. John Steinmeyer and his wife Holly. And to my friends and co-workers in Thoroughbred rescue for their support and knowledge, I add Elizabeth Stevenson, Barb Hutchinson, Deana Roark, Sierra Downs, Carrie Ramsey, and Glenn Youngman. Cathy Schenck at Keeneland Library, Cindy Grisolia at Old Friends, and Jackie Duke of *The Blood-Horse* also deserve sincere thanks for their support, insights, and help, as does Ethel Baker, for her tireless support. Philip Slein and Barry Leibman were helpful providing needed expertise about the art world. And finally, the book also gives a nod to two very special racehorses, John Henry and Kelso.

Virginia Slachman, St. Louis, Missouri

Prologue

Early October mornings lately had been cooler. Paris could sense fall finally settling in as she guided her horse slowly around the large pond, her happiness building as they both warmed to their work.

Paris moved her body ever so slightly atop the big gelding and Zydeco responded, turning to the left, breaking into a trot over the pasture, ears pricked forward in anticipation of the fence course they'd jump in the far field.

Approaching the fences, Paris rose and fell easily with the horse's motion, letting all thought go as she moved Zydeco into a canter. She measured his stride, planting her hands and arching over his mane's crest as he sailed high over the fences, one by one, the horse's front legs curled up beneath him, his back hooves clearing the wood boards with ease. As one, they cantered forward in rose-gold light across the fallow field where she brought Zydeco to a halt.

"Good boy, Zeke," she murmured, smiling at his eagerness, loving his willingness to please. "You're getting a bunch of carrots for that one!" She bent over the crest of his mane and patted his arched neck, thinking of the upcoming competition and how he would sweep through the course without effort.

"Okay, boy," she whispered finally, leaning forward to scratch his ears. "One more and then we're done. I'm taking it easy on

you today." Zydeco nodded his head as if in agreement and she grinned, nodding along with him.

Off they went at a trot, then again into the canter as they neared the next fence, the highest one, the one closest to the big sycamore and oak stand at the edge of the field.

Into the clear day they rose, well above the high jump. In flight, the horse saw a movement to his right as the long whip came out of nowhere, snapping at his flank.

Confused and stunned by the sound, Paris felt Zydeco's shuddering, physical fear as he convulsed, stumbling to his knees on the far side of the jump. Paris clung to him as he struggled to rise, her eyes searching to see who had cracked the whip. You're okay, she thought, not locating the person, "We're okay," she whispered, wanting to believe it though the horse's panicked snort said otherwise. Then that sound again—the whip's harsh crack. Hang on buddy, thought Paris, as Zydeco lunged up, bucking against the pain.

Paris leaned forward toward the chestnut's neck, searching the wood's edge for the culprit, clamping her legs to his heaving sides, panic and fear coursing through them both. She clung to Zydeco by will and instinct. "I'm right here," she whispered, trying to calm her horse. "Go, go!" she shouted then, legging him forward, but the whip stung his flank and he bucked hard sending Paris high in the air.

Disoriented, Paris twisted as she fell, seeing the figure, finally, whipping her horse, landing on her back hard, stunned and nauseous, repeating over and over "I'm ok, it's only a fall," willing herself up, as above her Zydeco bucked and kicked against the whip's stinging blows, trying to miss stepping on her.

The chestnut reared again and pawed the air, came down hard, charging the person standing threateningly before him, his head lowered. The figure rushed toward the gelding, both hands raised, snapping the whip at the chestnut's eyes. There was no sound, save the harsh crack, the whip stinging his head and chest again and again as Zydeco squealed and snorted, arching his neck, prancing in circles to avoid the whip, his tail flagged in anger, his hocks feeling the whip's bite until he fled finally, galloping away mindlessly, driven by instinct only prey know.

As she lay on the unyielding ground, filled with pain and panic, Paris whispered "You?" identifying the figure, her vision fading in and out of focus. "You?" she whispered again in disbelief, her terror so great it felt like awe. Gasping against it, she thought I have to get up, but her legs lay still. She squinted at the person hovering over her. Paris saw the huge rock held high and squeezed her eyes shut against the coming blow.

She felt the sun's slight warmth on her face. Just a dream, she thought, feeling the hard ground at her back, curling her finger around a tuft of grass. "Zeke," she whispered, "Come get me, boy," she pleaded, uttering her last words, losing consciousness as she turned her head away and the blow fell. She seemed to see herself from afar rising over the pasture fence, feeling her body at one with Zydeco's strength and grace as they cantered off into the bright distances.

The figure bent over the young woman, placed the large rock against her head. He rose and nodded, satisfied as a vast, unearthly silence filled the brightening field.

Blood in the Bluegrass

Chapter 1

The minister lumbered toward the small rise in his black suit, a book held in his left hand, his right tugging the hat down over his eyes. Harper watched his slow progress, feeling nothing. The setting sun was low on the horizon, sending scant rays of light from behind clouds and casting a luminescent glow that felt false and unworldly. The trees at the wood's edge seemed lit by some deep, interior fire Harper couldn't fathom.

Around her, the mourners stood quietly on the small rise, as the service began, October's gold and crimson leaves adding to an atmosphere more suited to a wedding than a funeral. Harper looked from face to face as the grief that had wracked her over the week since her younger sister's death welled up. The minister droned on, but Harper wasn't listening. Still stunned by disbelief, she replayed over and over Marshall's call telling her of Paris' accident.

She might have been comforted by the large crowd, but everyone realized that Harper's focus was an interior one and respected that. They'd all last gathered there seven years ago at her parents' funeral; everyone understood her grieving solitude.

As with her parents' car crash, Paris' death had been ruled an accident—a lethal head wound from the fall, noted the coroner's report—but everything in Harper rebelled at that; Paris was one of the best riders in Lexington.

She simply could not have fallen from Zydeco.

With effort, she raised her head, swept her blond hair from her eyes, and glanced around at the other mourners—friends, stud farm employees, clients—some with hats in hands or heads bowed. Paris' friends and Harper's . . . So many had shown up, so many had loved Paris.

Harper tried to nod her thanks in their direction but failed. Some of the elderly had known her grandfather; the family had been in Kentucky, racing and breeding Thoroughbreds, since he'd been alive, so they had plenty of connections in Bluegrass country.

Everyone stood quietly with eyes on the minister or looking off into the gently undulating pastures' soft glow in the low light. They all shared Harper's grief and disbelief, all stricken at the loss of such a young, vibrant woman who simply could not be replaced.

Though it was a large crowd, Harper felt alone before her sister's casket. She'd always had Paris to confide in and watch over, to celebrate joys with and puzzle through failures. And loss. Harper put both hands to the corners of her teal-blue eyes and wiped the lingering tears.

Paris, thought Harper, reaching out to her as one fumbles in the dark for something precious that's been lost.

Her sister had left the racetrack long ago, left the mists rising off the dirt at dawn and the silence punctuated by muffled hooves and the snorts of twelve-hundred-pound animals ready to run. It wasn't a life for the timid, or those unused to or unwilling to endure pain and injury. Paris had been a rising jockey, but she chose another life and Harper had respected that.

The crisp outlines of other limestone gravestones gleamed in the sun's last light. Beside her sister lay their parents and grandparents, all now gone to earth.

As the service ended, Harper struggled out of her dark reverie as one by one people moved toward her, embracing her, extending their arms, or taking her hand gently in their own. The minister closed his black book and stood off to the side, respectful of the mourners.

Harper made herself look into each face as she conveyed her thanks. It's such a busy time with the Keeneland race meet coming up, she thought; every one of these people set aside pressing concerns to be here. She focused on that realization and on gratitude for their presence and sincere condolences.

The gathering at the house after the service was a blur to Harper, but she got through it. By the time everyone had paid their respects, left their casseroles and pies and breads on the long table and departed, it was pitch dark.

Restless, she wandered out to the porch, gazing down the long drive lined by sentinel oaks, squinting toward Georgetown Road where her grandfather's hand-laid stone pillars stood to either side of the entranceway, a lighted lantern atop each. Over the entranceway, in wrought iron, the words *Eden Hill Stud* arched over the gate, the familiar logo at the apex.

Harper sank down on the top step. She and Paris had been inseparable, no matter how far apart they lived, sharing everything but most of all a love of their horses. Paris had been the flashy one—riding like the wind, traveling from show to show, jumping or eventing, following her stint as a jockey.

Harper's connection to equines was different. Though she loved riding, she'd never cared if the horses raced or not. What she loved was their intelligence and grace, their spirit, their incredible intuitiveness, their willingness to please.

Harper connected with them on a totally different level from most of those in the racing game—she respected the horses and wanted nothing more than to keep them safe and help them find a role they enjoyed, whether on the track or elsewhere.

She looked to her right, past the creek to "Grandpa's barn," the first barn her grandfather had built over a century ago, inhaling the subtle scent of sweet feed and hay drifting from it.

She loved so much at Eden Hill. It had been nearly impossible to leave five years ago. After their parents' deaths, Paris and Harper had run the stud together, but two years later, Harper felt compelled to move to New York City to give her painting a shot. The sisters agreed to continue running the stud together and, to everyone's surprise, it had worked. Eden Hill had increasingly prospered under their shared leadership.

Harper flourished, as well. Her single-minded devotion to the stud and to her sister was matched by a commitment to her art. She'd done well in New York, both at Chelsea's Arcadia Gallery where she worked, and in establishing a budding reputation as a collectable painter. But now she wondered if the move hadn't cost her nearly everything—the stud farm, her horses, and her last shred of family.

Harper breathed in the loamy scent of fallen leaves and brackish creek water, her eyes wide and luminous in the starlight. She listened quietly as the wind rustled through the big oaks lining the drive, hoping the sounds and scents of her home would settle her.

They didn't. It would take more than sense memory to make up for all that she'd lost.

When she'd moved to New York, JD Cole, her longtime lover, refused to follow her. She thought once that they'd marry. Everyone, in fact, had thought that. JD was the son of Red Cole who'd been in partnership with Eden Hill since Harper's father had been alive. Instead, JD had enlisted in the army shortly after she'd moved.

In spite of her continued involvement in the farm, the move had cost her almost everything. Only her art remained.

And now Paris, too, was gone. Gone irrevocably.

Her hands clasped, she pushed those thoughts aside; there was time enough to sort out whether what she had left was enough. At the moment, she needed to grieve and to honor her sister.

She knew the only way to truly do that was to ensure the stud's continued success on her own.

She rose slowly and stepped off the porch, still feeling the numbness part of her was grateful for. It would take a long time before Harper got used to her sister's absence. Maybe she'd never get used to it.

The path down the drive was silvered by a crescent moon. Harper stood quietly in the starlight, picturing what Paris' last ride must have been like in the crisp early fall morning, the grass filled with dew and the fog laying low in the fields.

Zydeco likely pawed and snorted as she'd saddled him up; he was always ready for a hard workout. Racehorse training. He loved having a job and pleasing Paris pleased him, too. They were so close. Zydeco could literally read Paris' mind. Harper shook her head. She knew accidents happened. But Zydeco would rather harm himself than hurt Paris.

In her mind's eye, she saw her sister smiling as she ran a light hand down Zydeco's muscled neck that last morning. There was no place she felt more at home—or more safe—than on his back, loping over the pastures or rising together over one show jump fence after another.

How happy the two of them must have been—Paris calm and composed, Zeke eager, steam flowing from his nostrils. She would have mentally urged him forward, as they moved off into the far distances, her face turned up to the new sun, washing the straw-colored field in beneficent light.

As she'd forever be in Harper's mind—moving forward into some future she couldn't envision or follow.

She struggled against feelings of loss and anger. She didn't feel betrayed as she'd heard some do when their loved ones died. The bond between the sisters was not broken by Paris' absence. Harper couldn't explain why she rebelled at the thought of an accident everyone else had accepted, but she did. Call it sisterly intuition.

There just had to be another explanation.

She stared unblinking down the drive then looked up past the far-off cedars. So many stars. They lay like shattered glass across the October sky.

She let the starlight shimmer over her as she rose and slowly walked toward the paddocks and pastures. Harper couldn't face going back to the empty house. Not yet. Instead, she passed horses drowsing in their night-cooled fields, the mist hovering low on the grass. The world was reduced to silver and darkness—motionless stillness at the center of things.

Chapter 2

Once home, Harper yawned and squinted at the clock. Nearing nine-thirty, she thought, feeling she should try to get some rest, early as it was. Instead, she collapsed in front of the fire, but soon heaved an exhausted sigh at the loud knock on the door. She debated ignoring it then hoisted herself off the couch to answer it.

On the porch stood Marshall, his sad face a commentary on their loss. He'd trained Eden Hill's racehorses on behalf of the stud since before Harper was born, and had been like a father to the sisters, especially after their parents' death. Harper knew he was worried about her.

He held his big Stetson in both hands and from his arm hung a bag, likely full of more food his wife Surrey had made.

"You left no more than an hour ago," Harper said, as Marshall's large frame ducked through the doorway.

Offering a casserole, he eyed Harper with appraising soft, brown eyes. "Surrey'll be along directly, just waiting on her bread."

"No, Marshall . . . please," Harper said. The last thing she wanted was company. She couldn't bear more talk. Not even sympathy from people closest to family she had left. "I appreciate it," she said, "but right now I just need to be alone."

Harper took the warm dish and put it on the counter with the rest of the condolence food she had no interest in eating. She had enough meals for a month, but after eating New York City take-out for two years, she'd take Surrey's home cooking in a heartbeat for whenever her appetite did return.

The two stood there awkwardly then Harper put her arms around Marshall's waist, just as his cell phone went off.

"We'll get through this, Sweet Pea," Marshall murmured, holding Harper close to his big, hard chest, patting her back softly, answering the phone with his free hand.

He'd called Harper Sweet Pea and Paris Rose Bud since the sisters were toddlers. Hearing her childhood name wrenched something deep inside her.

"Down past C Barn?" he said after listening a moment, nodding as he patted Harper's back. "On my way."

"We've got a fence down in the mare's pasture," he said, adding, "John Henry was coming from town and saw it."

Harper's face flushed as she felt a surge of urgency. They could lose their best mares in a heartbeat if the horses got through the downed fence and onto the highway. The thought of more loss sent a rush of fear through her.

Setting aside exhaustion, she grabbed her coat and flung it around her shoulders, but Marshall held up a palm to stop her. "No need, Harper, stay here. You've got enough going on."

Harper rushed past him, heading to the foyer. If someone had stolen them, the mares could be whisked quickly out of state, or worse. Slaughter was not out of the question. Harper knew they hadn't a second to lose.

"I'm coming," she said resolutely, and they were out the door, headed at a dead run for Marshall's truck.

Claiborne Farm had experienced the theft of a high-dollar broodmare in exactly the same way, though Fanfreluche had disappeared in broad daylight. Eden Hill's night watchman made

9

the rounds, but he couldn't be everywhere at once. Thefts could still happen—take down a fence under cover of darkness, load up an expensive mare, no one the wiser till morning.

The two turned down the road and saw John Henry's truck up ahead, his small frame picked out in moonlight standing oddly still at the fence line.

Marshall pulled onto the road's shoulder, threw the truck into park, and they both leapt out. In the pasture before Marshall, a low mist lay on the field, shifting eerily in the light wind. Just past the collapsed fence, Harper made out a dim figure prone on the grass, still as death in the moonlight.

Marshall took off his Stetson and hit his thigh in disgust, strode to the fence, then jumped the fallen boards and waded into the mist. Starlight flickered overhead as clouds shunted across the sky.

John Henry nodded politely to Harper. "Seemed like just a fence down when I drove up," he said, his dark head hung in apology.

Harper gazed at Marshall's back then headed toward the fence, her panic rising. Marshall reached the figure and turned toward her, waving her off as he knelt to the ground.

"Who is it?" yelled Harper, peering through the obscuring fog. Adrenaline gave way to horrendous images—a farm hand trampled by a running herd years back, a local trainer nearly killed by a rearing stallion coming down on her, a drug-crazed horse knocking his jockey to the ground and stomping him unconscious.

The images hurtled through her like electricity. "Marshall!" Harper commanded, leaping across the downed fence with singular purpose, terrified of what lay before her in the sparse grass.

10

Marshall turned his head slightly. "It's Steve," he said. "Steve Hamilton. He's dead," and he called the police.

Oh God, thought Harper, halting, momentarily disoriented. Steve? She'd just seen him at the funeral! Harper felt the dark night close in, the mist wrapping impenetrable arms around her. Glancing up, her face was graced by the moon's meager light; she stood a ghostly, solitary figure in the light-spattered darkness.

She found it suddenly hard to breathe and craned to see Steve, but Marshall blocked her view. Surely, he was wrong. Steve could not be dead.

The mares on the rise behind Steve's body, sensing the tension, stirred and began to trot back and forth, stopping to stamp and snort, their hooves lost in the knee-deep, shifting mist. Harper heard their cries mount as their confusion increased; soon agitation could cause them to bolt.

"John Henry, get up the rise!" yelled Harper. "Turn the mares!"

In the starlight, Harper watched the horses' increasing frenzy—necks arched and heads high, they began stiffly trotting along the crest, their tails switching in fear.

Soon there'd be no stopping them. A shudder ran through Harper. They could all be crushed under the pounding hooves if the mares bolted down the rise.

John Henry ran past Harper, waving his arms in the starlight to turn the herd. Harper could see the whites of the mares' eyes—there wasn't much time to keep them from thundering downhill if their instincts drove them toward freedom.

Startled into action, Harper ran to Marshall's side, squinting through the darkness at the horses one second and looking at Steve the next. The mares were calling to each other now, as John

11

Henry moved swiftly right and left above the three figures, keeping the herd in check, putting himself in danger.

Around the trio, the mist shifted and turned as the breeze picked up.

Harper shivered. She kneeled and looked into Steve's fixed stare. Taking a deep breath, she searched his face for signs of pain or anguish, but his countenance told her nothing. Her gaze turned to the gun at his left hand, then back to Steve's face; the back of his skull had been blown off.

She turned away, fighting down nausea. Steve Hamilton was a young man with a family, a man Harper's father had hired eight years ago, and Harper had promoted to farm manager seven months ago.

She spoke to Marshall quietly. "What do you think happened?" she said, still kneeling beside the dead man. She looked anxiously up the rise, wishing they could move Steve's body out of danger.

Marshall didn't answer for a moment, his eyes fixed on the farm manager. "Not sure," He looked Harper's way. "Looks like he could've shot himself."

Harper put her hands over her eyes as if to blot out the image. A few moments later, she let her hands drop. The sight of the dead man's still, prone figure seemed surreal. Harper touched his arm, thinking *I just spoke to you at Paris' funeral.*

Now they were both gone. Harper leaned into Marshall, who turned and put his arm around her. They rose slowly, standing, gazing at Steve's blank stare.

"Close his eyes, Marshall," whispered Harper, turning away. She looked toward John Henry and watched him suddenly charge the lead mare.

"Git up! Git up! Go on now!" he screamed, racing at her, his arms overhead. The old man was nearly hoarse, and close to spent.

The lead mare squared herself and stared down John Henry. For a few seconds, the scene could have turned horribly wrong for all of them. Then in a heartbeat the mare made her decision.

Screaming to her herd, she turned and raced off down the other side of the rise. As one, the other mares leapt forward, pounding away behind her lead into the darkness.

Harper sent a mental thank you to John Henry. At least one disaster had been averted, if only for the moment.

She breathed deeply to steady herself and for the second time that day, willed herself to set aside emotion and think about the scene before her.

What was Steve doing in the mares' pasture at this time of night? There was no earthly reason she could think of for his presence. He should have been home with his kids. Steve was a nice, gentle man, great at his job and adored by his two little boys.

"What the hell happened?" Harper said with force, turning to Marshall who had quickly complied with her request.

Marshall didn't reply—they both knew what the likely answer was. He rose slowly, his face a mask of horror and sadness. "He's still warm," was all he could muster, "couldn't have happened but a bit ago." He looked down at the grass as if some solace lay there in the silvery light. "Police are on their way."

Did he do this himself? she wondered in anguish, her eyes fixed on the gun just at his left hand, then dismissed the suggestion of suicide. Steve was not the type at all. He was a happy guy, a great family man—no way he killed himself.

Harper looked up as John Henry passed, oddly silent in the silver light. He wouldn't glance Steve's way.

Appalled, Harper realized the only plausible explanation was that someone had shot Steve and left the gun by his hand. Someone had tried to make it seem a suicide.

But why, and why in the mares' pasture?

John Henry got his toolbox from the truck, preparing to get the fence back up. Harper glanced his way. Always the practical one, she thought. They couldn't risk the mares returning and getting out on the road, then the highway.

"Leave it," called Marshall, seeing his intention. "We can't touch anything."

"Don't usually come this way," said John Henry again, more to himself than his bosses, shaking his old head, clearly dumbfounded by the sight of the farm manager lying dead in the moonlight.

"That's what they were counting on," said Marshall as he and Harper approached the old man and stepped over the downed fence. The trainer rubbed the back of his neck with a big hand. "You maybe scared them off."

Them! So, Marshall was thinking the same thing Harper was, that someone had done this to Steve.

They all got the same idea at once.

"I'll go," Harper insisted, putting her hand out for Marshall's keys. It was possible the culprits were still on the property.

"No, you stay." Marshall was just as insistent. "I can see to it. The police are coming, and somebody's got to watch that the mares don't get out."

Marshall jumped in his truck and sped away.

14

Harper nodded, glancing at the downed fence then up the rise where the horses had fled into the deeper recesses of the pasture.

"John Henry," she said to the groom, not taking her eyes off Steve, "please stay with him." It didn't seem right to leave the dead man alone.

Reluctantly, John Henry re-crossed the fence with Harper, walked toward the farm manager, and stood over him.

Harper headed on up the rise. Maybe someone had taken down the fence to steal the mares and Steve had surprised them, she thought. Maybe that's how he'd gotten shot.

But a staged suicide made no more sense than what Steve was doing there in the first place, no matter if he'd surprised thieves or not.

Harper strode up the slope and peered into the cool darkness. The mares were a short distance off, heads bent to the meager grass. The lead mare raised her head at Harper's approach but didn't send an alarm to the herd.

She headed down the slope for a count. Sure enough, three were missing.

So, someone had stolen the stud's mares. Harper stood there surveying the herd. She'd ask John Henry to determine which ones were missing in the morning.

She returned to Steve's body and told John Henry to go on home and get some rest; she'd stay and stand vigil. But John Henry wouldn't leave Harper's side.

She again noticed the gun by Steve's hand. It sent a shudder up her spine.

Paris' death, now this.

She knelt one last time to the body and, taking Steve's hand gently in her own, Harper looked up at the stars. Their far light seemed small and ineffectual. Useless.

She rested the farm manager's hand softly in the grass and rose to stand sentinel at the downed fence until the police arrived.

Chapter 3

Marshall called a bit later. He hadn't found the culprits, though he had seen a three-horse trailer passing the farm down Georgetown Road at a good pace. When Harper told him about the missing mares, he cursed a blue streak under his breath then said he was headed to the house and told Harper to meet him there.

Harper felt sure Steve's death was the result of being in the wrong place at the wrong time. Someone had come on the property to steal the stud's mares and Steve had stumbled upon them. That was only explanation that made sense. Anyhow, thought Harper sadly, better than thinking Steve had walked out into the dark pasture to put a bullet in his brain.

But why was he roaming around the mares' pasture at that time of night in the first place?

Harper finally asked John Henry to guard the fence and watch over Steve. He was to call her when the police arrived. The old groom seemed reluctantly grateful for the duty. Then Harper headed back to the house where Marshall waited for her on the porch. He escorted her inside. She wasn't looking forward to talking to the police and was glad of Marshall's company, especially when he offered to call Steve's wife.

He knew Harper so well. Tomorrow she might have the energy to pay her respects to Cynthia and speak to the police. But at the moment she was exhausted beyond measure.

Thank goodness for you, Marshall, Harper almost said out loud. The sisters literally could not have run the stud without him. Now, with Steve gone, a lot of the farm manager's workload would fall to him; Harper knew he'd not utter one word of complaint.

While Marshall called Steve's wife and broke the sad news, Harper trudged toward the living room where the fire had burned down to nearly ash. It gave off little heat in the cold October night.

She was suddenly almost too exhausted to stand, but Marshall came in and steered her to the couch in front of the fireplace. Clearly, he had more to say.

He perched on the raised hearth, feeding small twigs to the dying fire. Harper sank down across from him on the soft leather sofa, taking note of his salt and pepper head bent to the fire. She'd known him since his hair had been black as coal.

"Who would do this?" she said shaking her head, still trying to wrap her mind around Steve being dead.

"Why is also a question," said Marshall. "And exactly what happened is not at all clear."

They were both avoiding saying out loud that Steve had taken his own life.

Harper numbly watched Marshall stoke the fire.

Paris. Steve. The mares gone. In her mind's eye, it all spread out like a white canvas, blank and meaningless.

Harper's mind again went to Paris, and all they'd done to increase Eden Hill's success. It was no easy matter for two young women to run a successful racing enterprise in a business lorded over for centuries by men.

She was proud of all she and Paris had accomplished; she would see to the stud's continued prosperity no matter what it took.

And Steve had been a big part of their success. Now he was gone, too, and under suspicious circumstances. Just like Paris, thought Harper, again struggling to accept her sister had died of a riding accident.

Marshall pulled at his mustache laced with gray, waiting patiently for Harper's attention. She drifted away from the thought of death as a clean, earthy scent welled up in memory, bringing her father into palpable presence.

Marshall's voice broke through her reverie. "The place seems so empty . . ."

He was referring to Paris. Then, quickly, as he noticed Harper's reaction, "I'm sorry." He thought a moment. "I hope at least the horses are some comfort."

The horses. Harper closed her eyes, images of horses she and Paris had trained and ridden flashed through memory. There was a time when everything she did centered around them. Horses had taught her—in some ways—more than people or books ever had. They'll walk through fire for you if you earn their trust.

Harper opened her eyes and nodded sadly at Marshall. Yes, they were a comfort.

Then she yawned. Horses aside, if the police didn't arrive shortly, she was not going to be awake enough to form a coherent sentence. Not that Harper thought sleep would come. She eyed Marshall who seemed trying to piece together some measure of additional conversation.

He snapped a twig and brought Harper's focus back.

"Have you heard from Red?" he asked, changing the subject again for her benefit, she knew. He tossed the wood in the fire and folded his arms across his stomach. He was trying to keep Harper's thoughts occupied as they waited on the police. Red Cole, the stud's partner and JD's father, had the adjoining farm directly west of Eden Hill.

Marshall would have to tell him of the mares' theft in the morning.

Harper shook her head. He'd been at the funeral but left before they could speak. The two families' long-standing racing partnership was a success due to everyone's devoted efforts since before Harper and Paris were born. Red was surely as devastated as they all were at Paris' death.

Marshall opened the screen and tossed the first of three small logs on the fire.

"No," she said, "haven't heard from him yet." Red Cole was a hard man and not prone to chitchat. Harper understood why he'd left the funeral immediately after the service. The mention of his name again brought to mind JD, and with it an unsettled feeling.

When she'd moved to New York, JD had vanished into the army without a word. Neither of them made an effort to talk things through. Their ending was abrupt and, Harper knew, unresolved.

Well, there was nothing to do about that now, she thought. And she had more pressing issues to think about.

"I expect you'll hear from Red soon enough," said Marshall, with slight distaste; he'd never been a big fan of the man. Marshall reached over and drew the fire screen together. Now that the blaze was going, the room was quickly warming.

He stood and ran his hand over his silvering hair and squinted at Harper. "Well, Sweet Pea, you best go on to bed now. Cynthia will be here soon. You don't need to shoulder any more grief than you already got. I'll deal with Steve's wife and the police."

"No, I'll stay."

He stared at her, meeting her eyes with a frankness she'd always trusted. "You look like a beat-up old dog, darlin'. Get some rest. I'll deal with this."

He was right; she did feel like she'd been beaten.

"Leave your phone so I get John Henry's call." He looked at his watch. "Surrey's likely to show up soon with her bread, a peach pie from our summer crop, and who knows what else."

He stretched and picked up his big Stetson, waving Harper up the stairs with it. "Go on now. You need some rest."

She went to him and he hugged her, then planted himself in front of the fire. Harper walked up slowly and stood in the hall's darkness.

And so, she was home.

Chapter 4

Long before dawn the next morning, Harper woke up. Momentarily disoriented, it took a moment to remember where she was, and why. Once awareness descended, she couldn't go back to sleep, so in the darkness she made her way downstairs, put the coffee on and pulled her robe close to fend off the early morning chill.

Then, fuel in hand, she headed to the study to the right of the living room, noting last evening's fire still burned low. She stoked it and lay on a few logs, then entered the study.

If the horses dotting the now-dark paddocks and pastures were the spirit of the stud farm, the study was its heart and soul.

It's where she always went to find solace.

She flipped on the lights and leaned on the door, taking in the walls hung with photos and crops and shining copper and silver bits from the bridles of Eden Hill's most successful stallions. She stared at the walls for a long time, sipping coffee and looking from one photo to another. They reminded Harper of all she'd lost and that she was now solely responsible to carry on her family's legacy.

With three mares stolen and no clue about who'd killed Steve, she didn't feel off to a great start.

The desk phone rang, Startled, Harper checked her watch. Horse racing folk were early risers, but it was barely 4 a.m.

It was Cynthia. Harper supposed the new widow couldn't sleep, either. Cynthia thanked her for all the sisters had done for

Steve and her family. Harper said she was sorry then they both fell silent. Harper heard a sigh on the other end of the phone. Cynthia spoke barely above a whisper, saying that as soon as the coroner released the body, she was taking Steve and the kids home to Saratoga. Then she started crying and Harper wanted to ring off and save them both the added grief of talking, but through sobs Cynthia insisted she had one more thing to say.

Steve's widow took a deep, ragged breath and said that Steve had come home after a meeting with Paris just before her death and he was really upset. He wouldn't say why, only that he was worried about Paris and that he'd take care of it. What "it" was, Cynthia couldn't imagine, and Steve had refused to discuss it. She'd pressed him on it, and he'd gotten mad, repeating he had gotten Paris into it and he'd get her out. Cynthia assumed it was some farm concern and that, as usual, Steve would get things on the right track in short order. Then Cynthia broke down again, so Harper murmured more condolences, thanked her, said how much they'd all miss her and the kids, and hung up, feeling the weight of both their sorrow.

She sat back in her father's wood chair, his old rosewood desk spread out before her, then went through the papers Paris had left strewn on it, filing what she could in the folders located in the desk's lower drawer, all the while thinking of Cynthia's comments. They distracted her from her own internal turmoil.

They also made Harper wonder if the meeting she'd spoken of figured into the deaths of her husband and Paris. She didn't like the coincidence at all—not just that her sister and Steve were both gone, that was bad enough. But just after a meeting together? It had to mean something.

The unease she'd been feeling over Paris' death welled up again, only now Harper's conviction that Paris' death was no accident seemed more than sisterly intuition. A man who had just been murdered—she still couldn't fathom Steve would take his own life—had met with Paris and then been worried enough to cause his own wife concern.

Whatever "it" was had to be connected to both their deaths.

Harper sighed and yawned. But of course, she could be blowing the whole thing out of proportion. Paris' death might have really been an accident, and Steve might have surprised thieves in the pasture and gotten a bullet for his trouble. Harper had to face that possibility, no matter her feelings.

She stared out the window, but all she could see was her own reflection staring blankly back, framed by pre-dawn darkness.

Pretty soon Harper noted dawn's first light and glanced at her watch. She was due at the training track shortly to meet up with Marshall and his assistant trainer, Dylan, to survey their budding crop of two-year-olds.

So, after donning layers of clothes, Harper headed for the barn to tack up Zydeco. John Henry said he'd been standing, head down, facing the back wall of his stall since Paris' death. He'd not been eating, either, mourning Paris like the rest of them.

Harper soothed her hand down his big chestnut head and looked into his sad eyes. "Come on, boy," she said softly, offering a carrot. "We'll get through this together." Zydeco turned his head away from the treat. "Okay, let's head out, maybe that will perk us up."

She saddled him, and off they went in the new morning light. They both needed to get out of the funk they were in.

They walked and trotted, then cantered over the slow rises and trails, the sunlight gold and rose, into and out of pastures, the lime green maples shading to electric yellow, the oaks in their deep reds and flaming orange—all shining at the edges of still-green fields in the first light of day. Harper avoided the place of Paris' death for both their sakes; horses have incredible memories and clearly remember trauma and the place it occurred for years. Some of them never forget.

They found themselves finally at the oval track Harper's father had put in way out past the stallion complex. It's where Marshall did his magic, training Eden Hill's young colts and fillies, sorting out the potential stakes race prospects from those who ended up elsewhere, some in the family barn as the family's trail horses or jumpers.

It was also the scene of training injuries last spring. Then Eden Hill had suffered the sudden death of a young colt last summer on the track, and another who'd broken down and had to be destroyed. It was a suspicious amount of injuries and loss to Harper, and she wondered if those incidents were connected to whatever had gotten Steve—and quite possibly her sister—killed.

The early mist still laid on the track, bounded by white-painted four-planked fencing with timing poles and a freshly dragged, deep dirt track. As they approached, Harper saw the string of horses jogging along, two by two, steam streaming from their nostrils, riders perched like bent birds on their backs.

Zydeco began prancing in place, so she let him out to a trot, his ears pitched forward in anticipation, but pulled him up to a walk as they closed in on the track so not to disturb anyone at the rail.

Marshall's assistant Dylan stood with his back to them, watching and nodding and, once in a while, calling instructions to an exercise rider. They seemed at the end of the workout—a group of big, fit bays and a few grays, snorting and trotting now as they wound down to a walk.

Harper slid off Zydeco and handed him to a groom to walk, while she headed over to the rail.

"Morning," she said, rubbing her hands together, wishing she had a steaming insulated cup of coffee like Dylan had. "Marshall around?"

Harper had known Dylan since childhood. He was about her height—5'10'—with unruly brown hair, squinty brown eyes, and apple cheeks he'd not lost since childhood. He hadn't really grown out of the mischievous grin stage, either. Still, he was an attractive guy, just not Harper's type.

"He was here earlier, said he needed to change for some appointment at the police station," muttered Dylan, not taking his eyes off the horses. "Said he'd be back as soon as he could."

Harper thought it odd that Marshall would leave Dylan to finish out the morning exercise, given his recent record. The last horse Dylan had trained was the one who'd broken down right out of the gate and was euthanized. The stud had lost a two-year-old, a potential stakes horse, first time out.

Bad luck. Or so she thought at the time.

Dylan smiled, lifted the ball cap off his head and settled it back. "I think Tap Down's gonna do real good for us." He pointed out on the track to a mid-sized dark bay with a regal arch to his neck.

"Marshall said he had a good mind," she said, watching the colt come to a walk.

Dylan considered the colt a minute as he went by. "Yeah, he's a good one. Don't make many bad decisions."

Harper considered Dylan. In all the years she'd known him, he'd never struck her as someone with a lot of horse sense. Marshall said Dylan had a "good eye," but Harper hadn't seen it. He'd also mentioned Dylan was short on patience and, he'd added, wisdom. Other than being a childhood friend of the sisters, she wondered why Marshall had kept him on.

Harper jumped the fence and walked up to the colt as Marcie, his exercise rider, nodded her head at her. She had on a knit cap with a big ball on the top and her stick stuck straight up her back where she'd tucked it into her pants after Tap Down's workout.

Harper approached the colt quietly. "How'd he feel?" she asked, stroking his neck.

Marcie grinned. "He's just a big kid havin' fun out there."

Despite herself, Harper laughed. Marcie was quoting a line from the movie, *Secretariat*. "Yeah, don't we wish," she said, pulling a peppermint out of her pocket.

Tap Down bent his neck in Harper's direction at the smell and she let him nibble it up as she patted him softly. Sweet boy, she thought. He loved his job and ran hard every time Marshall sent him out.

She made her way back to Dylan, considering what Marcie'd said about the workout. Harper had been away from training for years, so maybe her assessment of Dylan was off, maybe he'd learned something. Harper decided it was best to leave the professional training to the professionals.

Until she was proved wrong.

"How you doing, Harp?" Dylan said once Harper returned, not taking his eyes off Tap Down.

"Fine, Dylan, I'm fine," she said.

A loud commotion to the left welled up suddenly, catching their attention.

Dylan cursed then let out a string of Spanish, yelling at Evan Mendoza, the stud's longtime jockey who stood toe to toe at the edge of the track with a blustering Cooley Edison, Eden Hill's vet. They were screaming at each other, red-faced, Evan poking a finger up at the larger man and spewing invectives in Spanish. Dylan went through the gate to their left and ran over to intervene. Couldn't have their vet and jockey coming to blows, that was for sure.

Harper was about to join Dylan, but her cell phone went off. It was Marshall. The police detective had asked more questions about last night's events, especially about the horse trailer he'd seen racing down Georgetown Road and any recent firings at the stud but had provided few answers. The lead detective wanted to speak with Harper and the preliminary findings were that Steve's death was a suicide, given that his were the only prints on the gun. The theft, they felt, may have occurred before or after he arrived, though he did concede Steve could have surprised the thieves and gotten shot. They'd be looking into that. As for the mares, the police said they shouldn't get their hopes up about finding the perpetrators.

Great, thought Harper, her attention again going to Cooley and Evan who were both swearing a blue streak at each other. She heard snippets of *"Estupido!"* and *"Te matare!"* from Evan. The jockey was shaking a fist at Cooley, who just shook his head and waved a dismissive hand, finally walking away. Evan ran after him and socked him in the jaw, and then they went at it. Didn't seem a fair fight to Harper; Cooley was twice as big as Evan.

28

Dylan got between them and sent Cooley off in one direction, Evan in the other. Before he left, Evan spit in the dirt, hitting Cooley's well-polished boot. That was odd, thought Harper. Cooley and Evan normally got along fine. But spats and bad feelings had a way of creeping into any enterprise when enough money was involved—horse racing was no different.

Harper took Dylan's proffered coffee when he returned, shaking his head. "Hot blood," he said. "No accounting for it." He turned his attention back to the track.

Harper glanced in the direction of Cooley and Evan, but it seemed they'd both left the scene. The spat had erupted and vanished quick as a Kentucky cloudburst.

She turned back to Dylan. It seemed a good moment to ask about the racing injuries and losses they'd had. She wanted to get his take before talking to Marshall or Cooley.

He turned to her at the question. "Yeah, that was bad," he said, his voice trailing off. "But we weren't the only ones," he added, the exercise riders' easy banter fading behind them. "You know how the game goes."

Harper did. She knew you never had a perfect season— breeding or racing. But she was beginning to think their losses were something other than bad luck. The numbers of injuries and deaths suggested inept training or, at the least, very little oversight.

But Marshall was a successful and much sought-after trainer, with Eden Hill for as long as Harper could remember. He was certainly not inept and had always kept a close eye on all the stud's colts and fillies. So, barring they'd had a catastrophically unlucky racing season, there had to be another explanation.

Seemed Dylan didn't think so.

He took his coffee back, sipping it through the steam rising from the cup, turning his attention back to the horses.

Conversation over, she decided, heading to the training office to review Marshall's notes on their newest crop.

Friend or not, in both Paris and Steve's absence Dylan was not someone Harper had a lot of faith in, even supervised by Marshall.

Chapter 5

As she made her way back to the house, Evan's anger came to mind. Though the argument had been short-lived, *Te matare* is no small threat to level at someone. It's a death threat. And spitting on their vet's boots was an act of derision and disrespect, not at all like the Evan Mendoza Harper knew. Something serious had set him off. Hopefully Evan's beef with Cooley wasn't bad enough to threaten him riding for them. On top of everything else, Harper couldn't afford to lose their best jockey, too. She made a mental note to ask Cooley about it, or maybe Evan himself, the next time she ran into him.

In a few hours Harper was due to meet up with Tim Bradford, the vet Paris had hoped to bring on after the first of the year when Cooley retired, so she cut her ride short. After swinging around to check on the mares' pasture fence, Harper trotted Zydeco toward the long entrance drive, thinking about the previous night's events. It seemed odd the police would jump to suicide as the most likely cause of Steve's death when there was a theft involved. They had said they'd look into the connection between Steve's death and the theft, but still. Harper thought she'd stop by the police station later, if time permitted. Maybe she could get them to take that connection more seriously.

Seeing the familiar hand-laid stone walls at Eden Hill's entrance, Harper turned up the drive, relaxing in anticipation of a bit of time and space to further sort out recent events. She hoped a cup of hot tea in front of the fire would help restore her before Bradford arrived.

But as she passed the last of the century oaks and approached the turn-around in front of the house, she saw little R&R in the offing. Big Red Cole sat on one of the green Adirondack chairs on the porch.

She wondered what he wanted; Red was not the visiting type.

Redford Gibson Cole had worked his small farm into one of the premier broodmare farms in Kentucky, specializing in bringing Argentinian studs in for Harper's father and broodmares for his Hawk Ridge. But he was never easy to deal with. His rural Texas roots showed in his gruff presence, but Harper had always respected his knowledge of horses and his commitment to their families' shared success.

And Red didn't have it easy. He'd battled prejudice from the high-brow racing world for years. He was what some in the Lexington hierarchy called a "good 'ole boy" and they didn't mean it as a compliment.

"Hey girl," he called as Harper hopped off Zydeco and gave him over to John Henry then mounted the steps. "Glad to catch you." He patted the chair next to him. "Sit a spell here and let's have us a little chat." He nodded at John Henry and moved his Hawk Ridge ball cap from the chair seat, beckoning Harper to sit.

It was mid-morning, but it was cool outside. October cool. Red didn't seem to notice.

"How about you come in for a minute? I was going to make some tea."

"Coffee'll do me, if you got any," he replied, rising and getting the storm door for her. He had on overalls, a flannel shirt with a Hawk Ridge navy blue fleece-lined jacket over it, and tread-soled work boots. "Let me give Cooley a holler on the cell phone. He's over to the stallion barn with Marshall." He pulled a cell phone off his belt and fiddled with it.

Red came in shortly after Harper had put the coffee on and took a seat on the stool at the kitchen's granite-topped cook island. She grabbed two thick mugs from the cabinet and waited to pour at the coffee maker. Might as well forego the tea, she thought, and get some jet fuel in her bloodstream. She knew the fatigue would catch up to her by mid-afternoon otherwise.

"I hope you know how durned sorry I was to hear about Paris. She was a good girl. Didn't deserve to go this young." Red placed his ball cap to his right and smoothed his sparse hair back with a meaty hand.

"Thanks, Red," said Harper. "That means a lot to me." She set some homemade macaroons and pound cake Surrey had brought after the funeral in front of Red.

"Yeah, and having JD due home soon, I just wish things hadda worked out different," he said.

JD again. Harper felt her face flush—an odd response; after their breakup Harper thought she'd put all that behind her. She waited a few beats until it subsided and focused on Red's comment. She wasn't sure what he was getting at. "Worked out how?"

He waited till Harper poured the coffee and stood across from him at the island. The light was bright, and gold tinged with blue in the kitchen—the clear sky and maples in the yard cast a warm glow.

"Well, now I told Paris around a month ago. She seemed a little, whut? Overwhelmed maybe. With the Keeneland fall meet, the season a comin' up on us . . . All of it. An' no one helping her."

"Well, I was helping her," Harper said a little too hotly. "I talked everything over with Paris. All the decisions. She wasn't alone."

Red's comment had also completely ignored Marshall's presence, she thought.

"Aw, honey, now, I didn't mean to upset you so," said Red, his small brown eyes peering at Harper. "No need for that. We're all family here, and you're not to suffer all by yourself. Don't pay no never mind to me."

He sipped his coffee patiently.

She didn't think he'd heard yet about Steve's death, so whatever he'd come to talk about couldn't be that. Harper filled the ceramic hen pitcher with water and poured some into the basil and tarragon at the window.

When she turned back, Red cleared his throat, popped a macaroon in his mouth and washed it down with a gulp of coffee.

Kelso, their golden retriever, barked on the porch then the doorbell rang, both announcing Anna Cole's arrival.

Harper smiled and welcomed her inside.

Red's ex-wife hadn't changed much over the years. Harper took in her tall, lanky frame, her skin stretched taut over Cherokee bone structure. With deep green eyes and thick auburn hair, Anna had always been a striking woman. No one could figure out what she'd seen in Red: they were as opposite as they come.

She'd left him after Harper and JD graduated from high school, setting her sights on the star-studded skies of LA. Why she'd returned was anyone's guess. Paris said she'd resumed her work as a bloodstock agent, a career Harper's father had encouraged her in many years ago.

Anna stepped through the door, her smile fading as she took in Red's presence. "Oh," she said, "Saw your truck. Thought you'd be down at the barn."

The two didn't appear to get along any better now than they had during their divorce.

Anna stayed planted at the door. "I just came to give you these," she said, holding out yet more flowers. "And to see if you needed anything." She glanced quickly at Red and then back to Harper.

"I'm fine, Anna. Thanks." She took the flowers to the counter and plunked them in a vase. "Coffee?"

"Just the restroom, if you don't mind."

She walked past them and down the hall.

As she passed, Red's eyes took in her every step. Harper recognized the emotions playing over his face—longing and anger. His small eyes swiveled toward Harper and, as their eyes met, the emotions vanished leaving his face a blank mask.

What was that all about?

That spark of anger, though, was something everyone had seen before. There had been speculation that his temper was what drove Anna to leave.

After returning and planting a quick peck on Harper's cheek, Anna left. Seemed she couldn't get out of Red's presence fast enough.

Harper shrugged. If Anna had come for something other than flowers, she assumed she'd be back in touch.

"So, you had words with Paris?" Harper said, picking up her conversation with Red. "What did you tell her?"

Red put his cup carefully on the counter. After a momentary lapse, he was back to all business. Anna's visit seemed to fade into the background.

"Well, like I said, with JD getting to the end of his tour, I had a mind he might want to take over for me so I been planning what the future might be."

"So, I *asked* Paris. Didn't tell her anything. That's not how it was. I asked Paris . . ." Red thought a moment, then went on "near two years ago . . ." He studied his coffee a moment. ". . . to think on maybe selling off Eden Hill to us."

"Sell the farm?" Harper's voice was low and modulated, but Red's small eyes narrowed; he'd picked up her incredulity. He'd known the entire family forever. He knew Harper's Grandpa started the stud and that none of them would ever sell it.

Red's offer. Along with her talk with Steve, another thing Paris hadn't mentioned. Harper frowned.

"Now, just listen a minute," he continued. "Just hear me out. I'm thinking it would help you and me both. You could make some money and have your life free as a bird up there in New York, like you always wanted." He nodded at the thought. "An' I could give my son a leg up on making his way in the racing game while I'm still around."

Red's logic notwithstanding, what struck Harper was that he'd discussed this with Paris two years ago. She thought about that. Two years. That's around the time Sugarland and Deacon were foaled. The stud's two best racing prospects. Interesting timing.

Harper stared at Red. Did he feel responsible for helping keep Eden Hill going, much as she did? Their families had, more or less, been as close as blood relatives since before Harper was born, so his concern for her welfare and JD's made sense. Or, given his drive, maybe he was just plain greedy and wanted the stud for himself.

But sell the family's legacy? Never, vowed Harper. That would never happen. And then her temper did get the best of her. "Good Lord, Red, what's wrong with you? You know we'd never sell Eden Hill," she blurted out, but instantly realized that was a mistake. Red was touchy about what folks thought of him. "I'd never sell," Harper said more softly, realizing there was no more "we"—she was the only Hill left.

"Sorry, Red," she nearly whispered. "I didn't mean that the way it sounded." She reached across to him, but he'd already clamped his Hawk Ridge cap on and was rising from the stool.

"No offense taken, girl. No offense taken," he said.

But clearly, he was mightily offended.

"I'll just be getting on back," he said, showing Harper his back. "When you're feeling better, maybe think on it."

And he was out the door.

Chapter 6

Harper stood in the hallway and watched through the vertical window as Red climbed into his peeling blue pick-up truck, flung it hard into drive and sped away, sending gravel flying.

She shook her head. Red Cole was a rough, direct, grating sort of person, but he'd stood by her father since before Harper was born. She could imagine he'd been thinking about JD's return, wanting to do something major, something that would keep JD and him connected—his son meant everything to him.

JD was so different, she thought, more like Anna, but there was no time for further musings.

Coming around the paddock were Marshall and Cooley, who seemed in quite a hurry. They approached the house, Marshall climbing the porch steps two at a time.

The closer they got, the more serious was the look on their faces.

Harper opened the door as Marshall rushed in followed by Cooley.

"What is it, Marshall? What happened?" Something had, that was apparent. Cooley moved to his side, and Marshall took off his hat and planted his foot as if bracing himself.

"Aw, Harper, it's that Sugarland colt."

"What about him?" But she knew already.

"I got the call from Dylan when we were looking at the California stallion."

Marshall looked stricken. "I told Dylan to work on his starts and he broke good from the gate, then pulled up. No telling why yet. Or how bad it is."

God, thought Harper, another injury. And this time to one of their two best colts.

"Dylan hasn't been working him hard," continued Marshall. "I was clear—just let him out a little, see where we're at." Marshall momentarily looked disgusted and Harper wondered if he thought Dylan was responsible.

Sugarland had done incredibly well in his juvenile races over the summer, showing enormous promise.

"I'll see to him, don't worry, Sweet Pea. Could be he'll be fine," said Marshall. But she knew they wouldn't be so worried and wouldn't have rushed up to the house if they thought Sugarland wasn't in danger.

Harper looked from Marshall to Cooley, noticing the vet shifting from one foot to the other, not meeting her eye. He was clearly agitated and uncomfortable.

A hefty man, Cooley had a long, lined face, and a fringe of dark hair below the few hairs sprouting above it. He'd been their vet for as long as Harper could remember but was retiring at the end of the year, which accounted for Tim Bradford's imminent visit. "I got a call from Red a minute ago. Seems he's got an emergency with one of his mares," he said. "I said I'd be right over."

That was odd; Red had just left. Harper wondered if he'd called Cooley on the way out. Clearly, it seemed their vet's allegiance lay elsewhere. Well, fine, she thought.

"You go on, Cooley. We'll see to Sugar."

Marshall started to protest, but Harper held up her hand. She'd made up her mind. Tim Bradford was due momentarily. She'd have him look at the colt.

The last time the sisters had talked, Paris was oddly enthusiastic about Bradford as Cooley's replacement, stressing he'd helped solve some suspicious deaths at Brookfield Stud Farm, owned by a friend of Marshall's.

At the time, Harper was perplexed at Paris' insistence that Bradford was the perfect replacement, but with her death, then Steve's, she had a growing suspicion that Paris' reasons were sound. Add to that the list of injured and destroyed horses last season, and the whole picture took on ominous overtones.

Harper looked forward to meeting Bradford and picking his brain. She checked her watch as Cooley shut the door. "I want Tim Bradford to look at Sugarland," she said to Marshall. "He's due here in a few minutes."

Marshall looked at her oddly, shrugged and nodded, not asking any questions. "I'll be down at the barn with the colt. Send the vet over as soon as he gets here," he said and left.

A short time later, she heard Kelso barking in the circle and figured Bradford had arrived. He mounted the steps as Harper stepped onto the porch and stuck out his hand. He looked directly at her—a trait she was fond of—and said, "You must be Harper. Good to meet you."

He was a bit taller than her, about six feet, had light brown hair and big, expressive brown eyes filled with intelligence. He looked to be in his early thirties.

"Your timing couldn't be better. I've got a colt needs looking at—a two-year-old. Good one, we think. I'd appreciate you looking at him if you have the time."

40

Kelso, tail wagging, trotted up the porch steps and planted himself, smiling, off to the side of them. The vet bent down and stroked his head, not taking his eyes off Harper. "Don't want to step on any toes here," he said, well aware that Cooley was with them till the end of the year. "And I didn't bring my equipment," he said, standing and glancing back at his white Lexus, "but sure, I'll be glad to have a look."

"Thanks, I'd appreciate it," Harper said. No need to go into details, she thought. Cooley had made his decision. And Bradford might be with them going forward, not Cooley.

They headed out to the 'Gator parked to the left of the house. Kelso jumped in the small flat bed and they headed around the first paddock, down the gravel road, across Bucks Creek, and up over the rise to the stallion and racing complex, arriving at the first European-styled stone and wrought iron stallion barn in short order.

The large breeding shed was about half a mile beyond, centered some distance between the mares' barn and the stallion complex. The layout made it easy for all the horses to be led up separately for breeding, thereby avoiding mishaps.

Harper cut the engine and Kelso bounded out, meeting Marshall at the aisle door. Marshall greeted Bradford with a handshake and led him to Sugarland's stall.

"Don't feel hot, but he did pull up pretty good, Dr. Bradford," said Marshall. The vet was at least twenty years younger than Marshall. Harper smiled at her trainer's sense of protocol and respect.

Bradford turned and smiled, too. "Tim's fine," he said, looking at Harper as well as Marshall.

He waited as the groom brought Sugarland out of his stall; the vet's calmness put the colt at ease, which made it easier to do the exam. Bradford removed the leg wrap, flexed the colt's leg and probed, ran his hand down Sugarland's leg, feeling along the cannon bone, down to the fetlock and pastern, probing a bit more. He watched as the groom led the colt down the aisle and back then turned and halted him. Bradford felt up from his knee to shoulder and back down again and nodded at the groom to put Sugarland back in his stall. Bradford followed and stood beside the colt.

Marshall and Harper waited outside the curved wrought-iron stall bars for his assessment.

"Well, he's lame, for sure. Wish I had my portable x-ray with me . . ." He paused. "I'm thinking an x-ray is the way to go—could be a condylar fracture," he said, gently patting Sugarland's neck. "Probably best to get him to the hospital to make sure. Could be something else. I can't really say yet, but it's not too bad, maybe." He ran his hand along the colt's withers, down his back and croup. "Fine horse," he said. "I can see why you're concerned."

A fracture sounded bad, but Harper knew if Tim was right and it was a condylar fracture, and the injury was mild, Sugarland could make a full recovery.

Marshall looked furious.

"Good news, right, Marshall?" she said. "Maybe?"

Tim jumped in. "If it's what I think it is, he could be just fine."

Still, Marshall glowered ominously. Sugarland shifted his big chestnut head toward the trainer as if to reassure him.

All of them knew an injury like that could stem from hard pounding on the track.

"I told Dylan to put a light ride on him," Marshall spat in disgust. "Told him that for the past two weeks." He stomped out of the barn, even angrier than before.

Harper looked at Tim, wondering what he thought.

"Yeah, that's been happening lately. Train too hard, especially the young ones," said Tim as he exited the stall. "And then some of them do get juiced."

She wondered if the vet's recent experience at Brookfield was coloring his comments. Did he think the colt's injury was due to Sugarland being drugged?

Harper walked down the aisle with him, past the feed room with its sweet feed and leather scent curling into the barn. He looked in on Deacon, the black colt they'd bred along with Sugarland, stopping a moment before his stall. "Impressive individual," said Tim, admiringly. They went on past Tap Down, Suffolk, Manhattan Beach, and the others. He smiled appreciatively, making his way to the barn door.

Once outside, she motioned toward the bench punctuated by purple mums planted on either side with a tall poplar towering over them. They sat. Behind them, at some distance, was the rock-walled horse cemetery where the family had been burying their horses since their Grandfather was alive.

"So, you think Sugarland might have been tampered with?" she said. He'd been discreet, but Harper wondered if that's what he was getting at.

"Naw," he said, "wouldn't make sense. You're not running him at Keeneland, right?"

She nodded. Okay, so she was wrong.

"We ran them in a few race meets this summer, testing him and Deacon out. They did better than we thought they would."

Tim nodded. "Frog juice, used to be cobra venom . . ." He seemed on a roll about illegal drugging. "There's always some new thing trainers will try till it gets detected. Used to run them on heroin, believe it or not."

All racehorses are examined by a vet at every race. Any illegal substance given to a horse to enhance performance disqualifies him. Harper knew Tim meant that at a good track, the vet would have picked up if Sugarland had been dosed with a banned substance. But drugs were the track's dirty little secret and these days not so little and not so secret. It was a disgusting reality and Harper's family had worked hard to race the right way.

"But drugs put the horse at risk," she said. It's why she and Paris had made the decision to run their horses as cleanly as possible.

"Exactly," said Tim. "And from what I hear of Marshall, that's not his style."

No, he was right. Not Marshall. But though she hated to admit it, maybe Dylan. She wondered about the colt he'd lost for them. With even big-name trainers getting busted for banned substances and Dylan desperate for a win, Harper had to consider he might resort to that.

She also wondered about the other horses they'd lost to injury and death last season. Horses it seemed her sister was looking into before she'd died: Harper had found some odd notes Paris had made in their Grandpa's studbook, but what she'd written made no sense to Harper.

Tim was thoughtful a moment, then changed the subject. "Don't feel you have to send Sugarland over. Call Cooley if you'd like. As I said, I'm not here to step on any toes."

Harper's intuition said go with Bradford, and this time she trusted it. She wasn't feeling so inclined toward Cooley at the moment, though she knew he wasn't having an easy time of it. His wife had battled cancer for the last three years; Harper and Paris had finally persuaded him to retire and care for her. But he'd been "retiring" for seven months and the sisters had finally forced December 31st on him as his last day. Harper shrugged. Everyone had challenges, and though Cooley had been with them a long time and her heart went out to him, the truth was he had just left one of their prized colts in the lurch to run when Red called.

The two headed back in the 'Gator. Harper said she'd send Sugarland to Rood and Riddle Equine Hospital right away then wait for Tim's diagnosis.

The coffee she'd had earlier with Red notwithstanding, she was suddenly exhausted.

Once back at the house, she walked Tim to his car, and he said he'd call first thing after the x-ray results were in.

"It's good to meet you, finally, though I'm sorry about the circumstances," said Tim. "Paris spoke often of you. She seemed like a good person. I was real sorry to hear about her accident."

Harper shuddered. She would never get used to being reminded of her sister's death. And she was growing more and more certain it was not an accident.

Harper thanked him and they shook hands.

She spent the rest of the day on farm errands—signing checks, returning calls, conferring with their bank and lawyer, and putting out feelers for a new farm manager. She had wanted to check in with Detective Walker, but by the time she'd put in a call, he'd left for the day.

She walked back to the house in the falling light, intending to spend more time going over Paris' studbook notes about the horses they'd raced last season. Paris had made a lot of notations and it seemed she was looking for something specific.

Harper pulled off her gloves once inside and hung her jacket on the coat rack by the door. She took Surrey's casserole from the refrigerator and popped it in the microwave, all the while pacing the kitchen between the island and the sink. She glanced out the kitchen window, down to the barn where she hoped Zydeco was eating his dinner.

The family had called the family barn Grandpa's barn for as long as Harper could remember. It stood, as it had for nearly a century, a long stone's throw from the house, over the bridge surmounting Bucks Creek. Their father had renovated all the other barns during the 1980s but left this one untouched. It still had Grandpa's hand-laid stone foundation, the wrought-iron fittings forged by his blacksmith friend, and the two paddocks adjacent were bounded by thick-cut cedar posts and boards from trees Grandpa had felled on the property. The girls had always stabled their riding horses in it, and it had been the scene of many of Harper and Paris' tearful young sobs and joys as well as days spent with their Grandpa mucking out stalls, feeding the horses, or just listening to him tell tales of his favorite stallions.

The microwave dinged, but Harper lingered a moment more at the window. John Henry had left the barn lights on and through the stall windows she could see the comforting sight of horses safely in their warm stalls, eating their dinner.

Time for mine, too, she thought. She slid Surrey's casserole onto a plate, opened a bottle of wine and poured herself a fruity Pinot Noir. She intended to eat and head straight to Paris' notes in Grandpa's studbook. But all she could manage was dinner. Harper's eyes literally could not stay open one more minute after she plunked her dishes in the sink, so she headed for bed.

Chapter 7

Harper gazed out the kitchen window the next morning, sipping coffee and watching John Henry turn out the horses in Grandpa's barn. She'd slept in, so Zydeco and the rest had already had their grain and morning hay. Now it was time for play. Harper loved watching John Henry lead a string of five ex-racehorses at once into the large turnout beyond the barn. Not many people had the internal calm to manage that.

She flipped on the TV to catch the news and saw a reporter step in front of the camera, gesturing to a man sitting behind her to the right on the curb. Harper turned up the volume and heard the reporter mention the suspect's name, one that seemed familiar to her. She stepped closer to the television just as the camera zoomed in on the man seated next to a restored '60s muscle car.

Abel Desormeaux. Harper set down her coffee and stared at the image. I know him, she thought. She listened to the news story, remembering that long ago he'd been an intricate part of the day-to-day life at the stud.

A Creole man of color, Harper recalled he was a Louisiana ex-con, who'd come to Kentucky and hired on at a number of Kentucky stud farms, Eden Hill included, when the sisters were small. As a young man he'd worked on a prison gang, picking hot garbage along the burnt-out sides of highways supervised, he'd told them, by a thick-armed beef of a man with a long gun hanging off his quarter horse in rural Concordia. Later Harper learned that Abel had a fifth-grade education and had done time for burglary plus possession with intent. He'd come to Eden Hill from Hawk Ridge and Rafe had put him to work renovating pastures. He was big, strong, spoke little, and did his work willingly. Harper recalled him as a polite, funny man who had always been nice to the sisters. He'd moved on after a time but evidently was still in the area. The news report of his arrest in Cincinnati's Over the Rhine district came as a surprise to Harper. He'd been found with one and a half kilos of heroin in the trunk of his car. The bust had an estimated street value of a million dollars.

She switched the news off, and Abel's sad face faded from view, leaving her wondering at the circular nature of his life; it had begun, more or less, in prison and looked like it would end there. *You never know how things will wind up, or where.* It seemed to her that the trajectory of Abel's life, no matter how different their cultures, was also her own; Harper had come back to her starting point, too. But whether her circle was complete or not remained to be seen.

After dumping the rest of her coffee in the sink, she made her way to the study and sat staring blankly at the walls, looking from photo to photo as if one of them held the secret to all that had recently gone on. Again, Harper was struck by how much they all had been through together—their parents, Red and his family, their grooms and horses, and of course she and Paris.

Harper hauled out her Grandpa's studbook, running her hand over its worn cover, carved and tooled, now in faded red, blue, and brown, shuffling all the loose pages back in neatly. Most bloodstock agents used online databases for nicking and to evaluate breeding matches these days, but Harper's Grandpa had begun this book in the early years of the stud, and it was their primer in the business, their bible. Harper flipped through it slowly, noting her Grandpa's faded script, her father's neat block letters. She saw the notes Paris had made when the sisters had bred for Deacon and Sugarland, two of the most talented colts they'd ever produced. So much history lay between the covers.

She went over the notes Paris had made in the margins of horses they'd bred in recent years, and again they made no sense to Harper. She'd especially targeted the colts and fillies they'd raced last season, looking into their bloodlines' turf and track records as well as their stamina and speed evaluations. What that information had to do with the runners the stud had lost last season eluded Harper.

Whatever it was her sister had been investigating seemed to have died with her.

She checked the time, and headed for the kitchen. The studbook would have to wait; she was due at her friend Mariel's Thoroughbred rescue shortly to help with her fundraiser.

Harper rummaged around for the horse portraits she'd painted last summer at Mariel's request. She'd been a close friend to both of the sisters and every year they did what they could to help Mariel raise money for her operation.

Harper located the two wrapped portraits and with those, plus her backpack in tow, she headed out, Abel Desormeaux and, at least for the moment, Paris' studbook notes far from thought.

Kelso sat on the porch, his big golden head tilted in question, his tail moving from side to side in anticipation. Clearly, he hoped for an invitation.

"Come on," Harper said, grinning at his expectant expression and waving him into the back seat of the Range Rover. Kelso loved visiting Cedar Run Rescue; he and his buddies shot through the pastures and waded in and out of the ponds in any weather.

So, the two of them bundled into the Rover and took off heading to Midway, where Mariel, Jen, and who knows who else, waited in the cool October morning.

The landscape fell away from the road in gentle rolls. Deceptively gentle, she thought, glancing out the window now and then. Beautiful, sometimes deadly, country.

Because of the money. It was always because of the money. Horses killed surreptitiously for the insurance payout. Horses drugged, clients swindled . . . there was no end to it. Bluegrass country was flashy and high-dollar, but there were always those, as in any business, who'd rather do it the easy way.

Not so easy for the horses, thought Harper, heading to the other end of the racing world—the "discards," a world of untreated fractures and horses too slow and headed for slaughter.

Cedar Run loomed up a few hundred yards to the right, so she slowed and made the turn, a sturdily built, sprawling log-cabin greeting her and Kelso as they made their way up the short drive.

To the left were the pastures and paddocks, and directly behind the house, up a small rise, stood the barn with a paddock attached.

As she exited the Range Rover, a pack of dogs greeted Harper, running toward them in full voice, who then took off once Kelso had leaped out and into their pack. Off they went, tails high and wagging,

Mariel and Jen came out of the house, the ubiquitous thermal cups of coffee steaming in their hands.

"Hey, my darling!" called Mariel. Her partner Jen waved and pulled at her ball cap. A woman of few words, which was fine with Harper.

Mariel's flame-red hair attempted to stay in a high ponytail, but strands escaped here and there, and by mid-morning, Harper knew, she'd look wild as a gypsy. Though she was all smiles, a lot of angst lay just below the surface. During her time working around Argentinian racetracks, she'd survived death threats and at least one knife-wound whose scar lay like a lump of rope just below her ribcage. Mariel knew as much about drugs and corruption in the Thoroughbred world as she did about surviving.

She popped her huge sunglasses back up her nose and took the porch steps in one bound to greet Harper with hugs and kisses on both cheeks.

"Ah, the paintings!" she said, as Harper pulled them out of the Range Rover, remnants of her Spanish accent adding a lilt to her pronunciation. Her eyes widened as Harper removed the brown paper protecting the front of the first one. "This is Seattle Slew, no?" she asked, knowing, of course, it was her rescue, Slew's grandson, not the Triple Crown winner. "Harper, so lovely," she said, taking Harper's hand and kissing it. "So beautiful. It will bring the high price, I know it."

From the house poured the volunteers, there to set up the cider, face painting, carriage rides, pony rides, horse photos, a silent auction, and bake sale in the barn aisle and all over the grounds lining the paddocks. Harper knew most of the people filing down the steps. Surrey and Lucas, Eden Hill's stallion manager, would be along in an hour or so. Marshall and Dylan would likely show up later; right now they were handling the morning exercise for the horses the stud would be racing at the upcoming Keeneland race meet.

Jen joined the two women, and Harper longed to ask her how things were going at Curwen's Bay Stud. Mariel, evidently, had recently made a scorching speech at the Farm Manager's club about drug use on the track, a subject no one wanted aired publicly. In retaliation, everyone pulled the horses Jen had in training—the old boy's network was solidly in place. Harper couldn't imagine Jen would be happy as a stallion groom—the only job she could get—handling stallions rather than training them.

Jen was stocky and a bit gruff, but Harper had known her a long time, so she got that she just wasn't a chatty person. She motioned to Harper who excused herself and followed Jen up towards the barn.

"Need anything?" Jen asked, her hands deep in her back pockets, her short, dark hair cupped behind her ears beneath her ball cap. She headed straight up to the barn, not looking at Harper as she talked.

"Thanks Jen, I'm ok." She trod along beside Jen in silence, wondering if the trainer had heard anything about the goings on at Eden Hill.

They got to the barn and Jen overturned a pickle bucket used to water the horses and sat on it, pulling out a cigarette. She lit it, drew on it, and let out a long stream of smoke before speaking.

"Y'all had a string of bad luck," she said, still not looking at Harper. She shrugged her shoulders under her forest green fleece and took another pull of her cigarette.

Harper guessed she was talking about the injuries and deaths on the track, since her mind always ran to horses first. Harper sensed she had something to say, so she sat on an overturned feed bucket next to Jen and folded her hands, her elbows resting on her knees. Both of them gazed out on the pastures and paddocks for a time, as below volunteers bustled all the fundraising activities into place.

"We did," said Harper. "Haven't talked to Marshall about it yet . . ."

Jen turned, squinting through the smoke. "Yeah, sorry. Of course, with the funeral. And then Steve. I didn't mean . . ."

"No problem," she said, attempting a reassuring smile. Jen would never knowingly offend anyone. "What's your take? You were there, right?" Harper glanced back down the slow rise to the pastures where twenty or so horses grazed on the last tufts of grass or meandered toward the fence.

Jen smoked and thought. "I was there a couple of race days. Been seein' to the stallions here lately." She stopped and looked at Harper with a crooked, wry grin.

"Mariel," the two said simultaneously. Harper smiled and Jen shook her head, though the small smile still played at the corner of her mouth. For all her flair and trouble-making ability, you couldn't argue with how committed Mariel was to the horses' welfare.

"But I was there when that colt died," Jen continued, her tone turning serious. "Didn't look good." She paused. "Didn't look right, I mean."

Jen had trained racehorses all her adult life, so Harper paid close attention to her comments. Plus, she'd pulled her aside first thing.

Below them, the volunteers were scurrying around setting up tables, putting out cakes and cookies, brewing coffee, arranging the silent auction items, and setting up photo stands. Things looked about ready to go.

She watched Glenn and his big Percheron, Max, bring the ornate white carriage with its purple velvet seats around to the front and wished Jen or Marshall or Paris or *somebody* had clued her in about the goings on at the stud farm.

The sun was bright, and the day promised to be clear and even slightly warm. The horses were now nearly all gathered at the rails of their pastures and paddocks, interested to see what all the fuss was about. In a few minutes, hopefully, the guests would begin arriving.

Harper turned to Jen. An odd conversation for such a festive occasion. "What didn't look right, Jen?"

She didn't answer right away. "Seems unlikely Marshall wouldn't have noticed," she said finally, squinting into the sun. "Maybe best to ask him."

But Harper persisted. "Jen, you brought it up. I will talk to Marshall. But right now, I'd like to know what you think."

She turned to Harper, pinched her cigarette between her thumb and index finger, and took a drag. "I knew that colt. Expected he'd fade or come up empty under pressure, especially at that distance. Not that time. Can't imagine Marshall didn't pick up on it. But anyway, it didn't sit right with me."

She was talking about the colt who'd dropped dead after the race—ruled a heart attack, which was odd in a young, healthy animal. The necropsy hadn't turned up anything suspicious, so the heart attack ruling stood. Harper assumed Jen had watched him run before; she had a good eye and knew what she was looking at more than most. Was Jen suggesting their colt could have been drugged?

Harper nodded. "Did you talk to Paris about it?"

"Didn't see her much," said Jen. "Been busy with the Curwen stallions."

They were both silent for a time.

"I'm not accusing Marshall of anything," Jen said, stabbing her cigarette for emphasis. "Or anyone. Could have just been a good day for that colt that turned out bad." She stood, flicked her cigarette, and ground it under her boot. "You best look into it, is all I'm saying."

Harper stood too. "I will, Jen." They walked down toward the smiling faces of Mariel and the rest of the volunteers. "Thanks for saying something," she added.

The two didn't talk on the way down, there not being much else to say.

Jen's comments made Harper even more concerned about drug involvement—it wasn't the first time it had come up . . . Too, as Jen implied, if the stud's horses had been doped, it seemed unlikely Marshall wouldn't have noticed. And that thought left a very bad possibility hanging in the air.

Harper glanced up at the pasture, watching the geldings and mares turn from the fence and head slowly out to the large round hay bale for a snack. Nodding to Jen to go on ahead, she ducked between fence rails, and followed, walking into the pasture under the warming sun as she had so many times before, sitting quietly in the cool grass.

One winter she'd spent many hours in that very spot. A big gray mare, almost pure white, had been dumped by a trainer along with the horse's companion—a dark bay with a knee as big as a cantaloupe. He'd broken it on the track and the trainer had done nothing. Willow, the big gray, must have been sorely abused; no one could get near her.

Harper had made her way out in the cold and snow for months that winter just to stand beside Willow, their faces to the wind as is the way with horses. She'd walk toward the mare slowly with her eyes averted so Willow wouldn't see Harper as a threat. It took a few months until she let Harper put her hand on her back, then her neck. She brought peppermints at first, since that's the only treat track horses usually know. Then came carrots. Willow never would approach Harper when she came to the pasture, but she wouldn't run away, either.

Come spring, Harper got a halter and lead rope on her, and after a time they made their way out of the pasture to the small arena. Harper let her smell the saddle pad there, and look over the saddle, her big dark eyes soft; she felt safe. She had the longest white eyelashes Harper had ever seen on a horse and a powerful body. She deserved a person to love and care for her, someone to take her forward into a new life.

And later that spring, she got that. A lovely young girl came one day and fell in love with her. Later, she sent Harper photos of herself standing on Willow's back, the mare's beautiful gray coat painted with hearts and flowers. Willow got her new life, thanks to Mariel's welcoming arms. Everyone on the track knew she'd never turn away any horse in need.

Harper looked back at all the folks come to help Mariel keep the place going, grateful so many shared her commitment to the care of horses who gave everything they had to do what trainers asked of them. Harper got up and brushed herself off, watching the quiet herd munching hay from the big bale. Feeling calm and a little bit hopeful, she headed back to Eden Hill.

Chapter 8

Harper was home by mid-morning. Her intention was to check in with Marshall about what Jen had said, attend to farm business, and stop by the police station. But she'd wait on Marshall a bit. She didn't want to jump to conclusions about the problems they'd had on the track; whatever "bad luck" Eden Hill had experienced could have been just that.

She needed to look in on Zydeco, so she poured some coffee, grabbed a few carrots and headed over Bucks Creek to the barn. It did her heart good to hear the chestnut nicker when he saw Harper and take some carrots from her hand at the aisle window. She threw two flakes of alfalfa in his hayrack, inhaling its fresh scent, and slowly ran her hand down the gelding's big, warm neck, happy to see him get right into it. He grabbed a mouthful and turned to look at Harper, tossing his head with pleasure, then went back to his meal.

She sat on a square bale in the aisle for a moment, glancing at the limestone rocks climbing the far wall, glittering in the early light, thinking again of her Grandpa and all he'd built.

But it was cool in the barn, so pretty soon, a bit more serene than she'd been of late, she headed back to the house.

Harper spent the rest of the morning more in the past than the present. So much had happened since her return, and she wasn't processing any of it well. She needed to focus if she was going to find out what really happened to her sister.

She got a box of photos down from the study's closet shelf and sifted through them, hoping something would settle her turbulent heart. Instead she came across a long-ago photo of Red and her father, Rafe, that gave her pause. They were so young, so . . . cocky. It was summer, the knee-high orchardgrass in the background gleamed in the heat, and Harper's father was grinning as he play-boxed with Red. Just beyond, in a circular enclosure, her mother was round-penning her horse, Miracle. Rafe's short-sleeved shirt was rolled up over his biceps, Red laughing and ducking under her father's wide swing. Both of them looked carefree and happy. Harper's mother had turned, and it looked as if she was mock scolding them both.

They had a right to their happiness. They'd all devoted themselves to their families' mutual success; they were at the top of their game. The world, Harper thought, sure looked bright— no obstacle ahead too formidable to surmount. It was a great time for all of them, and Paris, JD, and Harper were inseparable.

JD. Again, his presence rose from the past into the present . . . They'd been the best of friends as kids, then suddenly in high school and then through college, more than that. He was the star athlete, the brilliant student. Why he chose Harper was anyone's guess. He was tender, patient, and adoring. And Harper was . . . not. She wasn't as sure of herself as he was, and so she tested and tested his love and loyalty. Looking back, Harper couldn't believe he didn't tire of it. She tired of much less. But over and over, he waited her out, let her get angry over nothing, let her ignore him, let her choose horses over time with him.

59

Harper stared at the photo of her father and Red, then put it back.

It wasn't JD who'd ended things. Harper was the one who had left him. And Paris. She guessed she couldn't really blame Red for wanting to take it all back and start over again.

Harper was startled out of her reverie by the house phone's jarring blare. She stood there stupefied through three rings, unable to move so rooted was she in a past long gone.

She finally shut the box lid, her hand lingering over it, then picked up the phone.

It was Sean Holland, their building contractor. He'd done work for Red and Harper's father, so he'd been the logical choice when Harper and Paris decided to reward John Henry for his decades of service to their family by erecting a small house for him on the property. They'd chosen a lovely spot at a bend on Bucks Creek, a spot bounded by woods on two sides, a large gravel bar at the creek's edge, and a glowing meadow to the right of the house site. The sisters had loved the sound the water made rushing over the rocks and thought John Henry would feel right at home there. He could even fish if he liked, the creek was deep enough for a good-sized catch in the spring.

They'd broken ground a month or so ago, hoping to get up the modest home in time for John Henry to move in before Christmas. That, given the news Sean delivered, was not going to happen.

Harper drove to the site right away. Sean met her, his look grim. He'd dismissed the crew for the day. Likely for the foreseeable future.

The police and coroner were already there. They'd come prepared; an area back to the woods and out to the meadow's

60

edge had already been roped off. The coroner had called the forensic anthropologist in from Knoxville, and by the time Harper arrived, the crew had uncovered two more sets of remains in addition to the one Sean's team had unearthed. The police were carefully, even reverently, clearing away the debris from the rest of their sad find, mapping and photographing what turned out to be a burial site. By early afternoon, in all, seven skeletons were laid out side-by-side, as if they'd been carefully buried rather than thrown haphazardly into one large hole.

The coroner conferred with the police but had little use for Sean or Harper. They were both cautioned not to cross into the burial zone, so they stayed on the perimeter.

Harper walked over the spongy, moss-laden ground on the woods side of the excavation to get a better view and regain some composure, inhaling the scent of damp fall leaves and wondering if these were the remains of a family, buried one-by-one as they'd died over the course of a normal lifetime. It was odd if that was the case—there were no coffins and the gravesite did not include individual plots with headstones or markers. Harper wondered if that's why the forensic team had been called in—the scene did look suspicious.

She had no idea how old the remains might be—they were skeletons, so clearly they hadn't recently died. Conceivably they could have been part of the property settled long ago, much before her Grandfather had traveled from Virginia and purchased the land. They'd have to wait to find out about that.

Her thought that it might be a family was called into question when she looked at the remains more closely as the police and others moved quietly among the dead. As another skeleton was unearthed, Harper noted that three were obviously adults and one was quite a bit smaller. This one was not laid out ceremoniously on its back; it was on its side and curled around it was a larger set of bones. The coroner lifted a tin box from the two and handed it to the police.

Harper stood next to the policewoman as she opened the dented box and withdrew a necklace with a locket and a cross on it as well as a small bracelet. When the policewoman opened the locket, she craned to get a look, but couldn't see the contents. She glanced back to the gravesite; all the bodies were placed lying with their heads to the east and feet to the west, and it appeared that small, highly deteriorated pieces of cloth and leather were buried at the foot of each person.

Harper returned to the grave, kneeling on the moss to see the body closest to her. The ribs were crossed by what looked to be the remains of his or her arms. She looked up at Sean who stood guard above her, his clear blue eyes troubled.

Then, after giving her name and contact information, Harper told Sean to go home, intending to head for the stud office. The police said it might take weeks, even months for the forensic team to come up with information needed—in the end, they'd know the age, sex, even the ancestry of those in the grave. The team would also be able to tell if there was trauma involved in their deaths. But it would take time.

Harper sighed. More waiting. She took in the skeletons already visible, now somewhat cleaned and photographed, wondering who in the world those poor people were, especially the two that seemed entwined. They were particularly haunting, and Harper knew why. The protective curve of the larger, the vulnerable stature of the smaller seemed a metaphor for her and Paris. As a child, Paris had been the fragile one, always in need of someone to watch over her. Growing up, that had been Harper. But the truth was, Harper felt her efforts at protection had been as ineffectual as had that curved collection of bones in the grave.

It was a saddening scene. But there was nothing more Harper could do at the site and she had pressing stud farm duties to attend to plus Paris' studbook notes to puzzle out. So, pushing back thoughts of the poor souls before her, she climbed into the Range Rover with sober resolve, hoping something in the notes her sister had made would help her understand how Paris had ended up like those who had lain so quietly beside their rushing, sun-graced creek.

Farm and other duties took up most of the rest of the day. Harper made an appointment with the detective assigned to Steve's death, checked in on the mares barn briefly, got caught at the farm office again returning myriad phone calls, conferring with their lawyer about the new syndicate, and looking over the resumés for Steve's job that had already come in, then toward the end of the day she finally got to the dry cleaners.

It wasn't until just after dark that she settled at the old rosewood desk with her glass of wine, again opened the studbook, and pulled out the loose papers Paris had inserted, going through them first.

There was the *Chefs-de-race* list, listing the best sires in categories from those who might transfer speed to stamina. Paris had highlighted certain sires in both the speed and stamina categories. The other loose papers had pedigrees and racing results of predominant sires and dams in the lines of their runners.

Harper understood the basic idea behind inbreeding, which their bloodstock agent, Mary Edvers, had practiced on behalf of the stud since her father's mid-career. Of the many duties she had, Mary most enjoyed coming up with optimal breeding pairings. Paris and Mary were kindred souls when it came to the nuances of nicking and balanced sex inbreeding. They'd confer for hours and hours and had the patience to wait three years to see if the two-year-olds they produced had any chance of fulfilling the dreams everyone had for the stud's runners.

But why was Paris so interested in these horses? Harper wondered, flipping through her sister's notes. She could understand if Paris was investigating Sugar and Deacon—they'd been as close to perfect in terms of Mary's method as they'd been able to breed in years.

But the colts and fillies Paris had investigated were not nearly as well-bred as their two budding stars. Harper couldn't determine what her sister had been looking for. Well, she thought, the racing world is not an exact science, especially not breeding. Secretariat never sired his equal but was an incredible broodmare sire—no one could have predicted that.

Harper flipped through the studbook. Paris had made notes there, too, on some of the sires, adding in late racing results that had missed the printing. Her notes were numerous and thorough. And dated.

Harper compared the loose sheets of paper notes to the ones in the margins. Her sister's notations had stopped only a week before her death.

Harper glanced out the window. The moon shone among a smattering of stars. Inside, the lamp threw an eerie silhouette of her hunched over the desk, papers strewn among her parents' mementos.

Paris' notes brought up so many questions: Was she aiming to duplicate some breeding they'd already done? Was any of this related to the racetrack drugs that had so incensed Mariel, or any of the other ominous and deadly things that had occurred since Paris' death?

Harper had no idea. But she did know who might. She'd have to talk to Mary Edvers when she returned from the Caribbean cruise she took every year with her sister. She was due back sometime later that week.

Chapter 9

Harper got to the office especially early the next day because Tap Down and Deacon were due to run in the Keeneland race meet in the early afternoon. She was to meet Marshall, Surrey, and Dylan there. Lucas said he and his wife Alia would come too.

Early as she was, Pepper Hardy, their receptionist, was already at her desk when Harper arrived. The stud's majordomo, Pepper expedited all calls coming into Eden Hill as well as handled all the emergencies on the farm with efficiency. They'd be lost without her.

She'd already made coffee, set out the messages on the edge of the granite-topped high partition in front of her desk, and was busy answering calls as Harper walked through the door. She waved as Harper passed by, picked up her messages, and headed to Paris' office, depositing them in front of Harper.

Pepper had straightened the desk—all the papers Harper had left scattered everywhere were neat and orderly. As Pepper left, Harper decided she'd get to the calls and other duties in a moment. It was time to see if Paris had left her any clues.

She retrieved her sister's laptop from the bottom desk drawer, popped it open, turned it on, and realized she didn't know the password. She tried "stud," "racegirl" (her old one), "marypoppins" (her favorite movie), all without luck. Harper glanced out the door to see if Pepper was off the phone. Not yet.

After several more tries, including "Glenmorangie" (their favorite scotch), "Dakota" (their first dog), and "goodtrip,"

Harper hit gold with "Zydeco" and the laptop's desktop came on screen. Paris had several spreadsheets lined up on the desktop; one by one Harper opened them.

She had the summer races listed on the first one—Sugarland and Deacon's few races where highlighted, the purses they'd won noted. They'd done well, earning the stud money in their juvenile year. Harper made a mental note to call Tim Bradford about Sugarland's condition. She'd had Marshall trailer him to the hospital the day of the injury.

She hefted the heavy studbook from her briefcase and extracted the sheets on which Paris had run pedigrees of their other racers, comparing them to her spreadsheet. She studied both for about ten minutes, and slowly began to understand what her sister had been doing; the horses Paris had noted fell into two groups—the first were horses who'd done well on the track and the second were the several who'd been injured or who had died last spring. It seemed an odd combination.

Harper stared out the window, out past the bald cypresses' finely cut chestnut leaves, to the pond just beyond fringed in frost.

An odd combination . . . Unless Jen had been right. Maybe what she was looking at was Paris' investigation of doping. But Harper couldn't see the complete picture. She'd need to talk to Mary Edvers and Tim Bradford.

Funny how she'd so easily put aside Cooley Edison. Maybe she'd ask him first; after all, he was the stud's vet till the end of the year.

His heated argument with Evan came to mind. Harper would ask him about that, too.

"Pepper?" she called and looked up. Of course, Pepper was already at the door, her brown chin-length pageboy framing a face that looked about sixteen years old.

"How you holding up?" she said, folding her slim arms and coming over to sit on the black leather loveseat in front of Paris' desk.

Her desk now, Harper realized.

"I'm fine," she said. "You have some time for a couple of things?"

Pepper smiled. "Of course, I have time, what's up?"

Harper told Pepper to get Cooley on the phone and put a call in to Tim Bradford. She started to rise. "And when's Mary due in?" she said.

"She might be in this weekend," Pepper said, heading out the door. "I'll have her call you first thing." After a few moments, she buzzed Harper on the intercom to let her know Cooley was due at the farm in a few minutes and would stop by while Tim Bradford would return her call when he was finished his vet checks over at Brookfield.

Harper opened the financial spreadsheet next. Her first response was a short gasp. Her second was physical revulsion. Harper was used to looking at numbers and these were not good. She blinked, checked the document title thinking that she must not be looking at the quarterly reports for the last year. But that's exactly what it was.

She had no idea the stud had money problems. Paris had said nothing about Eden Hill being in financial jeopardy. But looking at the bottom line, clearly, they were in trouble.

Harper felt like she'd been dropped down a rabbit hole. Paris had not told her about the apparently deadly conversation with

Steve, said nothing about possible horse doping, and not one word about their financial straits.

Did she even know her sister?

Harper docked the spreadsheet, wondering what the hell else Paris had not told her, and opened the spreadsheet on their horse sales. Marshall generally oversaw what horses the stud acquired and which ones they sold and made recommendations to her and Paris. There were no significant acquisitions, but they seem to have sold off some fillies, colts, and yearlings—an unusual amount of horses had gone out the door in the past year, and especially in the last six months. Harper had heard nothing about it. Maybe Paris was trying to raise money to offset their financial difficulties. But the prices seemed like a fire sale—a six-month long fire sale.

Speaking with Marshall shot up on the priority list.

"Cooley's here." Pepper's tinny voice came on over the phone's intercom.

And in he walked. Or stomped might be the best way to describe it.

"So, was there some reason you didn't wait on me to look at Sugar?" he said, fiddling with his black-framed glasses. He was angry, that was clear. No pleasantries, no how are you doing. Cooley was all business.

"And good morning to you," Harper said, pushing back from the desk a bit. A confrontation seemed inevitable. "You seemed intent on looking in on Red's mare. If you recall. But we can discuss that in a minute," she said, glancing at the clock. "First I need to talk to you about something else." Might as well check out Jen's—and, she guessed now—Paris's suspicions.

He walked further into the room but did not sit down.

69

At the fundraiser, Harper had told Mariel she'd pick up Avalon, an old racehorse of her father and Red's that couldn't make it any longer in the pasture; she'd bring him home to live out his life in the comfort of his own, warm stall and turnout. Mariel had wanted Cooley to look at a wound on one of her mares, so it seemed they could kill two birds with one stone if they went together.

"I'm headed to Cedar Run. We can talk on the way over if you can spare the time for that mare now," Harper said and he nodded, but still had that hard set to his jaw.

In the waiting room, the two ran into Red.

"Check on that package I had sent up from Argentina, if you would, little girl," he was saying to Pepper who scowled at him then looked under the counter and shook her head.

"Hey, Red," said Cooley, squinting through his glasses.

"Well looky here," he said, turning to them both with a big grin. He raised his ball cap and settled it back on his balding head. "Where you off to now in such a rush?" he finished as Harper passed him.

"Picking up Avalon. I'm putting him in a stall," she replied, her hand on the doorknob.

"That old man? Nothin' but an ole pasture ornament," said Red, smirking. "Needs a bullet between them eyes is all."

The mention of shooting horses brought to mind the theft of their mares and made Harper shudder. Who knows where they might end up; slaughter was not at all out of the question.

"You mean that horse who brought you a check every time he hit the track?" she said, turning and motioning to Cooley who trailed behind her as she headed for the truck. Red's comment irritated her—whether it was his odd attempt at humor or not—

70

Avalon had run with heart and made that man a lot of money. Racehorses were not disposable commodities; that attitude led down a long, dark road ending in drugs, breakdowns, and a bad end for everyone.

The drive to Mariel's was marked by tension and silence. Cooley was clearly unhappy with Harper. They trudged up the hill to Mariel's barn and after Cooley examined the mare's leg wound, Harper helped him clean and wrap it. Seemed as good a time as any to ask him about the horses they'd lost.

"You think some of the horses who were injured and the colt we lost might have been drugged?" she said, handing him the cold-water hose. No use beating around the bush.

Anger flared on Cooley's long, lined face. "Who said that?" he demanded. He again fiddled with his glasses and seemed agitated.

Harper didn't say anything. He had to have heard it, if even Jen suspected it.

He hosed down the open wound and washed it while Harper stood at the horse's head, steadying her.

"Naw, that's ridiculous." Cooley waved his hand at Harper. "Not on my watch, girl." He looked up from his crouched position. "Coward's way of winning if you ask me," he said more quietly.

"Then what happened to them, Cooley?" she said, looking down at the top of his head. "We've never had so many losses."

"Put her in them cross ties," he said, and she moved to the cortisone tube and wraps after hooking the mare up. "Trained 'em too hard, maybe," he said, glancing back at her as she squeezed out some cortisone cream onto his finger. "Rode 'em wrong, bad trip, any number of reasons. You'll need to ask Marshall about that." He shifted his weight and dabbed on the cream. "It's a bad game sometimes, you know that." He

71

shrugged and reached back for the cotton wrap. "Bad luck. Hits everyone at some time or another."

Well, one thing was a certainty: it wasn't the jockey. Evan Mendoza, notwithstanding his fight with Cooley at the training track, was a cool customer who didn't make mistakes. At least not ones that got their horses killed.

Harper studied Cooley for a moment, poised to ask him about his fight with Evan but her intention gave way to pity. Cooley'd had a rough go these last few years with Emma. It couldn't be easy watching the love of your life waste away right before your eyes. They'd been married over forty years.

He stood up, unrolled the cotton wrap while Harper cut off a section, and patted the mare's neck. She stood quietly in the crossties, used to being handled.

Harper admitted she respected Cooley; he was good at his job and good with the horses. He looked at Harper, feet planted, hands on hips. He was shaped like a pear and looked slightly ridiculous.

"Let's finish," she said gently, motioning to the mare's leg. She'd save her questions about his spat with the jockey until later.

He sank down, checked to make sure the cream covered the wound, and vet-wrapped the bandage in place before putting the mare in her stall.

Then it was just the two of them in the barn aisle. Cooley's anger again surfaced.

Time to deal with Sugarland. "So, let's talk about the colt. You're upset, I take it." Actually, he seemed furious.

Harper's opening only stoked his anger. "I'm your vet of record. No need to be callin' in some youngster," he said, referring to Bradford, biting the last word off as if it left a bad taste in his mouth. "I'm not out the door yet."

"No, you're not," Harper agreed. She reminded him that he could have stayed but decided to leave their colt in the lurch to take care of Red's mare. Sugar had ended up in the hospital. "And since Paris had intended Tim to come on the first of the year after you retire, it seemed right he look at the colt," she finished.

Down the short drive, Harper saw Mariel's Audi making its way up to the house. They'd best finish the conversation. Not one she'd want Mariel a part of.

Cooley smirked. "So, it's Tim now." He rubbed his hands on his pants, smoothing out the nonexistent wrinkles. Suddenly his attitude changed. "I'd like to talk to you about that." His tone had lost its edge; he seemed furtive. "I'd like to renegotiate my retirement."

"Renegotiate, how?" Harper said when he paused and seemed unsure of how to proceed. She gazed at the stalls and the square bales in front of them. This was not the place to be having this conversation.

"I'm not ready to retire," he said, sticking his chin out a bit. "I'd prefer to stay on." The edge was back.

Lord, thought Harper, he was an emotional rollercoaster. In deference to his decades with them, she and Paris had discussed his retirement at length over the last year. Their conversations and her encouraging encounters with Tim Bradford coupled with the demands Cooley's wife's cancer made on his time, made it clear to Harper that keeping him on was not a good idea. Surely, he must realize how much Emma needed him at the moment.

Harper sighed. "Cooley," she began, her voice softer, "I don't think we'll be able to do that."

Around them, the horses shuffled in their stalls and issued a few snorts, picking up on the tension.

He shook his head. "I been with you all for thirty-odd years now. Or more. Devoted myself to you and Red. That means nothing?" The anger flared again. "I'm asking you. I would like to stay on." He seemed anxious now as well as angry.

"Cooley, Emma needs you," she said, trying to reason with him as Mariel exited her car and headed up to the barn.

Harper knew the stud was Cooley's main source of income, but the last time she'd seen Emma, the woman looked weak and pale. The cancer treatments were taking a huge toll. Cooley had a nice retirement income in the offing; surely, he could see his wife's needs took precedence.

"We all came to this decision together," Harper reminded him.

"You don't understand," he said, getting up. "You just use folks and throw 'em away." He waved his hands at Harper disgustedly.

"No, Cooley, you know that's not true," she said. This was very hard. Cooley had been with them for so long.

"Not true? All those nights I stayed up with your sick foals. All those nights your daddy called me and I came rushing over. And when I was needed, whenever you all needed me, did I not come? Did I not do right by you and your daddy?"

Cooley's voice was raised. Harper didn't think Mariel could be missing much.

"Of course, you did," she said softly, not knowing what to think of this outburst. "We always appreciated everything you've done. Over all the years."

A breeze wafted through the barn, lifting a few sparse hairs on Cooley's otherwise bald head.

"So that's it then," he said. "So now when I ask this one favor, something that would save you a lotta work—you wouldn't have to change a thing—you're not gonna help me out?"

Mariel stepped through the doorway and waved.

"Cooley, we can't do this," Harper said, stepping close to him. "We all talked this over—you, me, and Paris—and we all agreed. We have to bring on a new vet now, we can't have your attention sporadically or when Emma doesn't need you." Things were going to be hard enough without worrying if she could trust Cooley to be there when she needed him.

Evidently, him abandoning Sugar wasn't the first time that had happened; both Paris and Marshall had mentioned it. Right now, the stud was facing huge problems. Eden Hill needed a vet they could count on, and Bradford seemed a perfect fit.

Harper didn't want to insult Cooley, but somehow, he had to accept the change.

"This is painful for both of us," she said, "but we've got to do it. And we have to start the process now. Think about Emma. Think about how much she needs you right now. You have to think of yourself. Of her." Harper nearly pleaded with him.

Cooley suddenly seemed spent. His shoulders slumped and he stared at the floor with an air of resignation. "All right then," he said, "I won't beg." He drew himself up with some semblance of dignity. "Your daddy wouldn't do me like this," he said, pointing a finger at Harper. "He'd be ashamed of you. You know he would."

He glared at her, stomped out of the barn ignoring Mariel, jumped in the truck, and slammed the door. He sat in the passenger seat staring straight ahead.

Harper stared after him in silence.

Mariel eyed her sympathetically and gave Harper a quick hug. "Want to talk?"

She shook her head. "We cleaned the mare's wound. It looks ok. Just change the bandage every two days or so. She should be fine."

Mariel nodded and they both walked toward the pasture to retrieve Avalon, who stood at the fence trying to munch the last of his bucket of slurried senior feed. Harper appreciated that Mariel didn't push the conversation.

"Not many more teeth," she said, smiling at Avalon. He was close to thirty and looked terribly thin. He wouldn't make it another season in the pasture and deserved a warm, cozy stall come winter.

"We'll soak some alfalfa pellets for him. Been through this many times, Mariel."

She smiled. There was a prolonged silence, so Harper turned to her. "Something up?"

Still Mariel didn't say anything.

Harper waited, scratching Avalon's head as he bobbed it a bit, helping her efforts.

"What is it?" she said. Mariel was generally not reticent to speak her mind and the atmosphere had turned suddenly chilly.

She stared out past Avalon into the pasture where the other horses had their heads bent to the sparse grass. "When I get Avalon's papers together for you, I see the vet check when he first arrive." She turned to Harper. "Your dad and Red, they send three horses—Avalon, Sparrow, and Mitchell. All three, they retire. Two injured, one, he have serious injury." She smiled sadly at Avalon.

Harper knew all this. She remembered when her Dad and Red had retired them. "Right. Avalon had a career-ending fracture, Sparrow bowed a tendon, and Mitchell wasn't injured--they just thought he was losing a step and didn't want him to go down."

"Yes, but . . ." Mariel began. She pulled a sheath of papers out of her back pocket, and opened them, not looking at Harper.

She handed them over.

The first page was the vet's findings on all three horses. The two injured ones had tested positive for morphine.

"I not think too much at the time," she said, "I know Rafe."

Harper's father had an impeccable reputation. And horses back then, just as now, were given painkillers legitimately to aid in injury recovery. She glanced at the truck where Cooley sat rigid, his eyes fixed straight ahead.

But morphine?

"When I was in Argentina, they inject the horses' knees with morphine," she said, looking off toward the barn, a pained look on her face. "So they run. And how many broke down . . . Babies." She looked at Harper with anger. "They know and they run them anyway," she continued, holding Harper's gaze. "Then the season we have . . . I know what is happening. I see it before."

Harper knew she had. And she trusted Mariel's knowledge about corruption and drugs. She knew all the signs. But everyone in the racing world knew that drugs were the norm; Lasix and other drugs were legal in many states. But Mariel had darker ideas; she thought there was drug cartel involvement on South American tracks. Harper wondered if she thought it had made its way to the U.S. track. She also wondered if she was overreacting on both counts.

Harper nodded, not sure what to believe. She looked again at the papers Mariel had just handed her. Red. Marshall. Cooley. They'd all been with Eden Hill when Avalon and the others were retired. She didn't want to consider what that might mean. But no matter how it might look, Harper knew it was equally possible that the test results were legitimate efforts on the part of her father and Red to stem pain during the horses' recuperation.

"I'll get to the bottom of this."

"I hope so," Mariel said, turning back to the horses.

After they loaded Avalon, and Harper headed home with Cooley silent beside her, she thought about an even worse possibility; if Eden Hill's horses had been dosed last race season, perhaps the practice stretched back to when her father was still alive.

The idea that Rafe, Red, Cooley, and perhaps even Marshall, could have been involved in illegally doping horses seemed preposterous. Two weeks ago, Harper would have dismissed the notion categorically, but with Paris' and Steve's deaths and everything that had occurred since then, as much as she hated to admit it, she couldn't in all honesty rule that out.

After securing Avalon in his permanent stall and blanketing him, Cooley had stomped off without the courtesy of even a polite goodbye. Harper headed to the office, checked in with Pepper, returned some calls then left with more questions than answers.

She felt in the midst of an oceanic swirl of dark events that every now and then, broke the surface. But what tied them together beneath eluded her.

Chapter 10

She got to Keeneland late, no surprise there, with little time to mill around. This was the earliest part of the race meet, which lasted about three weeks and was primarily for 3-year-olds. The purses were huge, making it well worth the entry if you won. With only two races for two-year old colts, Eden Hill was fortunate they both ran on the same day, an oddity of this year's schedule.

Horse racing is called "The Sport of Kings" and coming to Keeneland always made Harper feel it was just that. In spring and fall, horses are saddled in front of the public under tall paddock trees, while in fall, the elegant, updated but still old-style, grandstands were warmed by the sun. Precisely sculpted green hedges spelled out *Keeneland* in the grassy infield. It was a place of history, founded by Jack Keene who established the track as a venue where beauty, grace, and spirit reigned. It angered Harper that at present the sport was horribly tarnished by drugs born of greed and fueled by corruption.

Deacon was up first, vying for the Claiborne Breeders' Futurity $500,000 purse. Tap Down was slated for the $250,000 Dixiana Bourbon. Both races were eight and a half furlongs—a little over a mile—so it would be a good prep for their 3-year-old racing season.

Given the stud's financial situation, Harper was hoping one of them hit the wire first.

She headed over to the paddock where Deacon was being saddled. It was hard to miss their colt. Whereas Sugarland was all elegant refinement with his finely sculpted head and long legs — he seemed to stretch out and float effortlessly over the track— Deacon was fierce, raw power. From his muscled stallion jaw, aggressive intelligent amber eye to his long neck, laid back shoulder, and that big, square hip that drove like a freight train, you didn't have to see him run to know he'd never back down from a fight. He had that X factor, the thing you can't breed for, what Harper's Grandpa called "the look of eagles," a tenacious, relentless, competitive heart saved for only the rarest of stallions.

She caught up with Marshall leading the colt and all of them walked past the huge sycamore to the walking ring as Evan and the others came out of the jockey room. Marshall gave Evan some last instructions and Harper gave him a thumbs-up. Their jockey, dressed in Eden Hill's pink and orange silks, saluted Harper as Marshall gave him a leg up onto the black colt. Evan was a highly respected jockey, but even he said he could barely keep Deacon under control. Harper had missed his summer races and had only seen a summer pre-race workout, when Marshall had the exercise rider blow him out. Deacon looked explosive.

She turned, searching for Surrey's portly figure and shoulder-length white-gray hair. There she was, right in front of the huge crowd, so Harper headed over through the throng of spectators lining black wrought iron rail.

"Mercy," Surrey said when she saw Harper, grabbing her hand. "I swear that colt takes my breath away." She grinned at Harper like a schoolgirl with a crush on the quarterback.

"He's something," she agreed, and the pair headed to the grandstands.

Harper chose to watch the race where her Grandma Eden had always taken the girls, to the grandstand, as close to the finish line as possible rather than in the members-only clubhouse. That's where Surrey and Harper headed, picking up Lucas and his wife Alia at the bottom step as they'd arranged earlier.

"Here to see that colt of ours make a mess of the field?" chirped Lucas, grinning. As stallion manager, he handled Deacon when Marshall didn't have him. Harper thought Lucas admired Deacon's bad attitude a bit too much.

Alia reminded her of Tinkerbelle. She was small-boned and finely featured, and with that short little bob Harper half expected her to flutter up off the steps as they mounted to their seats. Alia was in charge of all the farm plantings, season to season, and any designs for client brunches or meetings the stud had. Lucas and Alia looked an unlikely match—she was small and petite while he was built like a refrigerator, his big, strong body reflecting the South African wrestler he once was.

Alia punched her husband in the arm in response to his sassy comment about Deacon. He grabbed her as the group edged its way past patrons to their seats, tickling and grinning at her, the dimples at the corners of his mouth deepening. "Alia tagged along, as usual," he joked.

"Settle down, you two," said Surrey, who loved them both dearly. "No squabbling among the children."

Once they were seated, Alia passed Harper a large portfolio, whispering "Some ideas for the buffet and holiday plantings."

Eden Hill had a buffet for clients every year during the Keeneland meet when even those from abroad were in town. This year, of course, things were on hold. But maybe, thought Harper, they'd best try to schedule it given the financial straits the stud was in. Clients at the farm were more likely to leave some money behind, and they sorely needed it.

81

The stands were filled with the fancy and the favored—all the serious horsemen who'd surveyed this crop of 2-year-olds had taken notice of Deacon, now the odds-on favorite.

Marshall found them as the twelve hopefuls loaded into the starting gate. He scooted Alia over next to Lucas and plopped down between Surrey and Harper.

She asked Marshall where Dylan was; he shrugged and focused his binoculars on the starting gate just as they went off.

Deacon broke well from the outside post and dropped toward the middle of the track. Even this far away, Harper could see Evan was checking the big colt, keeping him well off the pace. Deacon switched leads into the turn and went up the far side in the middle of the track, getting boxed as the other horses closed in around him.

She looked at Marshall who seemed cool with it. He and Evan always had a plan.

"Fast quarter mile," Harper said softly, and Marshall nodded. The fractions seemed blazing.

"Speed horses up front," said Marshall. "I told Evan to keep Deacon in hand, watch for his move."

Holding Deacon back wasn't easy. "Good luck with that," Harper said, smiling to herself, watching the big screen in the infield as the pack rounded the far turn into the backstretch. Evan had Deacon in the center lane, his tiny pink and orange form riding still and composed atop Deacon's huge body. To Deacon's left, Hannondale, a California colt, seemed to come out of nowhere, heading up on the rail. In a moment he'd shot past the pack toward the clearing between the frontrunners and Deacon's boxed bunch.

Deacon saw Hannondale and there was nothing Evan could do. The black colt bolted outside as they rounded the far turn—he was making a very long trip for himself, yet eating up ground as he went. Marshall put the binoculars up to his eyes and pursed his lips.

"That is one head-strong colt," he said, taking them off and handing them to Harper. She tried to find the pack before they turned for home and located Deacon, finally, there on the outside moving like he had wings, Evan hunched over his neck just trying to hang on. Deacon was flying.

Then Hannondale and Deacon closed in on each other as Deacon passed the pack and the two frontrunners faded, sinking quickly behind the two new leaders. Hannondale was no slouch, but his rider was already showing the stick. Evan generally saved that for late in the stretch, but it didn't look like he'd need it this trip. As they rounded the turn, everyone rose to their feet, screaming for Deacon.

And then Evan turned him loose. It was as if Deacon had one moment been jogging and then somebody flipped his switch. Deacon lowered his center of gravity, dug in, and shot forward in a leaping bound, and Harper felt the world suddenly go into slow motion. Deacon was monstrous, stretched out, ears flat back, flying effortlessly down the track, his long, fine tail sailing out behind him, his muscles rippling as if the whole world boiled down to his fluid, effortless power and motion. Forward he charged, lengthening his lead, surging past the grandstands to a sound so loud Harper's eardrums vibrated.

Evan's hand shot up to the sky as they crossed the finish line, Deacon breathing white steam that could have been fire.

Surrey grabbed Marshall, and Marshall grabbed Harper, and they all flung themselves down the grandstand steps with Lucas and Alia racing behind as the crowd continued to scream and applaud. Deacon had demolished the field, just as Lucas had predicted. He'd won by four lengths and had the race been longer, his lead would have only increased.

They got to Evan as he dismounted. A photographer snapped a photo of them all as Evan reached around Deacon's huge neck and planted a big kiss on the colt's cheek while the rest of them looked on, grinning like crazy. Deacon turned regally toward the camera, his neck arched like a god. Which, at that moment, Harper could almost believe he was.

After they cooed over Deacon, who had only disdain for them, and sent him for his cool-down, clean up, hay, sweet feed, and his bottle of beer, they all bid Evan goodbye since he was due up on Tap Down race after next. The rest headed for food at the Lafayette Room. Marshall got slapped on the back any number of times on the way there, with Surrey looking demure and proud as she could be at the same time. Harper thought momentarily about pulling Marshall aside to talk about the "fire sale" among other things but changed her mind, putting that conversation off until later; they all needed the moment of joy—there'd been precious little of it lately.

Harper thought lunch might be a good time to talk with Alia and Surrey about getting the buffet together. With Deacon as a calling card, she felt they should definitely go forward with the client buffet if at all possible.

As they entered, she saw Red at a table by the window conferring with a South American client he'd recently garnered for the stud; Emilio Moreno, who looked to be a man of about thirty five, had sent one of his broodmares all the way from Argentina to breed to one of Eden Hill's premier studs since they weren't sending him abroad this year. Harper took it they had horses in upcoming races.

She hadn't met Moreno yet, so she excused herself and went to Red's table, offering her hand.

Moreno rose to take it while Red remained seated. "Sorry to intrude," she said to Red, who nodded with a brief, stiff smile. He still seemed miffed about their previous encounter. He was not a man who easily got over hurt feelings.

Harper turned to Moreno. "I'm happy to meet you. Paris mentioned you'd be in for the Keeneland meet."

Moreno nodded politely, but his eyes shifted to Red. He didn't seem comfortable meeting Harper's gaze. As if reading her thoughts, he turned back to her, his dark head shiny with gel, his eyes taking Harper's measure in a way that sent a slight chill up her spine.

"May I congratulate you on your win, just now," he said, bowing his head slightly. He had a formal way about him.

Red seemed intent on his food. He glanced up and added his own congratulations.

Harper smiled and thanked them both, reticent to mention the buffet they were about to plan, though as a new client, Moreno should certainly be there. Red fiddled with his drink.

Glancing down, the watch on Moreno's wrist caught Harper's eye. It looked eerily similar to the one she and Paris had given Steve Hamilton, including two silver links inserted next to the watch face in an otherwise gold band. Harper searched Moreno's face as he shot his cuff over the watch and smiled. Perplexed and a little unnerved, she excused herself and went to the table where her party had been seated.

Of course, the watch wasn't a commissioned design; Moreno could have purchased it at a jeweler, just as the sisters had. Still, something about the man made Harper uneasy. She turned back briefly to the two men; Moreno and Red seemed again deep in conversation and took no further note of her. Harper shrugged. Who knew what went on in Red's world.

As it turned out, the buffet planning lasted well past the next race, so Lucas and Marshall excused themselves, needing to meet up with Dylan so they could watch Tap Down's race together. This was Dylan's second, and Harper thought possibly last, chance to impress Marshall. She hoped for the best but was very happy with the winnings Deacon had just garnered for the stud.

The women sat at a window in the dining room, so they could watch the race and still finish their plans.

"Don't worry about a thing," Surrey said, patting Harper's hand as she always did. "I'll see to the food myself, and with Alia's flowers, and your mother's fine crystal and china, it's a no brainer." She grinned and looked pleased with herself for using such a catchy phrase.

Harper laughed. It felt good to laugh. Deacon's winnings and these two wonderful women did a lot to bolster her spirits. She nodded, Red and Moreno far from thought.

"Just a walk in the park," Harper added, since they were doing clichés.

Alia reached into her large portfolio and pulled out a blank sheet of paper and they began the guest list. Harper would call the stationery store they worked with first thing Saturday morning and get the invitations started. She knew Pepper would have no trouble discovering where everyone on their list was staying; she'd have the invitations delivered by early next week.

Harper's phone rang. Tim Bradford returning her call from that morning. She answered and he had a cheery, "Well, I have good news for you."

Harper so appreciated when people you're nervous to talk to let you know, up front, all is well. She sighed with relief. "Tell me," she said, and felt they were old friends.

"Sugarland's got just what I thought, a condylar fracture. And not too bad, really."

"Well, that's good news, Tim. Thanks so much for letting me know quickly." She looked from Alia to Surrey, giving them the thumbs up.

Tim continued. "It'd be an operation, stall rest after, some hand-walking—maybe two months total. Then a couple months of paddock exercise."

Harper was relieved beyond measure. She wasn't sure he'd get in much training next season, but she felt optimistic. They'd take it slow with Sugarland, not jeopardize his career. Deacon would have to shoulder the load, but Harper felt he was up to it. "Can I call you after we're done here at Keeneland?" she said. "I want to hear everything, but we're kind of in the middle . . ."

Tim said fine, and they were done. What good news after so much bad. Now they really would have two budding stars— Deacon and Sugar would be good to go sometime during next year's racing season if all went well.

Harper raised her glass of Chardonnay, looking at Alia and Surrey, happy for the first moment in what seemed like forever. They toasted, and she had the feeling that just maybe the tide had turned. Alia grinned and Surrey winked at her, clinking her glass of water.

A sudden cry from the clubhouse crowd caused Harper to turn toward the windows. Gasps made her rise and shouts sent her racing to see what happened on the track. She heard the ambulance siren, the bad feeling rising in her like a swift tide. Please, she thought, please let it not be . . . Then she saw Tap Down. He lay writhing on the track ahead of all the other injured horses who had evidently piled onto him as he went down. Evan's trampled body was just beyond, bloody and twisted in horrible angles.

Harper couldn't comprehend the scene. She saw it, but nothing registered. She stared without blinking. Her mind had frozen. She couldn't breathe. Her mouth opened to scream but nothing came out. Surrey grabbed her, trying to turn her away, but Harper wrenched out of her arms, transfixed by the carnage on the track. Photographers rushed from the sidelines, snapping shots, racing from one broken, screaming horse to another, while Evan's body lay still as stone on the track.

Marshall leaped the fence, Dylan behind him, Lucas already nearing Evan's body, as the ambulance pulled up and two medics leapt out. An hour before, he'd raised his hand in triumph and kissed his beloved colt. And now. And now, nothing.

The equine van arrived, and the vet set about doing the dark business of contacting owners, loading what horses he could, and euthanizing the rest on the spot.

Still, Harper couldn't speak or move. Around her, people talked, maybe to her, but she heard nothing. she could only see Evan, so still. And Tap Down, and all the other beautiful, courageous horses. All so still, so quiet.

There wasn't a sound in the world.

Chapter 11

Overnight the temperature dropped forty degrees. Snow fell and by morning the world was blue-white.

Harper spread the front page of the Lexington *Herald-Leader* on the kitchen's granite island, standing there in her robe, her palms planted on the cold stone, staring at the photo of Evan kissing Deacon's cheek, the rest of them crowding around, frozen smiles of victory on their faces.

She'd folded the other photos beneath. She didn't need to see them—the scene in her mind was so clearly etched it would never be erased.

Harper studied every detail of that photo: how Deacon's great neck bent to Evan's height; Evan's closed eyes and his gentle hand twined in Deacon's mane. Reverence and joy caught in its fleeting perfection.

Evan had made it halfway to the hospital. He'd been dead on arrival.

The phone rang incessantly. Mary Edvers called, leaving a message, then Marshall. The feed store wanted to know if they needed more senior feed for Zydeco. When John Henry called, Harper picked up, asked him to make sure Avalon was blanketed; he was too old and thin for such drops in temperature. Marshall showed up at the door, but she didn't move from the kitchen. Surrey called. Alia.

Harper folded the front page, dressed, stuck it in the pocket of her down coat, and walked through the quiet, snowy world to

Paris' grave. Someone had laid white lilies and Bells of Ireland across the low mound. Who could that have been? she wondered idly. Certainly someone who knew her well: those were her favorite flowers.

Harper sat in the snow and turned her face up, thinking of nothing, letting the large, cold flakes melt, one by one, until, like a cold rain, they ran down her face. The cold felt . . . right, somehow.

She wondered if Paris looked down on them all. Harper hoped not. She hoped her sister was somewhere filled with light so brilliant all this darkness couldn't penetrate.

She got up finally and walked to the painting studio her dad had built long ago, her hair wet with snow. Inside Harper put on Mozart and turned up the volume. She felt like she'd swum out on some huge unseen current so far, the land had dropped away. Even if she wanted to get back, she had no idea in which direction to go.

Harper walked to the wall-sized canvas she'd stretched last summer, bringing the Mason jar full of brushes and her oils along. She painted, submerged in the music, laying on color, imposing form on its chaos, painting over it all. She thought of Motherwell painting *Ode to the Spanish Republic* in a blinding New York snowstorm, and looked out the wall of windows onto her white world. A comforting view where all vitality was erased by blankness, a complete, colorless void.

She turned back to her painting—an act of beauty she could destroy at any moment.

After a time, Harper left, wandering the farm in the freezing temperatures, not wanting to go back to the house. At length, she found herself beside the small barn where quarantined horses were stalled when they first arrived. She saw Sheriff out in the attached paddock and supposed John Henry had turned him out for a bit, just to get his legs moving. He stood by himself, head lowered in the snowy cold.

He'd come from a Midwest racetrack, abused and so, like all beaten things, he was terrified and angry. Paris had retrieved him from Cedar Run shortly before her death. Evidently, she'd seen through how unmanageable he appeared, and felt there was something promising in him; she was excited about his prospects off the track.

As Harper passed through the barn door, Kelso came barking up to greet her, startling the big bay. He reared as Harper came through the barn and out to where he stood on his hind legs, his white blaze gleaming in the sunlight that had just broken through the gray snow clouds. She thought it an extreme response to a bit of barking, but then remembered Sheriff had recently come off the track and was likely on edge.

The familiar scent of alfalfa and sweet feed drifted over her. Only a short time ago, she'd been in a city full of bustle and business. Now, here in this place, she felt as disoriented as the horse in front of her. Sheriff came down heavily then raced around the plowed enclosure, rearing and squealing in fear, the whites of his eyes rolling toward and away from Harper.

Without thinking, she clicked the paddock gate open and entered. Sheriff's entire focus was on escape not on Harper. *Darling boy*, she thought, not knowing what horrid people had done to him; something that had hurt him deeply if Kelso's happy barks startled him into full flight. Sheriff didn't need to live this way—always on the brink of terror.

She watched as he wheeled and charged at will. She knew he might well charge her, given his panic. His nervous snorts came quickly as he cantered off in anxious circles.

Harper stood quietly, telegraphing her calm and willingness not to push him. Stepping to the middle of the paddock, she murmured quietly, "Whoa, boy, it's okay." She spoke softly and slowly. Standing still as she could in the circle's center, she tracked Sheriff's deep red-brown bay body as he raced the perimeter, snorting nervously, his tail flagged, his neck high and stiff.

Poor boy. She pivoted slowly as he continued his panicked fleeing, stepping as she could at an angle in front of his shoulder to slow him. In the brightening day, she watched him circle, continuing her soft murmur, assuring him he was safe. Finally, she saw his inside ear turn toward her as she spoke to him, and Harper quieted further. His stiff ears and high, tight neck began to soften a little as he sensed maybe she wasn't there to harm him.

He slowed to a trot, his head lowering a bit, his ear again twitching toward her.

His attention had finally gone to Harper, not to the fear running rampant inside him. She smiled, relieved. "It's okay, boy," she murmured, wishing she'd brought a carrot. Or a halter. "Nothing to fear here . . ." She continued pivoting as he trotted, keeping her body as still as possible, her voice calm. "No one's gonna hurt you here," she said, keeping up the calmness she hoped to instill in him.

Sheriff licked his lips and began the chewing motion Harper knew meant he was listening, calming, and maybe beginning to trust her a little.

93

She hadn't planned on this . . . But she'd been drawn by something. The need to help? The need to heal something?

"I get you, boy," she continued. "It's okay, you're going to be just fine. Good boy." After a few minutes more, she pivoted her shoulder away from him, hoping he'd respond.

He slowed and finally stopped, considering Harper. Then, head lowered, he quietly walked toward her, stopping at her shoulder.

She turned gently, speaking quietly to him, "What a good boy," she told him. Trust is the first step. It's always the first step in conquering fear. *And grief.* Again saddened by the loss of her sweet sister and all else that had gone on, Harper wanted so much to trust that something good would come of all this pain.

She ran her hand slowly and lightly down Sheriff's big bay neck, then up again, scratching him behind the ear and along the crest of his mane. He stretched out his neck, cocked his back leg and Harper knew he'd broken through his terror.

The first step on a long road back. She bedded him down in a stall, stayed with him until he began munching his hay then headed for the house.

An hour later, the florist stood on the doorstep with a tissue-wrapped bouquet. Once inside and unwrapped, Harper saw they were red roses. No one else had sent flowers after the track accident, so the gesture was singularly odd. The typed message accompanying them was simple, "Sorry to hear of your loss. Hope you're careful. Wouldn't want an accident happening to you, too."

Those last words chilled Harper. She flipped the card over; it wasn't signed on either side. She took the flowers to the sink, reluctant to find a vase. Red roses were something you'd send to a lover, not as a condolence. It angered Harper, but she wasn't sure why.

She opened the cabinet and found a vase but put the roses in an alcove off the kitchen where she wouldn't see them.

The next day was Sunday and Surrey came to stay with her. She did simple things, taking care to leave Harper alone, not speaking to her, sensing her need for silence. She mothered Harper—made fluffy eggs and bacon, served it with orange juice. She answered all the phone calls, made a fire, wrapped Harper in her grandmother's afghan. She slept there on the couch and woke, then dozed again. All day they did this—Surrey the comforter. She made tea with honey. Popcorn. Pasta with vegetables. Simple things. Warmth, food, comfort. Maybe love. If it was love, Harper couldn't feel it.

The world had simplified: sleep, safety, one day of peace.

Chapter 12

Monday arrived and found Harper headed up to Cincinnati to meet with the stud's bankers. Two balloon payments were soon coming due, which Deacon's winnings would help pay off, but they were also calling in a note Harper thought they'd have at least a year more to pay. She was hoping a face-to-face would head that off at the pass. She'd also made an appointment with her lawyer to see about a new will; she'd been putting that off, but it needed to be done.

On the drive, as fall rushed by in a blur, Harper spoke with Mary Edvers. Pepper put in the call and mentioned Mary had wafted into the stud office wearing a bright orange polyester caftan from her cruise, flipping her signature dyed black braid behind her back, and sporting a huge turquoise necklace that clanged against her hefty bosom. Harper laughed at the image, not at all surprised. Pepper chuckled before buzzing Mary and putting her on the phone.

Mary had come to the stud as a very young woman, a protégé of Harper's father, at the start of her bloodstock agent career. She'd developed a stunningly successful breeding system, but her arrogance made her a difficult person to be around. Rafe found her nearly impossible to deal with, but he was not one to argue with success, so Mary stayed on and Harper tried to stay out of her way.

She had gone over Paris' notes and agreed that she'd been right to be suspicious; in Mary's words there were a few too many "flashy finishers" in the group of winners Paris had listed. And, based on their breeding, conformation, and assessed potential, the ones that had been injured or died—those on Paris' other list—she felt could have had some illegal "help" or maybe been injured, put on a pain killer, and trained or raced anyway. Too, she noted, some of them were entered into longer races than they'd been bred for.

In short, she felt Paris' concerns about doping were warranted. But then, of course, Mary being Mary, she concluded with "Let me be clear. You can't tell everything by a pedigree or conformation . . . Attitude. Training. Luck. Heart. They all count. All those winners, they could be legit. You can't make an average horse run beyond its means. Then again, nothing's impossible in this business."

Harper sighed, maneuvering around a semi-tractor trailer and speeding on toward the bridge crossing the Ohio River. The day was bright and clear, with a slight chill. Though Mary hadn't confirmed anything, she had indicated their horses could have been dosed with illegal drugs—it would explain the unlikely winners as well as the injuries and deaths. And if Paris had discovered that their horses had been drugged and who was behind it, that would certainly have put her in danger.

The other call she had on the drive up was much the same. The police said they hadn't found anything new about Steve's death or the theft of Eden Hill's mares. Harper asked about the forensic anthropologist's progress, but they knew nothing about it. Finally, she mentioned the unnerving red roses and the note, but the police didn't take that seriously. All in all, the call was pointless.

Ahead Harper could see the bridge and the sparkling river dotted with barges chugging upriver with their loads of coal and lumber. Pleasure boaters made their way closer to the banks, getting in the few last outings before winter's cold set in. Beyond the river, the city spread out along its banks and Harper figured she'd better get her argument in order; their bankers' offices were in the downtown area.

She was mentally making her case when, out of nowhere, her left front tire blew, sending her SUV careening into the left lane. In an instant the entire scene changed from a normal commute into chaos as a dizzying wave of fear and disorientation washed over Harper. Suddenly, there were cars everywhere, swerving around her, horns blaring as, with a clenched jaw, Harper gripped the wheel and prayed the onrushing traffic could avoid her. The concrete median loomed ahead. The Range Rover headed toward it at high speed. She pumped the brakes trying to gain control. Scowling drivers sped up or slammed on their brakes to dodge a collision while Harper gasped with the effort to steady the wheel, her forearms straining in the midst of horns and screeching tires.

She glanced in the rear-view mirror in the midst of her death grip on the wheel, painfully trying to control a two-ton metal body careening toward a bad crash. The sun shone down serenely, casting a ghastly light on what she realized might be her last moments in one piece.

Harper saw the semi she'd just passed bearing down on her at an alarming speed. She held the wheel with all the strength she had, glancing again in the rear-view mirror to see if it was slowing, then back to the road trying to keep the car from catapulting into its path. At the speed she was going, the outcome would not be a good one.

She continued easing on and off the brakes, straining to urge the car to the right between slowing trucks and cars, maneuvering toward the shoulder, as the semi shot past her on the left, horn blaring and fading, and the cars behind slowed further to give her a path to the side of the road. By then the Range Rover was thump-thumping, jerking to the left even as she steered onto the shoulder, still going too fast for safety. She concentrated as gravel crunched beneath her three good tires and the SUV bumped and slowed, finally halting at the far edge of the road's shoulder. Harper slumped in the seat, her heart hammering inside her chest, her breath coming in gasps.

Harper's parents had died in a car wreck. Suddenly she was a young kid again, walking into the house with Paris, blithely discussing the day's events only to hear the news gently from her Grandpa, her Grandmother standing behind him sobbing.

Harper's stomach heaved. She opened the car door and vomited, wiped her mouth on her sleeve, and slowly sat back in the seat taking a few long, deep breaths.

She scanned the trees to her right, squeezing her eyes shut then open again, trying to focus on the rust and gold fall colors, trying to regain her composure. Around her cars raced north toward the city, no one paying the least attention to her predicament.

As Harper's heart stopped racing and her breathing slowed, rational thought attempted a return. She'd never blown a tire. But she did know how to change one.

A dirty Chevy pick-up pulled in behind her. Harper felt a small relief; someone had stopped to help. Grateful, she craned around to see two men in overalls, one on the phone, the other getting out and stuffing his hands in his pockets. They both sauntered toward the car, the driver flipping shut his old-style phone and pocketing it.

That one came to the driver's side, while the other walked to the passenger side. Harper glanced from one to the other, her relief evaporating, replaced by sudden fear. She couldn't figure out if she was overreacting or had some reason to feel suddenly trapped.

She relaxed. It was mid-morning and there was a lot of traffic. Surely no one would be fool enough to pull something in broad daylight.

The driver had on a worn straw hat, had a scruffy beard and watery gray eyes. The other guy had long, stringy black hair and smiled at Harper.

The driver leaned over, spat on the ground, sneered at the patch of vomit, and bent to look at the tire. Harper didn't know whether to get out or lock the doors.

He stood and smiled, his teeth stained, and knocked on the window. He motioned to the back of the Range Rover as if indicating he would get out the spare, then made a rolling motion with his hand indicating he wanted Harper to roll down the window. Presumably to talk.

Something told her to lock the doors; instead she pressed the down button and opened the window. Cold air shifted into the car as the guy leered at her, then turned to his friend and nodded. He leaned on the window so he was at eye level. "Stop stickin' yer nose inta whut's not yer business," he hissed. "This ain't nothin' compared ta whut'll happen if ye don't pay attention this time."

He stood back, opened the door, hauled Harper out of the SUV and punched her square in the stomach so hard she doubled over. Harper rose as best she could, stunned, but managed a right uppercut to his jaw, her adrenaline surging. He gasped in surprise and shoved Harper hard against the car, pinning her shoulders and heaving a knee into her already injured stomach. No one spoke.

Harper grimaced in pain but managed a stiff kick to his privates as she wrapped her forearms around his and heaved all the weight she could in downward pressure to break his grip. He held on, grinning, as he sidestepped the kick. He snickered at her and shook his head. Then he glanced again at his friend, smiled, and pushed Harper roughly back into the Range Rover. As if on cue, the two men strode to their pick-up, not looking back.

As they pulled out and passed Harper, the driver doffed his hat and sneered at her. Shocked and transfixed by pain, she fell back against the seat, holding her stomach, smelling the vomit on her shoes and, in a weirdly disconnected way wondered if she had internal bleeding. She saw stars then, literally, and passed out either from the shock or the sucker punches, she never did know which.

Harper woke up in the ambulance and instantly insisted on being taken home. Nothing doing, she was told. Evidently, she'd regained consciousness and called Marshall, who'd found her. Hence, the ambulance. Hence the trip to the hospital, which Marshall knew she would not appreciate.

One more thing to talk to him about.

Harper sat in a stark white room with gleaming silver trays and a scary antiseptic scent; hospitals had never been the site of good news to her. She was prodded and x-rayed, questioned, and probed, then released. Harper spoke to the detective on the phone; she wasn't waiting around for his visit. Once out, she felt at last she could breathe again, albeit with pain on the intake.

Everything had happened so fast, Harper hadn't had one moment to think through any of it. *I could have been killed.* And those two men—it didn't take a brain surgeon to realize they'd been following her. But they didn't seem the type to think up that little scheme on their own. Harper thought about the weird roses and saw now they were clearly a threat, not a condolence.

Marshall hadn't left the waiting room, and when Harper was released, he gingerly helped her into his truck where she sat stone-faced thinking through everything that had happened as he drove her home. He glanced at Harper, concern written all over his face.

She broke Marshall's stare and pointed to the highway. He turned his attention there, still the look of concern writ large on his features.

During Harper's phone conversation with the detective, he'd indicated that yes, she would have to come to the station to look at digitalized mug shots. She'd be keeping her appointment with him, it seemed, as soon as possible.

"Maybe best to take it easy for a—" Marshall began.

"Please take me to the office," Harper said. She had work to do, not the least of which was having a serious talk with Marshall. One she wouldn't put off any longer.

If those two slimy guys thought they'd deter her from what was—at least to Harper —clearly now the murder of her sister, probably Steve, and likely a string of doping incidents, they were dead wrong.

Once back in the office, Pepper gave Harper some time then popped in with a toasted bagel smeared with butter. "Thought you might be hungry," she said, placing the white paper plate on her desk.

She wasn't.

Pepper shuffled through a handful of messages and checked her watch. "Marshall said he'd be back in half an hour, and Tim Bradford can come by either around two or about four. What's best for you?" She looked up.

"I think four," said Harper, rubbing her stomach. No internal bleeding, and now that the hospital pain meds had kicked in, she wasn't feeling half bad. Physically—emotionally and mentally, it was a totally different story.

She wasn't sure how long her little talk with Marshall would take. Their history and recent events notwithstanding, what had happened on the track was inexcusable. And then there were all the horses out the door over the last six months. Their conversation would not be pleasant.

"I'll give him a call." She turned to go. "Oh, he said Sugarland should be back by the end of the week, if all goes as planned." She smiled, hoping, Harper knew, that the news would perk her up.

Harper smiled back, still too numb to feel anything.

Marshall arrived shortly after, walked in and sat in the loveseat, crossing his legs, turning slightly to his right as if to avoid Harper. He removed his big Stetson, placed it on the loveseat, ran a hand over the cushion, and folded his arms across his chest.

"Okay," she said, "let's get to it." She'd known Marshall all her life. No use pretending they were having a friendly chat.

Marshall sat forward. "Let me take you home. You're pale, Harper, let me . . ."

"I need to know about the horses we lost at the track," she said. ". . . the weirdly successful winners, the amount of horses sold for nearly nothing, and how in the hell you could allow Dylan to kill our colts."

Harper ticked each one of on the fingers of her left hand. Marshall had a lot of explaining to do and she was not going home until she had answers from him. "And how come no one told me the stud was going bankrupt?" Harper glared at Marshall. There would be no "Sweet Pea" today.

He stared at her, maybe to determine whether she'd give in, let him take her home and escape the conversation. That was not happening; they were having this out.

"Dylan's done," Marshall said, sitting back, lifting his hat off the loveseat and settling it on his knee. "Kept him on this long on account of Paris and your father."

"What do you mean?" As far as Harper knew, Dylan was just another one of the boys she and Paris had hung around with as kids. They'd all been close, especially in high school, but Dylan was not a favorite of her father's, certainly.

Marshall shifted toward Harper and squinted. "You sure you're feeling up to this?"

She shrugged. "I'm fine."

Marshall nodded but Harper knew he didn't believe her. "Paris said your dad expected me to give Dylan a chance. So, I did," he said in answer to Harper's question.

Well, that would be like my father. Rafe loved racing and did everything he could for most anyone who wanted to learn about it. Learn the right way, she reminded herself. At least she trusted that was the case.

"You were his boss," Harper said, stressing the past tense. "You trained him. You were supposed to make sure he did what you told him to. Not kill our damn horses." She was nearly shouting. "And Evan," she said more softly.

Marshall looked stricken. As he should.

"Sweet Pea," he began, but Harper cut him short with a look that sent daggers. He withered, looked down at his knees and was quiet.

"Why didn't you, of all people, call me when the stud was in trouble?"

"Paris—" he began again.

"What possessed you to recommend selling our horses at fire sale prices?" Harper cut in, again raising her voice at him. She cringed at the twinge of pain in her stomach, rustled in her backpack, and popped another pain pill. Marshall looked out the door. Pepper, and anyone within the building, for that matter, could have heard Harper.

"If you want answers," Marshall began, "If you want to hear my side of things . . . you're going to have to stop screaming." He spoke softly, which is always an effective way to get people to shut up.

"Fine, so tell me."

Marshall got up, picked up his hat, went to the coat rack and got Harper's parka. "Let's take a walk," he said, holding her coat open. "If you're up to it." She assumed he meant he wanted more privacy than the office afforded.

Harper acquiesced. He was right, of course. No use airing their dirty laundry in the office.

Out they walked into the brisk day. It was just above freezing, so nothing had thawed, but it wasn't that killing cold of the day before. The two headed over to the stallion complex in silence. The walk calmed Harper down. A little. By the time they reached it, she was ready to listen.

Marshall headed past the wrought iron bench where Harper had sat with Tim Bradford a few days before, and they ended up in the horse cemetery. Crumbling stone headstones lay in one corner—her grandfather's first stallions. She walked among the markers, remembering many of the horses who rested beneath the snow.

"You ready to listen?" said Marshall, bringing Harper to the present moment. He was sitting on the low stone wall surrounding the cemetery.

Harper sat beside him and was silent.

"First off, Dylan," he said, turning on the wall, talking directly to her while she stared straight ahead. "Paris stressed it had meant a lot to your father that I'd taken him on. He's not a bad sort. And after being with me for a few years, he was champing at the bit to try some runners himself. I thought he'd learned enough. My mistake." Here Marshall paused, pulling on the front of his Stetson. "So, I was loosening the reins on him over the past year, giving him more leeway, letting him train, make decisions, while still keeping an eye out."

Not a very focused eye.

"Those horses who went down—if you take the time to look—they were at the first of the racing season. When I saw it, I put the brakes on with Dylan. And at that time last season, no one was having an easy time of it. We all had a bad stretch there." He shuffled his boot in the snow. "Ask around if you don't believe me."

Harper recalled Mariel's speech about drugs at the Farm Managers' Club. Maybe there were more than the usual number of track "accidents" early in the season and that's what sent Mariel off the deep end at the Club. One rider had broken his back, she'd said, and would never race again.

"Okay, but if you didn't think it was all that odd, why put the brakes on Dylan?" she said, returning to the issues last season, her anger still palpable.

Marshall shook his head. "I don't know. I told you, I'm just not that keen on the kid as a trainer. He's got judgment issues. At the very least."

The air was cooler now that they weren't walking. Harper got up and paced, her arms crossed.

"And then we started getting some winners after that. I just thought it was because I was telling him more what to do than before." Marshall rose, too. "And, of course I had Sugarland and Deacon going, and they kinda stole the show." He paused. "So maybe I did miss something. I'm not saying I didn't."

Harper looked at him. His defensiveness was gone; he seemed horribly forlorn and sad.

She looked away. Marshall had been protective of her and Paris longer than Harper could remember. He was someone she talked to, someone she confided in. And, she reminded herself, it was Marshall she'd called when she was attacked; there was something in her that trusted him above anyone else.

Besides, Harper just couldn't bear to see him with that suffering look, mad as she was at him.

"Why didn't Paris call me about the finances? Why didn't you?" she asked, her anger welling again. "Why didn't anyone consult me on selling off all those horses? Why didn't you call me, Marshall, when you *knew* things were bad?"

Harper stomped over to the cemetery's far corner feeling a little childish, to the few crumbling headstones laced with snow. *Here Lay Viscount,* read one in worn script. Next to him were the others: Eddlethorpe, Sultan, and Truefit. All horses whose portraits hung in her home. She brushed off Fireaway's sinking headstone. These were the stud's foundation stallions, the ones her Grandpa had brought over from England. Without these stallions, none of them would be standing here. Marshall joined her.

It seemed to Harper that they'd been spending way too much time in cemeteries.

"Paris loved you, Harper," said Marshall. "She wasn't about to call you home from New York when she knew how happy you were there."

What was he talking about? Of course, she loved Harper. Harper loved Paris, too. Love wasn't the question. They were in business together; Paris had every right to call Harper home. Her sister didn't owe her anything but the truth. *Which she seemed to have gone to great pains to keep from me.*

Marshall put his arm around her. She didn't struggle out of it, but she didn't give in, either. "Paris was real good with breeding, and she could ride like the wind," he said, looking into Harper's face. "But she was no businesswoman," he continued. "She couldn't handle the finances, the decisions about how to run the stud, what horses to buy, which to sell . . ."

"That's why she needed me," Harper said quietly. "And you," she said, looking hard at him, then away.

Marshall turned her around, not allowing her to avoid his gaze. "She knew she needed you." He held Harper firmly by the shoulders. "But she also knew how hard it was for you to leave and she wasn't about to—in her words—'ruin' your life by telling you she was in trouble."

She was right. Harper needed how the art world fueled her painting. That's why she'd left everything to move to New York—to give her work a shot. Harper loved the city's art, its stimulation. It wasn't something you found in the middle of Kentucky. It had put an end to her and JD. Paris knew all that. Paris knew what an impossible choice Harper had made.

She took a deep breath. Paris, she realized, was trying to protect her. Harper had literally given up everything to move to New York. And she had made a success of it; her paintings were selling, and she'd become indispensable to the gallery she worked for.

Harper felt her resolve weakening.

"We argued about it," Marshall said. "But Paris said she could handle things. We could handle things. She knew you'd be back here in a minute if you realized the situation. She needed to prove to herself she was capable of running the stud. She wouldn't budge, no matter how many times I talked to her." He let his arms drop.

Harper glanced at the crumbling headstones, feeling herself going to pieces inside.

"Still," she said, remembering she was there to get to the bottom of Paris' death, "how could you let the farm get in this financial hole? You were here. You should have done something."

"I did," said Marshall. "What do you think the 'fire sale' was all about? I pleaded with folks to buy those horses, Harper, just to keep Eden Hill afloat."

Harper sighed. Against her wishes, her anger began slowly subsiding. She walked the perimeter of the cemetery, inhaling the sharp, cold air, watching a brilliant red cardinal dart in and out of the huge green cedar at the corner of the stallion barn. She hopped to the top of the stone wall as she'd done as a kid, dodging the icy spots, walking the perimeter, thinking, trying to put together the picture Marshall had drawn of the last year. *A year I should have been here. Paris had needed me.*

The fire sale. Marshall had kept Eden Hill solvent, even if by drastic measures. Harper saw that now. He'd always been the quiet one, the behind-the-scenes guy who held everything together. Her heart went out to him. How difficult to love them all so much and know the sisters had to do things on their own if they were to move forward. He could have gone behind Paris' back and filled her in. But he wouldn't do that. So he suffered right along with them, and did what he could to keep the stud going.

And Paris' stubbornness about not contacting Harper sounded just like her.

She looked at Marshall. She was still angry at all the events, but she did see the he'd been there for Paris and Eden Hill. And for her. Suddenly Harper realized what a terrible position they'd put him in. Paris insisting he keep Dylan on and not let her know how much she was struggling while trying to singlehandedly keep the stud afloat.

How could she have doubted him? Well, Harper reminded herself, there was still what happened to Paris to figure out. And

Steve. She was sure their deaths were tied to the doping issue. But, as for Marshall, Harper felt ashamed she'd lost trust in him. She hopped down from the wall and turned to him allowing his fatherly embrace, wishing he'd say those words she'd made him ashamed of earlier.

"What do we do now, Marshall?" she murmured, holding onto him as if for her life.

"Don't worry, Sweet Pea," he said. "We'll figure it out." He pulled back and looked at her. "We're in this together, just like we've always been."

Harper leaned into him, and they both stood there among the graves like two statues worn into one.

Chapter 13

Marshall and Harper agreed to move Deacon and, when he arrived, Sugarland to the stallion barn where Nico, the California stallion, was housed; Lucas could keep a watchful eye on all of them. He'd see to Deacon today.

That stallion barn had bigger stalls, larger paddocks than the others, and Harper had made the decision to put in a security system—something Marshall had been suggesting for some time. The farm had a system in place overall, but Harper wanted something specific for their high-value assets. They'd use part of Deacon's earnings. Until she figured out the doping issue, Harper wasn't taking any more chances with the stud's two best colts.

As it turned out, before she could meet with Tim Bradford, Harper had to run to the police station for her interview; Detective Walker called and said he was available. Harper felt she'd at least be able to get that over with.

The detective was a tall, big-lipped, blond, thoughtful guy who was courteous and took the attack on Harper seriously. They met in his sparsely furnished office, where he said they had a lot to talk about. He told Harper the inspection on the Range Rover revealed her tire had been slit. She'd either have had a blow out or a sudden flat tire.

Harper described what happened. He asked what "business" she was sticking her nose into that had gotten her attacked. She told him she had no idea who'd want to intimidate or attack her or why, which had a smidgen of truth to it—there were so many concerns it was hard to sort them out. Who knew which ones had provoked her being punched and warned off?

Harper looked through all the digitalized mug shots Walker had for her but came up empty. After that, they sat in his office while he flipped through the paperwork quietly; he had Harper's complete file, so she knew Paris' and Steve's deaths were noted there along with the theft of the stud's mares. And, likely, the seven skeletons found on the property. He glanced up momentarily, continued his progress through the file, then called up something on his computer and opened files there, too.

"So, you up for a few questions?" he asked, his eyes still on the computer. "I'd like to start at the beginning."

Harper nodded mutely. She didn't feel up to questions, to be honest, but they'd come now or later. She was there, so now was as good a time as any.

He turned back to the paper file, comparing something there with something on the computer. "Let's start with your sister," he said, glancing up at Harper to gauge her reaction.

Again, she nodded.

"The police and the coroner noted that her head was turned to the side, she had landed on her back, and it appeared that she'd either broken her back or her neck, and that she'd struck a large rock after falling, the one located to the side of her head. The trauma from that was determined to be lethal—the blow to the head just above and behind the ear." He lifted an eyebrow as he turned his computer around to show Harper photos of the scene.

She swallowed hard and turned away.

"Okay," he said. "That's fine," and he swiveled the computer back to himself. "Sorry, I didn't realize you hadn't seen these." He turned back to the computer, continuing, "The findings seem pretty cut and dried." He studied the computer again. "I see here your trainer and the groom, a John Henry, were spoken to about the horse's volatility. Seems he could be a handful?" He looked up at Harper.

"He was a racehorse," she said. But Paris was the best rider she knew. And she and Zeke had a bond. He was like butter in her hands, a dream under saddle when she was aboard.

"I get that," said Walker. "Still, the coroner felt–given the horse's rep—that this was, in fact, an accident." He studied her. "But I'd like to hear what you think." He sat back and folded his hands in his lap, keeping his gaze on Harper.

She wasn't sure how to respond. She didn't know this man. She didn't know how to put what she thought about Paris' death into words that made sense to anyone but her.

But she did know that Paris hadn't died an accidental death.

Whether to say that to Detective Walker was another thing, especially since she had no proof. And because she didn't feel sure about what to say, she said nothing.

He waited. He was a patient man, evidently. After some time, he sat forward, never breaking his gaze, and placed his folded hands on his desk.

"It's okay," he said with some sympathy. "When you feel like talking about it, I'm here." He shuffled some papers together, and turned a few pages, evidently meaning to take the conversation in a new direction.

Harper got up then. There was not going to be any more conversation, at least not today. The photo of Paris on the ground, the wound, the clinical nature of the shot . . . She'd only caught a glimpse, but it would never leave her.

He was not inclined to let Harper go that easily. "Look, I get this is hard, but I do have more questions. I've spoken to your trainer and others, and I've got a pretty good lay of the land, but you're central to all this so we do need to talk further. There are just too many incidents to overlook the clear indication that someone, or some people, have it out for you."

He turned to the computer. "Though the autopsy on your farm manager isn't finished . . ." Here he looked up and gestured to the chair.

Harper remained standing.

"We're waiting on lab tests, but the autopsy determined he died from a self-inflicted gunshot wound to the head. I'm not inclined to agree with that . . . the mares' theft suggest the culprits were surprised by Steve Hamilton and he got shot for his efforts, perhaps, to stop them."

He was quiet, inviting her to add her two cents.

"That's possible," said Harper. "That was my thought, too."

"And you have no idea who is behind this? Why someone tried to make it look like suicide?"

She thought a few moments, but in the end, just shrugged. What could she have said? She had no idea who was behind any of it.

Well, that wasn't exactly true. She had a lot of ideas. That was the problem—so many bad things had happened, and any number of people could be involved. Harper didn't mention the roses again or the weird note since evidently the police hadn't taken them seriously the first time she'd told them. She didn't mention her suspicions about drugs, either. Until she had proof of who was behind all this, or even proof of what was actually going on, there didn't seem a point in spilling her half-baked ideas.

115

Detective Walker nodded, evidently sensing Harper wasn't going to add anything else. He didn't push her further, which she was grateful for. But he did mention he'd be in touch as questions or findings arose. They would be talking again. He also noted he'd be having words with the coroner to see if the forensic pathologist's examination of the seven skeletons on her property could be expedited. He seemed to be covering all the bases, which Harper was glad about. She didn't relish the thought of more interviews, but she would like to know who those seven people were, and how they'd died.

Harper left with the detective staring thoughtfully after her and headed back to the stud, hopefully in time to meet with Tim Bradford; she now had more serious questions for him than in their previous conversation.

At four o'clock Harper was talking with Lucas at the stallion barn when Bradford arrived at the office. Pepper called to say she had sent him over, mentioning that a package had arrived for Steve Hamilton. Harper told her to put it on her desk; she'd see to it when she returned to the office.

She told Lucas to move a groom over to Zydeco's barn and put John Henry and Cheyenne, one of Lucas' best assistants, on 24-hour watch at the stallion barn until the security system went in. He gave Harper a crooked, isn't this over-the-top look, but her stare down said the question was settled.

No more catastrophes, she vowed.

Tim walked in as Harper was finishing up with Lucas.

The stallion manager put out his hand as Tim approached. They shook and Lucas gestured over to Nico who stuck his head out the stall window to see the newcomer.

"We'll be needing some measurements on him pretty soon," said Lucas, looking at Harper, then Tim.

He was talking about measuring Nico's "operative" stallion parts, and so grinned, pretty proud of his innuendo.

"Right," she said. Lucas had the luxury of humor. Right now, Harper did not. It occurred to her, too, that maybe she should have a talk with Cooley about early retirement. *Earlier,* she corrected herself.

Tim raised an eyebrow at Harper. She'd asked him to stop by for something; he seemed interested in getting to it.

The two excused themselves and walked out into what had become an overcast day. Showers soon, it looked like. One day snow, the next it could be balmy. Fickle weather.

Just like fate.

Tim and Harper headed up to the house and perched on the porch steps.

"Sugarland's doing well," he said, settling in on the hard wood. "Should be ready to come back by the end of the week."

At least there was something to be happy about. Behind them the porch and its chairs loomed. Odd they were sitting on the steps, like two kids.

"Yeah, he's going to bounce back fine," said Tim. "Best to take it slow with him, though."

Harper had already decided to do just that. Sugar had potential and possibly a long career ahead of him. They'd assess his future once his recovery was underway; if he needed to be retired, that's what they'd do. Harper wasn't going to jeopardize his health no matter how talented he was. Best case, he'd likely miss the Triple Crown prep races, but Eden Hill had Deacon for that. Harper wasn't worried.

Tim fell silent, waiting until she was ready to broach whatever subject she'd asked him there to discuss.

She pulled her legs up, folded her hands on her knees. "I'd like your opinion about something," she said, turning to look at him. Then it occurred to her he might be wondering about her plans for him as the stud's vet. "Oh, and also talk to you about formally coming on after the first of the year."

He smiled. "Sounds good."

Then Harper brought up the horses who'd been injured and the ones that had died at the track.

Tim was thoughtful a moment, his brown eyes roved over the holly bush at the side of the house. "So, were they fractures? Orthopedic issues, or was it something else?"

She'd talked to Marshall at length about the losses. They'd tried to piece together how the horses looked and acted, too. She'd called Jen and she'd also talked to Lucas. Everyone had the same story—some had gone down due to fractures and then there was the colt who'd died of a heart attack. And just recently, there had been Tap Down—barring evidence to the contrary, Harper was convinced he, too, had been drugged.

The training injuries seemed mostly orthopedic—a hind end bone fracture, scapular fracture, and a cracked sesamoid. Those were the ones she'd heard about. With rest and treatment, some might regain their form and some needed veterinary intervention. Certainly, the horses couldn't continue training. Tim nodded as Harper relayed all this, then his expression turned serious.

"Well, here's the thing. These days, one thing cheaters focus on is enhancing red blood cells to increase oxygenation—the more oxygen the better the breathing. The better the breathing, the more stamina, and the less deceleration the horse experiences. More staying power. Just like Lance Armstrong and the rest of them. Same deal."

Harper nodded, remembering what Jen had said about the horse she watched who'd died.

"Also, cobalt—horses naturally have it in their system. The horse gets dosed over time and when it runs, the vet check after doesn't reveal anything abnormal."

She nodded.

"And then there's the legal meds. Lasix, for instance. It's legal everywhere—it prevents bleeding in the lungs, but it's also a diuretic so some folks think it flushes out evidence of other drugs. And, of course, the labs can't detect all the illegal drugs out there." He shook his head. Seemed he was as disgusted as a lot of people in the racing industry.

He continued. "The real bad guys are using designer drugs— they're expensive, come mostly from Canada, China, and Mexico. They're EPOs, like what Armstrong used, and they aren't detectable. But they are really expensive, and you usually need a connection in the human medical system to get them."

Tim shifted around so he was facing Harper, his eyes now dark and very serious. "That's why I asked about the types of injuries they had. If a horse—especially a young horse—develops micro-damage, a slight injury, not a full-blown fracture . . . and you run that horse on a pain killer—either in training or racing him—could be that slight injury turns into a catastrophic fracture."

Harper wondered about Tap Down; she'd caught two of his wind-downs after workouts and the last time he looked off at the trot. Sounded exactly like what Tim was describing.

"So, let's say you're using an EPO on a horse and he develops a small problem. As a trainer, you've got a lot of money and time in him, so you want to run him anyway."

"We wouldn't do that," Harper said, interrupting. She wouldn't do that, she thought. Marshall wouldn't do that. . . .

Tim shrugged. "Well. That's what you're asking about."

He was right, of course. Harper looked down at her clasped hands.

"There's lots of stuff trainers do to push a horse," Tim said, reclaiming Harper's attention. "And it is mostly the trainers."

She suddenly remembered what Mariel's vet report had implied about Avalon all those years ago. Again, she considered whether Red or her father could have been involved in illegally drugging their horses all along. It seemed unlikely that could have happened, and nobody noticed.

"So, frog juice, for example," continued Tim, his voice bringing Harper out of her reverie. "*Dermorphin* is the medical term—it's more powerful than morphine. You can put that on the mucus membranes. No need for needles. And as early as the 1920s they actually used heroin. It metabolizes to morphine, which acts as both a stimulant and a pain killer."

Morphine was what Avalon and Sparrow had tested positive for. And what Mariel said they'd used in Argentina on the horses' knees.

The picture was looking pretty grim. Harper knew that good racehorses have a heart to win. They want to run, that's what they're born to do. And if they're on performance-enhancing drugs, get slightly injured and dosed with pain killers, that's exactly what they'll do—go all out, even if it kills them.

And, if their breeding focuses on turf sprinters but they're slotted to run in longer, dirt races, they'd need some added help to get the distance. That's where EPO factored in, Harper guessed. Her sister's stud book notes were beginning to make sense.

A wave of revulsion swept over her. What Tim described was exactly what she'd seen at Keeneland. She thought about the significance of all she was learning, but things still weren't adding up—Tap Down was Dylan's horse to train. Even if her father and Red had been dosing horses all those years ago, and that was a big "if," it still couldn't be Red now—he had nothing to do with the stud's runners at present and hadn't for years. It was all Marshall and Dylan. Red couldn't have been involved in drugging Tap Down, if that's what had happened.

And so, she thought, maybe she was wrong to consider her father and Red had been doping horses at all. Maybe Avalon and Sparrow had been administered morphine for the pain, as she'd thought—to help in their recoveries, not to run them while injured. Still, the idea rankled Harper—there was no excuse for morphine. There were other choices to control pain, legal ones, even back then, like Bute—*phenylbutazone*. It's an anti-inflammatory, Harper reasoned, but everyone used it to control pain. Why use morphine?

It was exasperating; Harper could put some of the pieces together, but still couldn't see the whole picture. It was impossible to know what had really gone on all those years ago since her father wasn't around to ask. Cooley had been on a two-year exchange to Argentina during that time, so there was no use asking him. And approaching Red was not an option; if all of Harper's previous attempts to get him to reminisce about the past still held, he'd simply change the subject.

Either way, the present situation was clearly different than it was back then. All the signs pointed in the same direction. What had happened to the horses last season—those who'd won against odds and those who'd been injured or died. What Mary had said Paris was up to with the studbook notes. What Jen had seen.

The most obvious culprit would be the trainer, but Harper knew Marshall wouldn't be involved in drugging horses. Cooley did have access to all the horses as Eden Hill's vet, but Harper couldn't believe a man who devoted his career to keeping their horses healthy would harm them. It had to be Dylan.

Well, she thought . . . maybe it was him.

Harper had known Dylan most of her life. He wasn't the sharpest tool in the shed. But, as Marshall said, he wasn't a bad sort. She couldn't imagine Dylan could do that to their horses. To the family. He wasn't that kind of person.

But then, Harper couldn't imagine Paris wouldn't confide in her about the stud farm's financial problems. Or whatever it was she'd spoken with Steve about. Or her suspicions about doping.

Just then, Kelso came bounding across the bridge and waggled up to Tim, who reached out and scratched behind his big golden ear. Kelso bent his huge head and couldn't get enough.

Tim grinned at Harper, breaking the seriousness. "He's not spoiled at all," he said, dropping his hand and then smiling as Kelso pawed him to continue.

Up the drive came Red's truck. That was a surprise. Harper hadn't seen him since Keeneland, and he hadn't been all that friendly then.

Tim stood as Red pulled up and got out. Kelso bounded away towards the creek.

Red looked up at the sky, then at Tim. "Might get that rain," he called, in what passed for conversation with Red. He slammed the truck door and started for the porch.

Tim nodded politely. "Just might."

"Just checking in, just seeing how things are settling in around here," Red said to Harper, finishing his walk up to the steps. He nodded again at Tim then looked hard at Harper.

She knew what he meant. "Settling in" so she could give him an answer about selling the stud farm.

Not a man for whom the words "social amenities" had much meaning.

"Things are fine, Red," Harper said. "Thanks." She stood, feeling a stab of pain; her stomach muscles were still protesting.

After her conversation with Tim, she needed time to sort through the dark implications. The truth was, Harper didn't have time to talk to Red.

As if on cue, Mariel's Audi pulled up the long drive. Like Red, she was an unexpected visitor. Once at the turnaround, she parked and breezed past Red, giving Harper her usual hug and turning with curiosity to Tim.

Harper introduced them while Red shuffled his work boot in the gravel, clearly uncomfortable at being left out of the conversation.

"We are going to dinner," announced Mariel, turning fully to Harper, who started to shake her head, but Mariel would have none of it. She invited Tim, as well, but pointedly left out Red.

Harper mouthed a "sorry" to Red; he nodded and glanced back at his truck. "Gonna meet Marshall over to Nico's barn anyhow," he said, turning to leave. They'd be talking about the syndicate for the stud's newest stallion.

Harper knew she should probably be present for that, but she'd rather not give Red another opportunity to press her about selling out.

"You go on now, girl," said Red. "Get your dinner."

What he meant was *Let us men folk do our business. No need for women meddling in men's affairs.*

Harper cringed.

Tim smiled. "I'll head over to the barn with Red. I'd like to take a closer look at Nico myself."

Fine, the less misogyny in my life, the better. She'd talk to Marshall later; right now, a little respite suddenly sounded like a good idea.

And food. And to think.

"It's not even five o'clock," she said to Mariel, checking her watch. "Dinner, really?"

Mariel smiled. "We go to Jen and my favorite restaurant. We go in time for the special for the old folks . . . .. How you say? . . . the 'early bird!'"

Harper grinned back at her. With all the tension she'd been carrying around lately, she did feel a bit like an old fogey ready for some mild mash at a ridiculously early hour. The early bird special sounded just fine to Harper. And there was only one restaurant around that served it.

Mariel was taking her to the Florence Café, known now as when Harper was a kid for its down-home cooking and incredible desserts. It was where all the "real" horse people went, and at this time of the day, they'd likely run into folks who'd long been out to pasture.

Chapter 14

But before dinner, Harper had a few things to clear up at the stud office. Pepper checked in about the buffet guest list and offered to hand deliver the invitations. It would take all morning, but it was a good idea. Monday and Tuesday were "dark days" at Keeneland when no races were run, so if Pepper got them delivered early enough, it was possible their guests might respond right away. It was hard to say no to Pepper.

Lucas let Harper know the security system would go in first thing next week. Until then, Cheyenne and John Henry were taking twelve-hour shifts, bedding down in the stallion office.

She had an odd call from Red's ex-wife, Anna Cole, asking to meet. For what, she wasn't quite clear, just said she thought it would be good to "talk over a few things," and wouldn't elaborate. Harper agreed, though Anna's tone roused her curiosity; Anna had been strangely insistent. They agreed to meet for lunch at Wilshire's the next day.

Alia dropped by just as Harper finished with the day's mail. She'd brought sketches to approve for the buffet set up. Harper looked at them briefly and finalized plans for flowers, tables, extra wine and water glasses, white cloths, and chairs. She'd finished the guest bags, making sure they had enough stallion and stud farm brochures for everyone they thought might attend. Harper made a mental note to put in the wine order and check in with Surrey on the food. They had plenty of Kentucky bourbon on hand.

The final task was a call to Marshall about picking up Sugarland on Friday; he said he'd call Tim later in the week and make a plan.

Then Harper remembered the package sent to Steve and retrieved it from the desk. Inside was a stallion bridle for the newest stud Red had sent from Argentina along with some of his old racing silks. That was nice. Unusual, but nice. There were also some printouts noting the colt's pedigree, and other assorted material associated with the stallion. She pulled it all out, thinking to go through it quickly, keeping the printouts and sending the rest over to Lucas at the stallion barn.

She thumbed through the pages—racing results, purse winnings, pedigree, potential breeding matches. There was also a page with a list of shipment dates, some kilo measurements, and initials.

None of the information on the last sheet made sense. The weight measurements were way out of whack for stallions, and the dates made no sense—their breeding program ran from February to May for optimal foaling during January through April of the next year; these were the first months listed but given the stud's planned mating and foaling schedules, Harper couldn't see the connection. She looked over the initials but they, too, didn't register. She knew of no one associated with the stud with any of them. Harper flipped the printed sheet over, but the blank back held no clues either.

She shrugged. Maybe a mistake. A loose sheet of paper that somehow had been inserted in error. She folded it, put it in her purse, and set the rest of the printed material to the side, along with the CD likely containing the same information. Finally, she packed the silks, bridle, and other material back in the box for Lucas.

Harper placed her hands flat on the box and sighed. Done. At least for the moment.

With all that, after changing clothes, and calling Mariel, it was close to 7:00 when the two women pulled into the Florence Café's parking lot, jammed as usual. Mariel parked the silver Audi at the far end of the lot. Harper glanced over at her South American friend, wondering what she had up her sleeve. Her dinner invitation likely came with a hidden agenda. Harper smiled inwardly considering what sort of scheme she'd come up with this time . . . something that benefited her beloved horses, that was certain.

Ah well, she thought, everyone needs to eat. As her stomach, sucker punch and all, vociferously reminded her.

Tim's comments about doping and fractures came again to mind. Haunting thoughts. She pushed them aside and set off with Mariel for a satisfying dinner with a good friend—a rare event these days.

The café had been updated many times since she and Paris were kids, but Harper wasn't prepared for its current iteration.

When they walked through the door, Harper's mouth dropped open, literally. This was hardly the Florence Café of her youth. Or even the café of last year. Gone were the vinyl-covered booths, the Formica tabletops. The café was now all dark wood, slate gray banquettes and booths, brass light fixtures with small frosted globes and a great big, glistening dark wood bar backed by a huge mirror along the far wall. A maître'd check-in podium, complete with computer, graced the front entrance.

127

Mariel laughed out loud at Harper's reaction. "You see? Best place, no?"

She saw a few friends across the dining room and raised her hand before the two were seated at one of the booths, the table covered by a crisp white cloth and topped with flowers, dark wood salt and pepper grinders and an assortment of wine and water glasses. The silver gleamed in the low light.

Mariel adjusted the silverware while Harper settled in to survey the room. She was glad Mariel had suggested she wear something special; she'd donned a simple black dress and her big silver cuff courtesy of Dahlia, one of the metal artists represented by Arcadia, the Chelsea art gallery where Harper worked. Mariel's insistence seemed ridiculously formal for the old Florence Café, but was right at home here.

As were Mariel's red cowboy boots. She scooted around in her seat, seemingly preparing for an announcement.

"How'd the fundraiser turn out?" Harper asked, signaling for the waiter. Menus and a wine list miraculously appeared, and Harper looked over the selection.

"We raise a lot of money," said Mariel. Heads of the other patrons bent close in conversation; a low murmur filled the room. "Thanks, Jen and me say, to the paintings."

She thought a moment then sheepishly confessed. "The Slew painting I keep for myself."

Harper smiled. Of course, she kept it. Mariel's house was crammed full of horse portraits. Where she'd hang Slew's grandson was anyone's guess.

Mariel fiddled with her loose, low bun and adjusted her hot pink and neon blue scarf. Somehow the outrageous colors worked on her.

"So, I get the calls . . . they come from Arkansas, then from New York . . . Chicago," she began, catching glimpses of Harper and looking down at the fork, which she turned over and over. "And today, I am speaking from a man in California."

Yes, of course—the reason for the dinner invitation.

The waiter came by and Mariel ordered a Knob Creek bourbon, neat, while Harper had a glass of house red wine.

Every year, Mariel agreed to take in more rescues than she had room for. Several years ago, Eden Hill had set aside a far pasture for "Mariel's extras," complete with a run-in shelter so the Thoroughbreds could get out of the bad weather. The stud supplied hay and a bit of feed, but only horses who were healthy and could keep their weight on were candidates. Harper was sure Mariel wanted to send over new rescues, so she waited, knowing Mariel had likely rehearsed her speech on the drive over to pick up Harper.

Part of her wanted to smile and tell her of course she'd help, as the stud always had. Instead Harper gave her space—Mariel flipped over spoons and forks, thinking.

Low music and the murmur of guests washed over their silence as Harper grinned affectionately at her friend then took in the room. At the bar she saw Dylan bent over his draft beer. He looked up and caught Harper's eye in the mirror.

Great. Not high on the list of folks Harper wanted to see.

She turned back to Mariel, dividing her attention between Mariel and buttering her torn French bread. She stuffed and sipped and listened, nodding.

Mariel finally made her request, as Harper stole another look at the bar. Dylan was still there.

"I'm sure we'll have enough room," said Harper, again glancing tensely in Dylan's direction. "Just let Marshall or Lucas know when they're coming."

Mariel gave her a look of quiet, sincere gratitude. "You are an angel," she said earnestly. "I am having no better friend in the world."

"This is true," said Harper, turning back to her, chuckling, "but you, my dear, are the one with wings."

Mariel smiled with what passed for demurely, accepting the compliment with a little good humor; she and Harper had done this dance before.

Ignoring Dylan's presence, Harper decided to ask Mariel more about her South American track experience. Though she'd intended to have a quiet dinner without one thought about deaths of any sort, something nagged at her about the drugs. Maybe Mariel could shed some light on things.

Everything pointed to Eden Hill's horses being doped. Then there was the new client from Argentina who seemed a bit off, and Red's role in securing him. Steve's death. Paris' suspicions. Harper fingered her purse. And that weird set of dates that came up from Argentina—kilos obviously suggested drugs, especially since the dates noted couldn't relate to anything in the stud's breeding program. There seemed a confluence of drugs, horses, and South America in the works. But Harper needed specifics. So, she asked Mariel about her time in Colombia and on racetracks in Argentina.

"Oh, yes," Mariel said, turning very serious. "In Colombia is bad enough. They abduct fathers, children . . . my family put up walls. We had dogs. We were never safe. Ever."

Harper asked her about the Argentinian racetrack; she knew Mariel's family had sent her away for her safety.

Mariel took a sip of her bourbon. "I thought I become a trainer, even though I am a woman." She looked at Harper, thinking no doubt about Jen.

Harper realized suddenly how conflicted Mariel must have been to speak at the Farm Managers' Club. Without a doubt she knew the consequences would not affect her—she had no stake in the track, being on the back end. But she surely knew Jen would pay the price. It occurred to Harper that her public stand was taken at great personal cost, one she had to be cognizant of at the time. Her heart went out to Mariel; she must have felt she had no choice but to speak out. And while she wasn't the only one speaking her mind about drugs at the racetrack, she could have remained silent, as had so many others.

She was staring at Harper.

"You couldn't train because you're a woman?" she said.

Mariel shrugged, took a long gulp this time of her Knob Creek. "Guzman has a home in Argentina before he was found first time. Other drug lords, they come from north, from Mexico. They are bad men, very bad. I think their monies are on the track. I tole you about the morphine in the knees. They don't care, they run babies—two-year-olds—into the ground. Horrible." She shook her head.

The scenario was familiar. Harper knew of one Kentucky track vet who had quit because trainers ignored news that their horses had micro fractures and had trained them too hard anyway. She couldn't take so many young horses breaking down and euthanized even before they could run their first race.

That could have happened to her horses, Harper realized. Given what she was uncovering, she saw how easily that could have occurred at Eden Hill. But not due to neglect on Marshall's part; there had to be another explanation.

"Not like in Mexico. No, no, no. The cartels, they no compete in Argentina. They divide, they cooperate." Mariel looked hard at Harper. "The government men help the drug lords. No one stop them. Even the churches, they invade."

"It must have been awful for you," she said, seeing for the first time how pervasive the drug cartels were in South America. No wonder Mariel sensed cartel involvement under every rock.

"They say 'we have no drug problem,'" she continued, speaking of Argentina. "They say I am crazy—*Usted es una mujer loca!*—this they say everywhere. I get no job. I am arrested."

Mariel was getting so agitated, her English was fracturing. In fact, she added, she'd been arrested twice.

She nodded soberly. "Once I serve my time in the filthy jail. The second, it would be a very long time I will spend with the bad men *en la cárcel.*"

She looked around for the waiter, raised her empty glass for another.

"But now you are safe," said Harper, seeing how much anguish the conversation was causing her. "You're out of that world."

Mariel looked at Harper and her face said it all—she thought her naïve. "No, my darling," she said softly. "What is stopping them from sending these monies, the drugs, now to America? So easy they go through the *hipodromo* . . . how you say . . .*las carreras de caballos.*"

Mariel stumbled around for words, lapsing into Spanish—a sure sign of her anxiety.

Harper clarified. "So, you're saying they may send the drugs here, launder money . . . they may drug the horses here? Through the racetrack here?"

Mariel nodded again, mutely.

She'd spoken to Harper about this before and had intimated it when she'd picked up Avalon. Now she was more direct; her fear that cartels had infiltrated Kentucky tracks was palpable. Harper wondered if she'd mentioned this at the Farm Managers' Club; if so, likely she'd seriously undermined her credibility. Though Harper knew those charged with protecting the integrity of racing were not stepping up when it came to drugs, attributing racing problems to drug cartels did seem a bit overboard. She bet the Farm Managers' members would feel the same way.

Harper touched Mariel's shoulder; she'd been through more than Harper could possibly imagine. It was obvious, too, that she felt far from safe. It was understandable her experiences in her homeland would color her outlook.

But Harper realized she was right about one thing. Harper had been naïve. That would change.

She picked up her menu and pretended to study it, thinking over recent events and Mariel's revelations. She was quiet a long time.

Mariel sipped her fresh drink in silence, entertaining her own dark thoughts.

They considered what to order, attempting to regain the mood they'd had going before Harper had broached the South American track subject.

She surveyed the crowd, her eyes again resting on Dylan who still sat at the bar, hunched over his beer. He seemed not to have moved a muscle.

"I see him, too," Mariel said quietly. "Not to worry, I will run the interference."

Harper smiled. Mariel may have her own dark past, but she had a strength Harper admired.

"So, you are having what?" she asked, putting aside her recent comments and trying to get Harper to think of something besides Dylan's presence.

They ordered shortly after. Mariel had the salmon and Harper ordered the bouillabaisse. They each ordered a different glass of wine as accompaniment.

"So, we are wondering, Jen and me. You miss Manhattan?" she asked, her English returning now that her focus was to divert Harper's attention from Dylan.

Harper did miss the city. She missed the gallery, the snobs and eccentrics. She missed her favorite hole-in-the wall Italian restaurant. She missed the art and the artists. She missed her friends, her apartment, her painting, her corner grocery, the light in the city at dusk, the Asian couple who ran the cleaners across the street. The cabbies, the streetlights. She missed the glut of people everywhere. She missed walking.

Yes, thought Harper sadly, *I do miss Manhattan.*

Mariel was quiet, watching Harper. "You have decided, yes, about going back?" She could see Harper's hesitancy, and how much she missed the city. And Mariel's look of concern showed she understood, which Harper was grateful for; she wouldn't get any pressure from Mariel to stay.

"If I did go back, I'm not sure what it would mean for the stud," she said, finally, picking at the salad the waiter had brought. Field greens, pine nuts, blue cheese.

Mariel dipped bread in seasoned olive oil, and Harper watched her face soften, though her eyes were alert. "I don't want you go," she said. "And Jen feel the same." She expertly swirled her white wine, watched the legs drift down the glass. "No one wishes that." She looked at Harper. "But happiness . . . is for you to decide. Only you."

Happiness. An odd word in the present context of things, thought Harper. She hadn't thought seriously about the decision—moving back to New York or staying on at the farm. Certainly, she hadn't thought about it in terms of what would make her happy. She didn't have much idea about what comprised that anymore. Accomplishment? Family? Work? Love? Until she found out what had really happened to Paris, she couldn't think in terms of her own happiness.

And hanging out there, complicating things, was JD's imminent return.

The waiter again appeared, whisked away their salad plates, replenished the bread and water. He raised an eyebrow and, getting no response, left to pick up the entrées.

Across the way, Harper saw Dylan hop off the barstool. He headed their way, weaving through the tables crowded with people, a singular figure intent on having it out with Harper, she guessed.

Harper gulped her white wine, checked the exits, and realized there was nowhere to go.

"Mind if I join you?" Dylan asked, his cheeks flushed. His eyes were a little too bright and Harper wondered how many drafts he'd had.

She did mind if he joined them.

But Mariel, not being one to avoid confrontation, motioned to an empty chair at a nearby table, and Dylan grabbed it. "Sit," she said as if talking to a five-year-old.

There was a prolonged silence, punctuated by the waiter bringing their entrées and both women declining more wine.

Harper sat stark still, her appetite gone. Her mind blazed with the horrific Keeneland crash, wondering if Dylan was mixed up in its cause.

Still, no one spoke.

"Harper," said Dylan, and hung his head. "God," he whispered. Suddenly, he couldn't meet her eyes.

Well, right, there is a hell of a lot you have to answer for.

Around them, patrons rose and sat, laughed and chatted. The trio seemed in a sealed bubble.

"You have apology, Dylan?" Mariel said between bites. Nothing stopped that woman from eating.

Harper had yet to touch her food. She took a small sip of wine.

"Harper, I'm sorry," Dylan said, looking at Harper. The pain in his eyes was clear. Harper thought he might actually cry. "It's all my fault," he said.

Her throat dry, Harper blurted out, "And that's supposed to fix things? You think an apology is enough?"

Dylan's presence was the last thing she needed. Harper made herself sip some hot, spicy bouillabaisse broth, the ocean's salty scent mixed with lemon wafted up from the large bowl.

"No, I didn't mean that," he said. "I can't understand what happened. I did the best I could." He looked up. "I tried, I really tried. I'm just sorry, that's all. That's all I wanted to say." Dylan looked like a little boy. A stricken little boy. He clasped his hands so tightly his knuckles were white. "Marshall was right. I'm no good at it." He shook his head, the beer blazing in his eyes. "I'm no good at anything."

Harper supposed he meant he wasn't a good trainer. That was a given, she thought. But she wondered if his apology had to do with more than that.

"Did you drug Tap Down?" Harper asked. That's what was on her mind, after all.

He looked at Harper, shocked at her accusation. Sorrowful and shocked. "God no!" he nearly shouted. His eyes went wide. "Is that what you think?"

"Is best not to scream," Mariel reminded Dylan.

Maybe Dylan was innocent. Harper sighed. It was so damned hard to tell what was really going on.

She changed the subject. "Dylan," she said, and he blinked finally. "Do you know what was going on with Paris before she died?"

His lips trembled. Goodness, she thought, this is one person who should not be drinking. If she could handle this, certainly he could.

"Do you think Paris' death was an accident?" she said.

"No," he whispered. "I know it wasn't." His shoulders hunched and he could hardly lift his head.

A chill passed over Harper. So, she wasn't the only one convinced that Paris' death was no accident.

Was it Dylan? Though the room around them hummed with conversation, and though the waiters and food and wine all came and went, for Harper the whole world had stopped.

"Dylan, did you kill my sister?" she whispered.

He looked up. "Kill her?" he said, tears streaming down his face. "How could I kill her? I loved her."

Needless to say, given Dylan's bombshell, dinner was over. Getting out of the restaurant was a blur; she leaned heavily on Mariel who somehow got her to the Audi.

Safely inside, Harper stared straight ahead into the darkness.

Dylan had been Paris' lover. Harper had not seen that one coming.

He was sure Paris hadn't died accidently because just before her death, she'd confided she was close to discovering who was the mastermind behind their horses being doped.

Harper looked over at Mariel's stern profile in the dashboard lights and the grim set to her jaw as ahead the headlights penetrated the dark road. Gone was the measure of conviviality she'd regained during dinner; Dylan's revelation had shocked them both into silence.

Neither of them spoke the whole way home.

Chapter 15

It was one of those brilliant October days. The sun shone, the air was clean and sharp, the trees were arrayed in brilliant amber, crimson, gold, and burnt orange. The countryside was a divine palette of color. Harper bundled up and took Zydeco out for a long ride. She wanted time to think through recent events, especially Dylan's revelation.

Just being in the presence of all that beauty nourished her soul, but she found as she rode that her mind wouldn't hold one thought longer than a few seconds. Maybe what she needed was some semblance of normalcy. A mundane, ho-hum, nothing of a day—cooking, maybe reading in front of the fire.

Anything but pushing against all the darkness swirling around her.

So, she tried to do nothing. She rode Zeke all over the farm, refusing to think about anything. She focused on being in the moment, on Zydeco's big chestnut body beneath her—his gait, his warmth, his willingness to please. She gazed out over the quiet fields, sensing the benevolent presence there, letting its peace settle over her.

They waded across Bucks Creek. They trotted and cantered, and once Zydeco stretched out in long strides at full gallop through a big open pasture, racing along the hill's crest as Harper relaxed into his gait, breathing as he breathed, alone in the big, wide world.

She mucked out all the stalls in his barn once they were back and turned out Oliver and Elle, then Claire Byee, Bernard, Sherlock, and Peyton. Each of them enjoyed their time in the paddock, racing up and back, kicking their heels, then settling down. A few nipped playfully at each other, then they crowded over to Harper for apples and peppermints. Oliver, a new addition, was thriving in his new home with his new family. Harper grinned at him as he nuzzled Claire Byee; he even had a girlfriend.

Restored somewhat, she headed back to the house to change for her lunch with Anna Cole.

After changing, she had a call from Detective Walker who said there were some findings regarding the unearthed remains. Images of the seven skeletons had continually recurred to Harper. She saw them in sunlight and last night had woken to a vision of them in their misty, dark grave. They wouldn't let her rest any more than would Paris' death.

The detective said they'd been Hispanic; the pathologist felt they were from a region in Mexico not far over the Texas border. This she'd determined from analyzing the bones. Their ages ranged from mid-twenties to early forties, excepting the smallest set of bones. That was a child of approximately seven years old. The coroner would have to rule on the official cause of death, but the pathologist noted that four had been shot in the back of the head. The remaining three had been bludgeoned to death, including the child. She didn't yet feel comfortable dating the bones, so they'd have to wait on that determination. The pathologist would continue her work and report on additional findings.

So, these were officially homicides, said the detective. He also had one other bit of news. The cross in the tin box had a Catholic religious order of nuns etched on the back. The locket contained a photograph, but over the years it had faded so much there was not much to recognize. Walker felt the necklace belonged to the larger of the two entwined figures and that possibly she'd been a member of the religious order, a nun. He would be following up on that to see if he could get a line on who she and the rest of the people were.

Detective Walker's information did not come as a surprise; if Harper was being honest, she'd known there was something terribly wrong with the burial site.

As she thought about the departed, she no longer pictured them merely as skeletons. They were people; they had lives, intentions, purpose, and family. And perhaps they were religious people. At least that seemed true of one of them.

Harper wondered if some had worked for the stud. They'd been hiring Hispanics for a long time, one of the first in Lexington to do so. She thought back to when they'd first brought them on. It had been a heady time for both families. After a run of five really great racing seasons and their studs establishing themselves as sires of winning runners, Eden Hill had seen the first flush of major attention. The success both families had worked so hard for had suddenly appeared on the track and in the breeding shed and everyone was happy and busy as they could be. They'd had to hire a lot of folks quickly one foaling and breeding season as the stud began making its mark and Eden Hill's stallions came into high demand.

Harper paused. Those early successes . . . they'd attributed them to their hard work, year after year. Now Harper wondered if some of that wasn't due to drugs. Drugs her father and Red had used on their colts and fillies . . . a winning track record based on lies and corruption.

Harper realized she might never know the truth about what happened all those years ago. But she did know one thing for certain: she and Paris had been intimidated by some of the Mexicans Rafe and Red had hired off local tobacco farms, and unnerved by a few Argentinians Red began importing not too long after that. Could those folks buried on the property have been among those first hires? Rafe had the foresight to hire Mexicans long before they became a staple of stud farms in the area; Eden Hill had plenty of Argentinians and other Hispanics on staff at the moment.

She remembered them as competent horse handlers, though a few had made her and Paris feel extremely uneasy. But they were kids, and Harper realized their discomfort could have amounted to little more than the cultural differences between them and the workers. She hadn't thought about them in years. Maybe she should have. But, then again, maybe there was nothing at all, really, to think about.

She'd wait on what the detective might find out about the religious order noted on the cross; maybe he could track down who these folks had been. What a Catholic nun would be doing on the stud farm was as much a mystery to Harper as everything else.

With nothing else to do but wait for more information about her, Harper turned her attention to Paris. She'd told Marshall about her sister and Dylan. He'd had no idea. Harper asked him to put Dylan in the lay-up barn; he could walk a colicky horse, give meds, change bandages, hand walk . . . whatever a sick or injured horse needed. It was a job he could handle.

Better to keep Dylan close. Until proven otherwise, his heartbreak had convinced Harper he was telling the truth. She longed to talk to him about Paris, but emotionally she didn't think she could bear to hear it. She had to focus on one thing—who had killed her sister.

The words still horrified Harper.

As did the possibility that drug trafficking was involved. Emilio Moreno, the client Red had gotten for Eden Hill, came to mind. His tête á-tête with Red seemed worth looking into.

Her thought went back to Dylan. The fact that he knew about Paris' last days plagued Harper. She called Marshall to find out Dylan's schedule, determined to be at the lay-up barn the minute he was at work. Though it would be tough, she really needed to know more about Paris just before her death.

But first, she was due at Wilshire's to meet Anna Cole and talk about God knows what. Harper thought she might be enjoying her woman-of-mystery role a little too much. She piled her blond hair into a scruffy high bun and headed out for lunch.

So much for a day of "normalcy," or whatever passed for that these days.

Anna was sipping her cocktail as Harper slid in next to her in Wilshire's crowded dining room. The bar was crowded, too, with a pretty bartender in large silvery earrings jogging this way and that attending to drink orders. Anna ordered a chef salad, while Harper opted for country-fried chicken. That about summed up the difference between them.

Anna set down her Cosmopolitan and began with what she'd come to say. "Paris came to see me in September," she said. "I thought, in light of what's happened, you should know what we discussed."

143

Harper gulped some water and was thinking about how to respond when two men approached the table in suits and ties. Anna rose and shook both their hands, smiling, introducing Harper as a friend she hadn't seen in years.

Well, okay, she thought. Go with it. Friends it was.

The older man shook her hand and said he'd be in touch soon. Then they moved off to a table to the far right. Clients, no doubt, or potential ones. With Anna, business was always on the menu.

So, Paris had talked with Anna. Harper wondered if she'd asked Anna's opinion about the horses they'd lost on the track. Mary had been the stud's go-to bloodstock agent for as long as Harper could remember and, though a hefty presence, literally and personality-wise, she'd never let the Eden Hill down. Harper wondered why Paris would feel the need to consult another breeding specialist.

Anna pulled some papers out of her briefcase. Her long, slim fingers and large hands reminded Harper of JD. They were so much alike—in looks, in composure, in style . . . She turned those big eyes on Harper and smiled sadly.

"I'm just sorry it had to come . . . this way," she said, laboring to find a kind way to preface the blow she was about to give Harper. She handed over the papers.

They weren't what Harper expected. They weren't pedigrees. They weren't breeding or performance results.

They were adoption papers. Or, rather, they were copied pages of information about types of adoptions a pregnant woman might consider. And at the end was a generic prenuptial agreement. Harper leafed through them with fingers like ice. Adoptions. Pre-nuptial agreement.

Anna reached across the table to me. "I'm so sorry, Harper," she said, pulling back as the waiter delivered her salad and plopped her entrée down in front of Harper.

"Paris was pregnant?" was all Harper could say. She pushed the plate away. The odor of the fried chicken was suddenly nauseating. Well, that and the news.

How could Anna eat? She nibbled her lettuce like the two were lunching at a Santa Fe spa.

"Yes," she said, dabbing her mouth with a starched napkin. "And very confused."

Harper could imagine. *Why hadn't she talked to me? Why Anna?*

And why were they having this conversation at a Georgetown restaurant?

"And excited," she added, her expression sad. "I so wanted to tell you this earlier."

Harper recalled her visit the day she and Red had that awful conversation about selling the stud.

Harper glanced around the restaurant, feeling confused. She wasn't up to talking about this among all these people. Was Paris' pregnancy and death Anna's version of a business lunch?

She turned back, steeling herself to finish the conversation, and asked what her sister had planned to do. She hoped Anna knew. She hoped there was some good reason Paris had confided in her and not in Harper. "Why did she come to you?" Harper said. *And not to me?*

Again, nausea threatened, and she sipped water. Her face felt cold, drained of blood.

Anna picked up her cocktail and took a deep drink, setting it down carefully. "She knew I'd had a child in . . . similar circumstances," she said softly, picking her words carefully. "It was some time ago." Anna shook her head as she saw Harper try to form words. "I don't know how she knew, but she did."

Harper felt herself collapse inside, her soul fold in on itself. "She didn't want her child?"

"No," said Anna. "I think she did want it. Very much."

"Then . . ." Harper picked up the papers, fluttered them in her hand. "Why these?"

Around them, the crowd murmured, punctuated by gentle laughter. The horse crowd over a business lunch.

"As I said, she was confused," Anna said. "She wanted to talk through her feelings with someone who'd been there."

Harper nodded. She got that. She got it intellectually, but not where it counted, down deep in the emotional bedrock she'd built with her kid sister over decades of sharing everything about every facet of their lives.

Harper gazed up at Anna, but she was a blur.

"What was she going to do?" Harper asked again.

Anna shook her head. "I don't know, sweetheart," she said quietly. "She didn't get the chance to decide."

Harper took her time driving home, meandering through the back roads, hoping the long fence lines, hand laid rock walls, and maternal rolling hills might soothe her.

They didn't.

She'd tried hard to be the best sister to Paris she could possibly be—always there for her, always watching over her, caring for her, making sure she had every opportunity to succeed in whatever she wanted to do. All those years . . . all the devotion and love Harper had for Paris . . . That she'd had to go to Anna, someone like Anna, and not Harper, spoke volumes about how much distance had grown between them. And Harper had not been aware of it at all.

She pulled over to the side of the two-lane road, trying to collect herself. Staring out the window, she didn't do a good job of it, feeling alternately numb and in the next moment, overwhelmed by sadness and confusion. How many nights in the past weeks had she wakened startled, her eyes wide in the darkness, picturing Paris in her last moments, horror overwhelming any hope of rest . . . and now this. Harper sobbed, her head resting on the steering wheel, her hands clutching it as if to fend off her heartbreak.

Finally, she forced herself to lift her head and take in slow, deep breaths; after a while she felt her emotions slip back to their dark depths. Then, for what seemed like the hundredth time in the last several hours and days, she forced herself to focus on the task at hand.

She had to talk to Dylan. Right away, if possible. So, at the time he was due at work she took the Range Rover over to the lay-up barn. She found him sliding open the back stall door to turn out an injured mare. Harper waited as he stroked the mare's neck, removed her halter, and returned to the stall.

He saw Harper and walked over, sober and serious.

"I was hoping to speak with you," he said, rolling the white leg wrap up as he spoke. " . . . to apologize for my behavior the other night." He looked embarrassed. "And to thank you for the job."

"Yeah, well, it's been a hard time for all of us," Harper said, drawing in a deep breath, pushing down the pain. She slid open the front stall door so Dylan could enter the aisle.

147

They walked past the feed room, the scent of hay mingling with cedar shavings and the sweet smell of grain.

She took stock of Dylan, the father of Paris' child. He seemed to have grown up in the last few days. Gone was the mischievous, careless attitude, replaced by a look of serious purpose. "I'd like to know more about Paris and . . . you," she said with a slight catch in her voice. *And your plans for your baby.* Harper wondered if he knew.

There would be a right time to ask him about that, she thought. But now wasn't it.

He smiled, but it was a smile tinged with sadness. "We thought we were hiding some big secret," he said. "Like we had this huge forbidden love affair going."

They left the barn and sat by the bronze statue of Persimmon, one of her mother's favorite broodmares. To their left, a host of tiny, unseen birds chirped, hidden in the deep recesses of the large holly bush.

"Beautiful stud farm heiress falls in love with a lowly apprentice trainer," he said, placing the wrap to his side, looking out at the paddocks. He turned and smiled. "Some love story."

Harper looked at her hands, thinking it sounded just like Paris, the idiot. She'd always been a sappy romantic.

"But once she died, why didn't you say something?" Harper said. Dylan had kept their relationship and the fact that Paris had suspicions about doping completely to himself.

"After I lost that first colt and Marshall tightened things up on me . . . And then with Paris gone, then Tap Down and Evan . . ." Sadness again played over his face. "I don't know . . . I just felt like I needed to do something right, figure out one thing on my own."

"Like what happened to Paris?"

"Yeah, and the horses, too. For her," He looked off. "For Paris . . ." He took a deep breath. "I mean, when you asked me if I'd juiced Tap Down . . ." He seemed unable to continue.

Harper put a gentle hand on his back. It made sense. Dylan wanted to find out who'd killed his lover, maybe the mother of his child. And he wanted to bring that person to justice himself.

Harper could relate to that.

She asked him about who he thought was behind the doping, what Paris had discovered that had gotten her killed.

Dylan stuck his hands in his olive-green fleece vest and thought a few moments. He looked at his watch.

"I got to put that medicine in White Heat's eye," he said. "You mind?"

They walked back into the barn and Dylan got the syringe and meds out of the refrigerator in the lounge.

He slid open White Heat's stall door and injected meds into the tube that ran over the horse's neck and into his right eye.

"Where this guy found a branch to run into, I have no idea," he said, sliding the stall door closed after him.

Dylan seemed ready to drop the subject of doping altogether as they walked back to the lounge in the middle of the barn and he disposed of the syringe.

Harper sat on the folding chair at the card table. "Dylan, you must have thought about it."

"Yeah, I've thought a lot about it," he said, sitting down across from her, kicking his flimsy chair back and then letting it fall into place on all fours. He folded his hands in his lap and shook his head.

"You do know Red was all over Paris to sell the farm, right?" Harper nodded. "And with JD due home soon . . . who knows what those two are up to."

"You think JD was involved?" Maybe that's why Dylan was reluctant to talk about it. He knew about their relationship.

"Yeah, well, you know JD's been in a special operations unit over there in Afghanistan. Maybe intelligence, maybe something else, I don't really know."

Well, no, Harper did not know that. Her stomach did a somersault. To think he was in danger was worrisome. Odd, she thought, to feel that after so many years.

"Who told you that?" she said, knowing it wouldn't be like JD to talk about himself in those terms. To Dylan or anyone else.

The refrigerator suddenly kicked on, the low hum a soothing sound.

"Red." Dylan shuffled his chair up to the table and leaned over it, again serious. "You know about Red's past, how he drove JD's mom away. Who knows what he did to her—he's got that temper." He was quiet for a moment. "And I don't know what JD might be doing over there in Afghanistan."

Harper considered the possibility that JD was involved in drug trafficking, and it wasn't South American drugs at all, but those from Afghanistan being funneled through Eden Hill, father to son.

She shook her head. JD had never been the type. But, she supposed, you never know what the pressures of war might do to a person. Still, she couldn't fathom what Red would gain by putting either of their farms in jeopardy.

Dylan leaned back. "And then there's Cooley. He's not happy about closing up shop. Especially with Emma's bills."

That was true. Three years of cancer treatments and the bills could be astronomical.

Dylan had no more to say on the subject, so Harper left him to his work. Which he seemed competent at and happy to do.

After she left Dylan, Harper went to the stud farm office. Pepper was not yet back from delivering the invitations. She glanced up at the clock behind her desk; she'd likely be a few more hours.

Down the hall, Harper heard Dave and Gretchen on their phones, probably fielding breeding submissions questions or answering inquiries about breeding stock they'd be sending to the November sales, what this year's crop might be like . . . any number of calls came in and Harper was glad to have the two of them holding down the fort in her pronounced absence.

She went in the office and sat at the desk, smoothing her hands over its worn surface, aware again of the history they had on this land, breeding and racing.

Living and dying.

All the baby clothes, all the birthday parties for Paris' child . . . Harper couldn't think about that at the moment.

She called Cyril at Arcadia Gallery in New York, just to give her mind something completely different to think about. She did her normal art gallery check-in—what sold and to whom, what new torture tactics had the artists come up with, any galleries in high scandal mode . . . all the mundane, day-to-day questions she'd ask if she was in Manhattan.

She gave Cyril a brief update on things at the farm, since he asked. He said they'd finally gotten the show up the two of them had planned; it was due to open in a few days. The artist, Cyril lamented, had just insisted the entire show be rehung.

Harper smiled. It was a small smile, which was good, considering. Cyril would head to Trestle on Tenth, pour his heart out to Uma behind the bar, sip a warmed cognac, and all would be well.

Harper sighed. The call only made her aware of how much she really did miss Manhattan.

But missing the city was not going to solve the murder of her sister so she set her other life aside and turned her attention to the task at hand.

Strangely, her first thought was of the skeletons buried by Bucks Creek. The information Detective Walker had shared came next and along with it, Mariel's mention that Argentine churches were, if not involved, at least complicit in the heroin trade.

Harper sat back at the desk and folded her arms, considering the implications. She wondered if what was true in Argentina was also true for Mexico, if either persecution or church complicity could have driven the Mexicans to the United States and to their deaths at Eden Hill. It was possible, she supposed; a lot depended upon how old the bones were.

The skeletons on the property remained a mystery for the time being. Purveyors of drugs or persecuted Catholics or merely stud farm employees, the questions remained. As did whether or not any of that had to do with her sister's death.

She sighed and got on with Eden Hill's daily business, sorting through the mail, returning calls, confirming sale horses, and reviewing the newest applications for Steve's job. Harper hadn't gotten around to interviewing people, but she needed to.

When she'd gotten through the "in" box, and the "out" box was full, she sat back again, staring out the window to the now-bare bald cypress trees set at the edge of the far pond. The ice

152

from the weekend rimming the water's edge had melted, leaving the deep indigo green surface gently rippling now and then by the wind or a very cold, very large koi.

She pulled out the weird South American list that had been addressed to Steve, and looked again at the dates. January through April . . . and then a break with some totals. Then farther down the page, May through July . . . regular dates, every four weeks. And the initials next to each date were listed in a particular order, four sets repeating themselves in the same order throughout the months. And the weight measurements were insignificant—a mere 35 kilos in one instance, 50 kilos in another . . . or a bit over seventy-five and one hundred ten pounds per notation. Negligible; they couldn't refer to horse weights or anything associated with the stud's stallions. And Eden Hill wouldn't be regularly importing anything from Argentina, so the recurring dates made no sense, either.

But, as Harper had felt initially, the weights could well refer to drugs. In fact, she realized, the most obvious way the list made sense was if what she was looking at were kilos, say, of heroin— as Mariel had indicated the cartels traded in—being shipped to the stud. It appeared that what she held in her hands was a delivery list. She paused. The package was addressed to Steve.

But like everything else, that didn't make sense. From what Tim had said, heroin and morphine were not the current drugs of choice for the track—they were easily detected. How the apparent drug shipment list connected to the horses' injuries and deaths remained a mystery.

And she'd known Steve a long time and always considered him a principled guy. Still, if he did commit suicide as the scene at his death suggested, Harper could well imagine his conscience catching up with him in the event he had stooped to drug involvement. Or, she considered, perhaps like Paris, that involvement had gotten him killed and it had been made to look like a suicide.

The regular intervals, the weights . . . drugs would explain that. And the initials. Perhaps they were the distributors, four people noted by initials—M.R., C.T., S.D., and A.D.

If that's what Paris had discovered, that there was a drug ring operating right under her nose, it would also explain why she was killed. Eden Hill functioning as one, or maybe one of many, distribution sites in the Kentucky Thoroughbred world, was cause for concern to whomever was behind this.

Red was their Argentinian contact, had been for decades. Maybe, as Dylan intimated, JD and Red were the conduits on both ends; heroin was as prevalent in Afghanistan as it was in the world of South American drugs. Some version of Harper's musings was plausible.

But she still balked at the notion. It made no sense that Red would jeopardize both the stud and his own operation, not to mention the decades he and her father had worked so hard, hand in hand, to build both of them. And she couldn't imagine he'd put JD's future in jeopardy.

Harper brought her attention back to Paris. She'd tried to handle way too much by herself. She'd been suspicious of their track wins and breakdowns and had gotten the stud into serious financial difficulties. And yet, she'd also pieced together something from the pedigrees and racing results she'd been investigating, and Dylan indicated she'd figured out—or was close to knowing—who was behind the injuries and the deaths of their colts.

Dylan. Harper had to agree with Marshall that he was inept as a trainer. And it made sense, now, why Paris insisted Marshall keep him on. She didn't want to lose her lover and the father of her child.

But was Dylan capable of murder? She didn't think so, but someone had caused Paris' death, quite possibly been involved in drug distribution, and just as likely had dosed their horses—whether legally or illegally seemed of little interest to her; neither was how Eden Hill operated.

As Dylan had noted, there was also Cooley. Another person who'd been with the stud for decades. He was as competent as they come, if a little old school. And he needed to retire. Emma was in and out of the hospital all the time. If a wife ever needed her husband at her side, Emma needed Cooley, now more than ever.

Yet, the Edisons had likely racked up huge bills. Harper wondered if bills alone were enough to drive Cooley to do the unthinkable, to commit acts jeopardizing the health of their horses, something he'd devoted himself to maintaining his whole professional life. Drugs were highly lucrative. Harper had to concede it was possible.

And finally, she did have to consider Steven Hamilton. The distribution list—if that's what it was—had been addressed to him. It seemed unlikely, though, that he could mastermind such a complex, secret, and evidently ongoing operation all by himself. And if not a suicide—which Harper still found hard to believe—his death seemed illogical if he was involved in the drug trade. Why do away with a central cog in your distribution organization?

Someone else was involved, possibly several people.

Emilio Moreno came to mind. Harper had a bad feeling about him. But then, she'd been wrong about so many things and about so many people lately, it was hard to have conviction about any of it.

She sat there in the growing dusk as the light changed from bright blue to lilac and pink. Again, she looked out at the pond, the trees, the pastures, the barns in the distance . . . such serenity beside such turmoil and death.

She sighed and headed home, intending to have a simple dinner and maybe figure out where to put all the folks she hoped accepted Pepper's invitations. She'd hit a brick wall—lots of suspects, lots of questions, and no answers in sight.

Harper was cutting veggies for a salad in the kitchen and planned a nice quiet dinner—grilled cheese with mustard and pickles plus a simple salad when Surrey and Marshall pulled up the drive. Kelso, parked on the porch, announced their arrival.

They stepped in together and Marshall hung his hat on the rack by the door and gave Harper a perfunctory hug. Surrey followed with the fixings for a peach and raspberry cobbler. With little fanfare, they cooked and chatted, and ate dinner together, speaking only of good things. They allowed themselves one evening of contentment, mimicking a past they all knew would never return.

Chapter 16

Harper woke to a sun that was way too bright way too early in the morning. She groaned and rolled on her side, plopping a big feather pillow solidly over her head.

There it was again. That sound. She yawned and squinted into the sunlight streaming through the windows. Men, she heard men's voices. For a moment, Harper didn't know where she was. Slamming doors, men's voices.

Thursday morning . . . she yawned again and gazed out the window.

And by the looks of the strong light, she'd slept in. Maybe from exhaustion or the simple food and good company of the night she before. Maybe a hint of normal home life had relaxed her.

Oh, good Lord, she thought suddenly, sitting straight up in bed. Wednesday. The buffet. That was today!

She flopped back anyway then groaned again. Might as well get up and get to work. Then, unbidden, Anna Cole came to mind. For some reason, their lunch together had drifted into her jumbled thoughts the night before as Harper had fallen asleep. And there it was again, still on her mind in the morning.

Her news had been so shocking. Paris, pregnant.

During their lunch, Harper hadn't had the presence of mind to ask more about her conversation with Paris. She propped herself up against the headboard, wondering what else her sister had confided in her. Perhaps something that shed light on her death. Harper decided to speak to Anna again; she felt ready for that.

Throwing off the covers, she trotted over to her closet. She'd call Anna, see if she could stop by today before the buffet. It felt urgent.

Down the steps she trundled in her bunny slippers and robe, heading to the coffee but stopped at the sight of large men carrying tables and chairs, a bar on rollers, assorted boxes, tall cardboard cylinders, and other things she couldn't quite recognize into the living room, dining room, and around the fireplace to the family room.

Through the open door, she saw Alia and Pepper walk up the steps, heads together, nodding at the clipboard in Pepper's hands. The event twins looked like they had everything under control. Beyond them in the drive were three trucks from which the large men were still emerging. Kelso meandered from one truck to another, his tail wagging slowly, sniffing out any treat that might fall his way.

Alia smiled when she saw Harper, while Pepper pinched her lips and studied her notes.

"Well, good morning," Alia said. "Sleepyhead."

Harper nodded. She didn't speak prior to caffeine.

She steered herself into the kitchen where one of the two had made coffee, which she nearly inhaled between stifling yawns.

"The caterer will be here at two, the ice sculptures arrive at four," said Pepper, apparently to herself, as she surveyed the continually arriving paraphernalia.

Harper hoped she knew what to do with all this stuff. She moved among the tables and chairs, nodding and checking, making sure the tablecloths and linens had arrived.

"I'll have the flowers over by three thirty," Alia said, "and Surrey will be here to look after the caterers . . ." She stopped and stared at Harper.

"Why don't you go do something fun today?" she said. "Let us handle this."

Having had sufficient caffeine, Harper was able to speak. "Alia, no. I've already bailed on you . . ." She and Pepper had set up the whole buffet themselves.

Pepper walked up, her short bob curving perfectly at her chin. "No, no, no, on the contrary," she said, laughing. "We were glad to have you out of the way." She grinned, joking with Harper, but did she imagine a surreptitious look passing between Pepper and Alia?

"Really," said Alia, giving Pepper a look, "we'd love to surprise you. Even Surrey said to see if we could talk you into doing something fun today."

"You need a break," added Pepper.

"Go wait on Sugar. Tim said he could come home a day early. Lucas and Marshall are getting him around one," Alia said.

Harper wasn't sure how she felt about this push out the door. Of her house, she silently reminded them. She'd just gotten up, after all. But Harper did want to see to Sugarland, and check on Cheyenne and John Henry to make sure they were doing okay sleeping in the barn office. And meet with Anna Cole if she had time.

"You two sure about this?" Harper said. "I mean, I'm kind of in charge."

At which point they both burst out laughing.

"Well, ladies," she said, "if *that's* how you feel, I'll take you up on your offer." Harper gratefully hugged each of them. They made her smile and reminded her there was still a lot of good in the world, even among all the dark currents swirling around them all.

Taking her coffee with her, Harper headed toward the stairs to prepare for the day—for her talk with Anna, she hoped, and for her lovely colt's arrival.

As it turned out, Anna was free around lunchtime and agreed to meet Harper at the mares' barn; she'd had enough conversations over food lately. Harper wanted to check on the stud's pregnant stock; there hadn't been time to look in on them all in her initial, cursory inspection. And she should.

Cooley had made his rounds earlier, so he'd seen to each of the bred mares. Harper had received reports from Megan, who supervised the stud's broodmares, but Harper wanted to get a look at them herself.

The barn door was open, so she walked in followed by Kelso. Big-bellied soon-to-be mothers lined the barn aisle, some peering out the stall windows, some turned out in the adjacent paddocks.

She'd brought carrots, and fed them to the mares, one by one. Sophie stuck her delicately featured gray head out of her stall and nibbled politely, her black tail switching behind her. Down the aisle, Risky, Silver Song, and Misfit nickered softly.

Kelso turned at the sound of Anna's car, and Harper darted into Megan's office to pick up the printout she said she'd leave there. That, plus a few screen shots of Cooley's ultrasounds, would give Harper a comprehensive look at where they were with the mares. Some were Eden Hill's, some were clients'; it was Harper's job to see all the foals safely on the ground.

She passed Emilio Moreno's mare, Lopata, and again had that unsettled feeling about him.

She flipped through the pages on her way out to meet Anna. She'd arrived earlier than Harper had expected. She'd have to save the mares' review for later.

Dressed in forest green designer jeans and a deep brown sweater, Anna looked casual but, as usual, elegant. Her green eyes were startling.

"Brought you a present," she said, holding out a professionally wrapped box. "Thought you could use a pick-me-up."

Harper thanked her, opened the present, and pulled out a beautiful, very long teal-blue and peach silk scarf. She wasn't much of a scarf person, but the pattern and colors were lovely. And it was thoughtful of her to make the effort.

Harper smiled and set the box in the Range Rover. "Thanks," she said nodding at the box, "for the present and for coming." She turned back to the barn. "Hadn't had a chance to spend enough quality time with the girls until now. I appreciate you coming all the way over."

They walked toward the picnic table and chairs. "Do you feel like walking, or would you like to sit?"

"Let's walk," said Anna, glancing at the high clouds. "We should enjoy the weather while we have it."

They walked, passing the paddocks where mares grazed on the last tufts of grass, their necks stretched to the ground, their tails still or slowly moving as they stepped forward quietly.

"I know Paris talked about her pregnancy with you," Harper began, "but I wondered if she'd discussed anything else."

"Like what?" Anna said, her tone curious. She stopped a moment, thinking, then continued. "She mentioned Dylan, of course. She was a little unsure of what to do about him as well as the baby." A look of concern crossed her face. Harper thought she didn't want to cause her more heartache than she already had to deal with.

Harper walked to a paddock fence and leaned on it. Anna followed.

"I was thinking more about the stud farm. I know she was concerned about something going on with the colts and fillies we had in training and on the track last season."

Anna stood to her right but didn't lean on the fence. "Well, there'd been some talk about drug problems at the track. More than a few people mentioned it." She paused. "Paris was one of them. But only in passing."

Harper studied her. Something in her tone made her think there was more to it than that.

Anna turned to look out into the paddock where a Cozzene mare grazed, a pretty gray just like her sire. The mare looked up at them and trotted over. Harper pulled out a carrot from her back pocket and gave it to Anna. The mare bit off a piece and chewed, her big, soft eyes taking them both in.

"Paris also mentioned Red had offered to buy the farm," said Anna, breaking the carrot in two and holding it under the mare's muzzle. Anna turned to Harper, and she noticed the lines at the corners of her eyes. Not laugh lines. Ones put there by strain, Harper thought.

"Red is an evil man," Anna said bluntly. "I told Paris to watch out for him."

"He made the same offer to me," Harper said.

162

"Then I'll say the same thing to you," she replied quickly, her voice filled with concern.

Harper wondered what she meant by "evil." She knew his temper had gotten the best of him at times, especially with his wife. Or, anyway, that's what Harper, and everyone else, had heard. She'd run off immediately after JD and Harper graduated and everyone thought she'd stayed with Red long enough to see her son safely off to college. So, it made sense she'd not hold a high opinion of him. But of all the words to describe her ex-husband, evil was pretty harsh. And if she actually thought of him as evil, why come back?

"Evil?" Harper repeated, and she nodded. Harper was quiet, hoping Anna would elaborate, but she didn't.

Harper's parents and the Coles had spent a lot of time together. Vacationed, had dinners and parties all the time. They'd all grown up together. Harper had always thought Red was a little rough around the edges. Wiley. Out for his own interests. But evil?

She chalked her comment up to a bad breakup until she learned otherwise and took a different tack. "What made you return, Anna?"

She smiled. "I bet you could guess the answer to that."

Harper didn't have the slightest idea. So again, she was quiet.

"I came back for my son," she said. "For JD." She turned suddenly sad. "But that didn't work out so well."

She fed the last piece of carrot to the mare and turned around, leaning on the fence. The mare nuzzled her hair. It didn't bring a smile to her face.

"When I got back," she began, "JD wouldn't speak to me. He was home for a short time. Actually, he's been back and forth between tours."

She sighed and folded her arms. "He'd never give me a chance. That boy's carrying a lot of anger around. He thinks I left Red in the lurch." She smiled. "Broke his heart. That's a laugh. That man doesn't have a heart."

Anna seemed lost in her own thoughts, so Harper didn't intrude.

She wondered about her comment regarding JD's visits. Could they have something to do with drug smuggling?

"He's a smart boy," Anna said after a long silence. "I just have to trust he'll see through Red sooner or later."

She'd clearly not let go of lingering feelings about her ex.

How odd, thought Harper. She'd asked Anna there to learn about Paris. Yet what she learned had more to do with JD and his family than her own. She wondered about JD's trips home, how many times he'd been back, and if those trips coincided with other shipment lists she had yet to discover.

"He'll be home soon, right?" Harper said.

Anna nodded. "Yes, he's finally leaving the service for good." She sighed. "Maybe I'll give it another shot."

She seemed to be speaking more to herself than to Harper.

Anna stirred, hefted her bag to her shoulder and Harper gathered their conversation was about over. She smiled encouragingly at Anna. JD had never struck Harper as the vindictive type, so she hoped Anna would give their relationship another chance. But, Harper realized, it's possible she didn't know him anymore at all.

But Red. Anna's comments made Harper consider whether Red had some role in what was looking more and more like a drug distribution ring. But he was a prideful man who had focused for years on the stud and his broodmare business becoming top racing and breeding operations in the Bluegrass. It would be stupid to jeopardize what he and Harper's family had achieved. And Red was certainly not stupid.

After a few moments of silence, Harper hooked her arm in Anna's and pulled them forward, resuming their walk into the light-filled October day.

Enough dark thoughts.

After comforting Anna—not the outcome Harper expected from the visit at all—and seeing her off in her car, Harper returned to the office and sorted through mail, returned calls, and signed yet more checks. By the time that was done, Sugar was already snuggly ensconced in his stall.

Lucas had just loaded hay in for him as Harper entered the barn, but the colt seemed too disoriented to have much interest in food.

Understandable, given he'd been at the hospital, had some screws put in, and was now settled into a new place he'd never seen before. Good to have Deacon next to him, at least there was one stable thing in his life.

Cantankerous as that one thing was.

Deacon's "welcome to our new home" gesture was to flatten his ears, bare his teeth, arch his neck and, as Lucas described it, growl at Sugar.

Well, she considered, Deacon was also a new arrival. They'd both just have to get used to their new home, at least for the time being.

Marshall joined her at Sugar's stall.

"Tim said he did real good, better than he expected." He rubbed Sugarland's blaze. "Four months, total, he thinks."

Harper peered down at Sugarland's leg, now housed in a fiberglass cast. "For the entire rehab?" she asked as she fed the horse a peppermint.

Marshall nodded. John Henry joined them, after saying hello to Deacon. He was one person Deacon didn't try to bite. Bad stallion manners.

Harper was the other. She moved over to Deacon who came to her for a peppermint. He'd seen Sugar get a treat, so felt he should have his due.

"You and Cheyenne doing okay here?" she asked, knowing that John Henry would never complain. He loved the horses, loved the farm, and Harper could call on him to do anything needed. At any hour of the day or night.

His old, lined face, creased with years in the sun tending their horses, turned from Deacon to Sugarland, then to Harper. "We're just fine, Miss Harper. Don't you worry about a thing on our account." He smiled, and they both stroked Deacon's neck. The big colt puffed up and stared down from the great internal height he inhabited.

Fractious as he was, Harper loved that horse with all her heart.

"Okay, good, good," she said to John Henry. "You know if you need anything, you just have to ask."

John Henry didn't reply. He didn't need to. He'd never asked for a thing in the fifty years he'd been with Eden Hill. Harper doubted he'd start now.

Marshall walked her down the aisle and stopped at the barn entrance.

He put his arm around her in that fatherly way that was so comforting. "I'll be up to the show on time, Sweet Pea, don't have to say anything," he said, grinning.

Marshall hated events like this evening's buffet, and would rather be in the barn, or nearly anyplace else. But Surrey would have him spit polished and dressed to kill, right on time. Between the Harper and Surrey, Marshall had no chance at all.

She patted his arm and walked up to the house to get ready for the "show" herself. Passing through the entranceway, she saw things were coming together well and sent silent kisses and hugs of thanks to Alia and Pepper. They'd handled things expertly. She was grateful for that. Her best Eden Hill hostess demeanor needed to be on full throttle tonight. Their work would set the stage perfectly.

Harper just hoped she could tease out some bit of new information from Red or Emilio Moreno to verify what amounted right now to mere conjecture.

At 4:30 Harper descended the stairs in a black, form-fitting Susanna Monaco dress and her mother's large aquamarine earrings. She'd gathered her hair loosely up for the night—a tad more formal, she thought—and took a few swipes at her eyelids with some blue-green shadow to complement her eyes.

She stood at the foot of the steps and surveyed Alia's handiwork. Genius, she thought. Alia had transformed the rambling family home into a frosted blue and gleaming silver paradise. From the polished silver chafing dishes to the horse head ice sculpture on the buffet, to the myriad flower arrangements in white, ice blue, and Paris' favorite, Bells of Ireland, their family home glittered and gleamed in light.

My home, Harper thought, realizing again she was the only one left.

She gazed around. White cloths with slate black cushioned chairs, small silver name plates next to bud vases, brochures at every table, crystal and silver . . . the scene was pure opulence and grace. How Alia did it on the budget Harper provided her was beyond comprehension.

As she moved through the rooms, she noticed that Alia had thoughtfully seated the stud's newest clients with their old reliables, the foreign visitors with those in adjoining countries, single men and women in close proximity. She and Pepper had done a great job.

Surrey rushed over to Harper like a little kid with a new toy. "Look at this!" she said, dragging Harper to the buffet where a tiered silver tower holding canapés rested next to her mother's covered silver casserole.

"Is that magnificent, or what?" she said, beaming.

Harper assumed this was one of Surrey's antique shop finds and so nodded appreciatively. Surrey then launched into what was being served, when, how, and on what silver platter, in what bowl or dish . . . she was in her element. Once she'd filled Harper in, back to the butler's pantry she went to take charge of the catering staff.

Harper's heart went out to them.

At four forty-five, Marshall dutifully marched up the porch steps, disgruntled and uncomfortable looking in his camel hair blazer and deep brown slacks.

Get over it, Harper mouthed, grinning, as he walked through the door and trudged toward Surrey for feeding and her last-minute check of his apparel.

When the guests began to trickle in, Harper planted herself at the door and greeted everyone with handshakes and pecks on the cheek.

To their credit, pretty much all who'd responded showed up and on time. Honoria and Cassidy Beal, Fitz Glazer, Neil and Miranda Whitney . . . they all filed past Harper, picking up canapés and wine from the silver-trays gracefully offered by the black-clad catering crew. Alia and Pepper moved through the gathering crowd, showing folks their seats, or just talking.

Whatever it took, seemed their motto.

Emilio Moreno walked through the door alone, stopped in front of Harper to kiss her hand and gaze into her eyes.

"Welcome," she said, "good to see you again." Harper gestured toward the table she recalled held his nametag and turned as quickly as she could to another guest. Moreno moved off, mingling with a couple to her right.

Tim Bradford arrived wearing a deep blue blazer over charcoal slacks and a blue and gray pinstriped shirt. Very pulled together, Harper thought, grateful for his friendly smile and genuine warmth—quite a contrast to Moreno.

Since he was to be their vet going forward, Harper thought it a good time to meet the clients, so she walked him over to a couple from Japan and introduced them.

Red had sent word he'd be a bit late. He always struggled with any attire other than overalls. Which sometimes went with a neon orange sweatshirt normally worn by road crew.

When Harper turned back to the door, she saw Mary Edvers heft herself out of her Honda Civic and hand the keys to the valet. She could afford any car she wanted yet insisted on her Civic. She "distained ostentation," as she was fond of letting everyone know. She might take a peek in the mirror, thought Harper, smiling inwardly, stiffening for the Edvers onslaught.

She entered, sliding a ratty fur thing with a stuffed head on the end off her shoulders and handing it to Harper. Beneath she wore a tight, green polyester number that made her look like an unadorned Christmas tree. A red slash of lipstick and a huge glittery barrette completed her ensemble.

"Lovely to see you," Harper whispered, kissing her rouged cheek, trying to mean it. The consultant would attract a lot of attention and she knew it; as one of the best bloodstock agents in the area, lots of folks would want her free advice.

Harper turned and, except for the Green Hornet, the room shimmered, as the crowd of people mingled and chatted, drinking and eating, and finding their seats. She moved to the family room, where Pepper had set up a projector showing a montage of stallions, races, fenced pastures and paddocks, mares and foals . . . it was captivating.

Tim stood at a table, talking with Iris Cramer and her husband Walt, who'd joined Eden Hill's Japanese clients. Iris and Walt had lived in Japan for decades and had come on board long ago as clients of Harper's parents. She sent them both a silent thank you. Though clients, they were also a lot like family.

She separated herself from the scene for a moment, thinking of Paris, seeing her sister in her mind's eye as she might have been at this gathering. As she should have been . . . The convivial mood Harper had awakened with vanished, leaving behind the sober resolve she'd grown used to.

Blue Lessaro, a long-time client from Virginia, trod over with his wine and a long-stemmed white rose, plucked no doubt from

Alia's display, when Harper's phone rang. She accepted the rose and put the phone to her ear.

But she could only hear mumbling. She looked at the caller ID; it was John Henry. Fear switched through her. She darted to the porch, held the phone to her other ear and yelled, "John Henry, what is it?"

More mumbling, but she heard, "Deacon . . . after Deacon" plain as day. Then an audible, pain-filled moan.

Something was wrong, really wrong.

Harper glanced back at the house and decided there was no time to locate Marshall—John Henry needed her at the stallion barn immediately. She looked out over the circle of cars searching frantically for her Range Rover, but it was boxed in, so she jumped in the 'Gator, fumbled in the glove box for the key, and set off for the stallion barn.

Coming over the rise, she saw flames.

Her father's '80's renovations included stone reconstruction for the major barns and tile roofs to guard against fire, one of the worst catastrophes for a stud farm. He'd installed sensors, too, so Harper knew the fire department had already been alerted. There were so many sorts of fires, though, that her father had opted not to install sprinklers since water was the worst thing for some fires.

Which meant that the fire department was on its way, but the barn still burned. Harper knew she had to get the horses out or the smoke would kill them before the fire did.

Once there, she leaped out, ran into the barn, flames flaring around her. The horses were in full panic, screaming, climbing the walls of their stalls, wild eyed. Her first priority was Sugar; with his bad leg, he was in the most danger.

She peered through the smoke, frantically trying to locate John Henry but didn't see him. It was so dark, except for the flames and billowing smoke.

The stud had protocols in place, so there were blinkers in the tack room, and halters with lead ropes at every stall. Harper could hear Nico kicking and snorting in the far stall. When she got there, flames shone in his eyes, his nostrils flared, his teeth bared as the smoke curled down from the ceiling.

She had a hard time breathing and ducked into the tack room for the blinkers and any piece of cloth she could find.

She dunked the rag she found in a water bucket and clamped it over her mouth, hearing the sirens far off mixing with the terrorized cries of her stallions, the smoke thickening. The flames seemed confined to the hay bales someone had pulled into the aisles and set alight. The smoke went straight up then curled down along the walls.

Kelso barked like crazy just outside, though Harper had no idea where he'd come from.

As calmly as she could, she entered Sugarland's stall; he stood in the corner with his head craned up. She had to get him out fast before he inhaled the dangerous smoke. With his leg, he couldn't scrabble up the wall well, but Harper knew he'd try. She wrestled the blinkers on, then threw a lead rope over his neck, soothing him, speaking with a calm she didn't feel. She led him out of the stall and out the barn door. He was surprisingly compliant amid the chaos.

She turned him into the pen adjacent to the barn and raced back. Inside, she could hear Deacon roaring—no panic in his voice. His was fury.

Then in the aisle she saw John Henry, prone and still on the floor by the office door.

"John Henry!" she screamed, racing over and bending to him. His eyes fluttered open, the whites glowing in the growing orange light.

"He shot me," he whispered. "He done shot me," he said again and his eyes closed.

Harper called Marshall on the phone, screamed "Call an ambulance, John Henry's been shot! Fire!" and hung up, dragging John Henry by his collar step-by-step out the barn door, laying him gently to the right of the water pump, checking his clothes for blood.

It appeared he'd been shot twice, just below his right shoulder. Harper pressed a wad of his coat into the wound to stop the blood. Weakly he opened his eyes again.

"Get Deacon," he breathed. "He was after Deacon." His eyes pleaded with Harper as he brought his left hand up and pressed his bunched coat into the wound. "Go on, now."

The flames leaped out of the barn aisle and Harper heard the horses' increasing frenzy, the pounding at the stall doors, and their heart-wrenching, terrorized screams.

Headlights shown over the rise. She saw Marshall's Navigator followed by a line of cars racing for the barn. He arrived in a moment with Surrey, leapt out, a blanket furled out behind him, as their guests piled out of Mercedes, Audis, and Porsches, all running toward the barn.

Harper hailed Iris as Tim Bradford raced past and asked her to watch over John Henry until the ambulance arrived, making sure to keep pressure on his seeping wounds.

173

Marshall distributed towels and horse pads; they soaked them at the pump outside. She saw Blue and Walt head into the barn for the horses. Everyone Harper saw look determined and focused. She ran back down the aisle, as from the hay bales on either side, rose flames.

Harper flung a saddle pad over Deacon's eyes and ran with him out of the barn, the ends of his mane singed. It was all she could do to keep up with his enormous strides. Marshall rushed up from somewhere, smothered his mane with a wet towel as they willed him toward the paddock, the saddle pad sliding from him.

Deacon's great head thrashed against the halter, the whites of his eyes flashing as he roared and rolled his head. They managed to get him into the near paddock and he galloped off in a panic.

Inside the barn, the stud's clients, some in furs, some bare-armed, raced everywhere beating down flames with wet blankets. Harper watched Marshall lead two stallions out of the barn, Lucas not far behind with Nico.

Harper sighed. They were all out.

She raced back to John Henry, cradling his head in her arms, his eyes fluttering open as the ambulance rolled up the drive followed by the fire truck, drawn toward the flames. Iris went to join her husband, pounding out the flames.

The paramedics jumped out, looking for the victim and Harper waved them over. They carefully lifted the bloodied coat from John Henry's chest, assessed the damage, loaded him on a stretcher, as from the fire truck men flew into the barn carrying canisters.

Harper watched her friends and clients beat back the last of the flames.

The firemen finished dousing the area, checked the barn thoroughly and gave Harper a verbal report on the way out. They'd be sending an arson team in, they said. Harper nodded her thanks.

As their clients straggled out of the barn, Harper had tears in her eyes. So much damage, so many disasters . . . she could hardly catch her breath. But as she saw Cassidy and Miranda walk by, looking exhausted, their partners behind, brushing the debris off their clothes, their faces smudged and strained, Harper was momentarily overwhelmed with gratitude.

These folks had put themselves in harm's way for her, and for the horses. They could have stayed at the house, eating, talking . . . but they didn't. They'd run straight into danger. Harper smiled weakly as they passed, thanking them each in turn.

Neither Emilio Moreno nor Red Cole was present.

As the paramedics were about to close the ambulance doors, Marshall came up behind Harper, patting her shoulder. She pulled away and ran to the ambulance, jumping in beside the medic.

"Can't be in here, ma'am," he said, working on John Henry. He turned to Harper "You can meet us at the hospital."

She bent over John Henry. "You'll be fine," she said into his dark, frightened eyes.

He smiled weakly. "I will, Miss Harper," he said softly. "I surely will."

She watched the ambulance all the way down the drive, vowing that she would not lose John Henry. She would not lose one more person in her life.

Chapter 17

Marshall and Harper waited in the lobby. He paced nearly the entire time John Henry was in the operating room. Harper was not a fan of hospitals, but given Marshall's anxiety, she called up calmness from somewhere, but it did little to settle Marshall down. Surrey called, then Lucas, and Harper updated them with the little she knew. Which was, essentially, nothing.

"Sit down," Harper said, folding the magazine she'd been leafing through and placing it on the chair next to her. If she was uncomfortable in hospitals, Marshall had her beat by a mile. Maybe she'd gone numb again, who knows.

He glared at Harper and kept pacing and checking his watch as if these activities could somehow hasten the outcome. Of course, he was close to John Henry. They all were. When she thought five hours must have passed, she looked at the clock and saw it had been barely an hour and a half. Marshall paced. She stared at a magazine, not comprehending a single word. They'd just have to wait.

Lucas called again, asked if she knew anything. She again said she knew nothing. He told her Detective Walker needed to question her about the fire so she had to go by the police station as soon as she could. Obviously, he'd want Harper's thoughts about who had set it and shot John Henry.

Though she had her suspicions, Harper didn't think she'd be much help. It was John Henry who could tell the police all they needed to know, not Harper.

Her thoughts drifted to Moreno and Red's absence. She'd place money on Moreno as the culprit. He had a look about him suggesting shooting an unarmed man wasn't something he'd be squeamish about.

Harper rose, spoke to Marshall. "Going for coffee. Want anything?"

The family to their left rose all at once as a doctor came through the doors, their faces expectant.

Harper considered whether she'd mention Moreno to the detective but dismissed it. Without proof or even a credible reason for her suspicions, it would do little good to turn attention to him. Besides, she didn't want him alerted to her interest in his activities.

Marshall shook his head and kept up his moving vigil.

Harper walked past the teenager sleeping on his arm, past the mother gently bouncing her baby, her eyes bloodshot, past young twins putting a puzzle together on the green carpeted floor . . . got a cup of awful vending machine coffee and returned to see a nurse in white tennis shoes pat Marshall on the arm.

"He's out of surgery," she said and walked away as Harper approached.

Marshall pointed to the nurse. "Find out," was all he could manage.

Harper chased her down as she conferred with the doctor who'd just walked through the door. He reported John Henry's wounds were not life threatening; they'd missed vital organs. But he had lost a lot of blood. He'd survive, that's all that counted. He'd be in the hospital for some time, then if all went well, good as new.

Harper felt relieved. It would take time, but their groom would fully recover. She told the nurse the police wanted to speak with him right away. The earliest that might be possible, the nurse said, may be sometime tomorrow.

By sheer force of will, Harper got permission to look in the door of intensive care. John Henry was asleep, a mass of tubes attached to him. She wished him a peaceful slumber, and to wake with the knowledge he was safe.

First thing the next morning she was at the hospital. The police hadn't called her in yet but she thought she might see them there.

John Henry was out of intensive care and in an antiseptic white room with a metal tree to the right of the bed filled with hanging bags and tubes. Monitors beeped encouragingly. The nurse told Harper, "Mr. Henry had a comfortable night."

Who knows if he had? He would not have complained had it been otherwise.

Harper, Marshall, Alia, and Surrey took turns going into his room when they were allowed. Detective Walker arrived in a dark suit and skinny tie. He greeted Harper first. She told him what she could.

He moved on to John Henry's room. Harper followed, but the nurse would only let her stand quietly by the door. Pen in hand, the detective stood next to John Henry's bed as the patient tried to scoot himself up with his one good arm so as to see the detective better.

Harper could tell John Henry felt intimidated by the guy, though Walker's friendly face, sandy hair, and fair complexion didn't rate high on Harper's scale of threatening presences. Still, he had a badge, and she guessed that's all that counted.

Detective Walker asked John Henry who'd shot him. Harper couldn't resist stepping into the room. John Henry turned his head to her, then back to the detective.

"It was the vet, Cooley Edison. He done it." John Henry laid his head back on the pillow, looking disappointed and exhausted.

Harper was utterly shocked.

Both of them looked at her as if she could provide an explanation. Cooley Edison had only crossed Harper's mind in terms of reliability, not arson and murder. She shook her head, completely flummoxed. She had been so sure it was Moreno.

Just when things seemed falling into place, Cooley turns out to be the bad guy. Harper smiled encouragingly at John Henry, nodded to the detective and left.

Cooley Edison. How confusing. If he was capable of shooting John Henry, not to mention attempting to murder the stallions he'd been caring for, Harper had to believe him capable of murdering Paris.

She reported John Henry's revelation to everyone in the waiting room. Detective Walker left quickly to locate Cooley.

Surrey recovered first, focusing herself on trying, for some reason, to give Harper water. She didn't want water. She also didn't want to leave, but Surrey and the others reminded her that she'd said John Henry was doing fine—he'd been awake, alert, and all he needed was rest. That's what Harper had told them, and they parroted it back to her until she reluctantly gave in.

Marshal insisted on taking her home, but she agreed only after making sure Surrey would text with updates if anything changed.

Once in the car, Red, not Cooley, came to mind first.

"Marshall, where was Red?"

179

He shifted the truck into gear and shrugged. "Last night?" he said, noting Harper's nod. "Don't know." He looked at her with concern, his brows furrowed. "Likely showed up at the house when we were at the barn." He shifted his hands on the wheel. "Haven't seen him since yesterday."

She dropped it. It was Cooley who should be occupying her thoughts at the moment, not Red.

It seemed inconceivable that Cooley, who'd been with Eden Hill for decades . . . and there she paused. Well, she had earlier considered Cooley could have been involved, but certainly she hadn't taken it seriously.

Harper knew someone had perpetrated the atrocities on her family, but when it came right down to hearing John Henry utter Cooley's name, it was hard to accept.

She had to talk to him. Yes, he was probably desperate. She got that, but what she felt was disgust. Plenty of people were in worse financial shape than he was and didn't attempt murder. Didn't betray folks who'd been like family.

Marshall sped through the sunlight, not saying anything or putting his hand on hers. There wasn't any comfort to be had in this situation. He knew best just to let Harper talk or not talk, as she needed to.

Harper picked her quarters off the floor for the second time and plugged them into the machine, choosing peanuts. The wood doors of the police bullpen looked like something out of a 1940's movie, scuffed and scarred.

Beyond the doors, Detective Walker stood beside his desk in his office, talking to a woman with a brown braid and a crisp blue uniform. After a few days stewing about Cooley, that morning, she'd made some calls to friends with more political clout than her and gotten permission to talk to him. He'd been taken into custody over the weekend without fuss. In fact, the detective said he'd been ready to turn himself in.

Full of remorse, Harper was told.

Who cares? was her mental response.

Cooley sat at the metal desk in the greenish light. Harper supposed detectives were watching through the two-way, which didn't bother her. Cooley did look mournful. But then, his long, lined face and sparse crop of hair could hardly look otherwise. He stared straight ahead across the table, as if some indelible ink there was about to reveal what had gone wrong with his life.

Harper sat, placed her hands on the table, and didn't say a word.

"I'm sorry," he whispered.

"You shot John Henry," Harper said quietly. "You set my barn on fire and nearly killed my stallions."

He merely nodded, still not meeting her eyes.

"Did you kill my sister, too?" she demanded.

He looked up at that. He seemed surprised at the question. "No, no of course not," he said.

Like murderous intent had degrees. John Henry was okay, but Paris was off-limits? Harper leaned over the table. Sweat broke out on her forehead and trickled down her sides. Her blouse was sticky with it. She'd finagled her way into this room, yet suddenly she felt at a loss for words.

In a weird moment, she thought about what strange creatures humans are. She supposed rationality and emotions were designed to work hand in hand, but really—when did they? Maybe Freud was right; maybe we're just the site of a war between conscience and impulses, with a puny ego not at all equipped to handle the two heavyweights, vying eternally for some smidgen of control.

"I could never do that to Paris," Cooley said.

The detective entered the room and said Harper had about fifteen minutes with Cooley.

She turned back to him, taking a deep, slow breath and letting it out in a stream. She slid her hands off the table and pressed them together in her lap.

"Okay, why don't you just tell me why you did all this," she said, leaning forward. Then, as a lawyer had once instructed her, Harper gently bit her tongue so she'd be quiet and let Cooley speak.

He shook his head. After a time, Harper wondered if he actually would speak. He just kept slowly shaking his head back and forth, back and forth.

She bit her tongue again.

"It was Emma," he said finally, looking at Harper, his eyes clear. She sensed something inside him was glad to be getting this off his chest.

"When Dylan was so damned stupid with those horses last spring, I thought I could just give 'em a little boost and maybe make some money on a couple of long shots." He paused. "Had a guy placing the bets for me." He opened his arms, his palms up in supplication.

So, he had not only tried to kill Harper's high-asset stallions, he'd dosed her horses, too. And he'd dosed more than "a couple."

"What did you give the horses?" Harper said.

Cooley shook his head, looked at a spot on the table between them. He couldn't meet her eye.

"Stuff I got from Steve," he said quietly. "Sold that and bought drugs from my brother in Canada."

Cooley's brother was a chemist. Harper remembered Tim Bradford's comments about blood-doping—EPOs were expensive and you needed a medical connection to get them. Okay, she thought, EPOs and probably pain meds, given the fractures . . . both were undetectable if properly administered.

Say, by a vet.

"But you know what Steve sold you," Harper said—it was a statement, not a question.

"Yeah," he said. "I do."

"It was heroin. You sold the heroin and doped my horses," she said flatly.

"Yeah," he said softly. "I did."

"And the ones in training? Did you mess with them, too?"

Cooley sighed. "Only the ones Dylan had, the ones he was gonna run," he nearly whispered.

The carnage when Tap Down died came to mind; that scene was seared into her.

"Did Dylan know? Did Evan?" she said. Harper doubted it, but she had to be certain.

"Dylan?" Cooley smirked. "'Course not."

"Evan?"

"Evan didn't know," said Cooley, "but I think he was catching on there at the end."

Nearly uncontrollable anger welled up in Harper. Everyone knew that drugs put more than the horses at risk. That fight Evan had with Cooley the morning after Steve's death, the death threat Evan had leveled at Cooley . . . now it made sense. Of all people, Cooley knew exactly how much jeopardy he was putting their jockey in. And Evan had paid with his life.

"How could you do this?" Harper said, after gathering herself. She wondered if he cared about all the harm he'd done. Not only had he doped the horses, he'd been responsible for the injuries and deaths of so many of them. Tried to murder the stud's best stallions and John Henry. And clearly Cooley was responsible for Evan's death.

All for money.

And then there was Steve, Cooley's supplier. And Steve's death, and his ties to Argentina. The drug ring again surfaced. Argentina. Emilio Moreno. Things kept shifting in and out of focus.

And though Harper was interested in the doping, she needed to know if Cooley had killed Paris. He'd denied it, but he'd just tried to kill John Henry—how could she believe anything he said?

"I just don't understand how you could do this."

Cooley bowed his head. "I can't say," he said. Then, so softly Harper hardly heard it, "I don't really know." He looked up, his eyes pleading. "Emma's dying." He looked at his hands. "It just made sense at the time. Get us out of debt, no one the wiser."

"But what about the barn? And John Henry?" Harper sat back, nearly overwhelmed with disgust. "And Evan." She took a deep breath and was quiet.

She'd start there and work back to Paris.

Cooley rubbed the back of his neck. "I just can't say. I snapped, I guess." He looked up at Harper, tears welling in his eyes.

Someone knocked on the door. A young woman brought in water, set it to Harper's right, and exited.

Sorrow and confusion rose in Cooley's eyes. "You fired me. After all I did for your father. All them years. And I near pleaded with you to keep me on." He looked away. "I needed the money. You know how bad off Emma is."

A wave of sadness momentarily washed over her. He'd been in a desperate situation. But he'd shot a man—a man who had been his friend for decades—and tried to murder Harper's stallions. She couldn't understand how a man who'd devoted his life to caring for their horses could drug them and then try to kill them, no matter how desperate he felt. It was baffling.

And seriously . . . after all he'd done for her father? Harper's father had given him a job, control over some of racing's best stallions early in his career. Cooley's arrangement with the family had benefited him just as much or more than it benefited Eden Hill.

Harper asked her last question.

"Who killed Paris, Cooley?" she said. "Was it you?"

Cooley mutely shook his head.

"If it wasn't you, then who?"

The light went from his eyes. "I don't know," he said. "I thought it was an accident just like everybody else." He sat there a while, looking at Harper. "Until Dylan told me about him and Paris. And how he knew somebody had done that to her."

Then he looked at Harper with such a deep sorrow that, despite everything, touched her. "Now I can't be there for Emma," he said, slumping. He took a few ragged breaths, then peered up at Harper. "Could you see to her? Look in on her once in a while? Till . . . till . . ." He looked down at the table and couldn't finish. He meant until she died.

Harper sighed. "Of course, Cooley. Of course, I can." What a broken old man, she thought. He'd made a mess of his own life and put everyone through a hell she couldn't forgive.

185

But Emma had nothing to do with that. Harper would visit her as soon as she could. She planted her hands on the table and pushed herself up, then left.

She still had no answers about Paris.

Outside, she searched the hall for the detective, but didn't see him. She walked toward the bullpen, noted him approaching her, his eyebrows raised in question.

"Get what you wanted?" he asked, without an attitude, she was glad to see. Harper had gone over his head, after all. His light blond beard was trying to come in, a lost cause apparently. "Unfortunately, we couldn't get anything out of him on the attack on you after the blown tire or Steve Hamilton's death or the theft of your mares. Struck out on all of them. Just the fire. And the attempted murder." He paused. "And drugs, thanks to you. I'll look into that—the connection to your murdered farm manager."

Murder. So he'd finally settled on the same conclusion Harper had. Steve's death was not suicide as the preliminary findings suggested.

He continued, gesturing toward his office. Harper stayed where she was.

"Also. . . I haven't made much more headway about those folks buried on your property, I'm afraid. I'll let you know when I do."

Harper nodded her thanks. She started toward the doors and he kept pace with her. Harper wanted to leave, but she did want to ask him about Paris.

"Cooley said he didn't murder my sister," she began. The detective stopped.

"That was ruled an accident," Detective Walker said, studying her seriously. "Are you saying it wasn't?"

Harper made a gallant attempt to curb her frustration. All that had happened wasn't the detective's fault. Buying time, she sipped her water, looked down at the yellowed linoleum floor just behind the detective, then brought her eyes to his.

"I'd just appreciate it if you'd check out where Cooley was when my sister died," she said, sidestepping his question.

"So, you do think it was foul play."

Harper silently reviewed her "evidence." All the suspicions she had made sense to her, just as they had in her initial conversation with Walker. Harper's own investigations coupled with Dylan's conviction Paris hadn't died accidently were compelling. And the Argentinian notations sent with the stallion paraphernalia made sense as a drug shipment list. But, again, to Harper. Not necessarily to the "beyond a reasonable doubt" crowd. Until she had solid proof, she'd keep her conviction and suspicions to herself.

"I'd just really like to know where Cooley was when Paris died," she replied. *No more questions*, she mentally shot his way.

He considered her for a few heartbeats then shrugged. Harper had the sense he'd be keeping an eye on her. Kook or no, her question had roused his interest. "Sure, why not," he said. "I'll let you know what I find out."

Once back home, Harper headed for the office. Pepper updated her about John Henry; she'd called Surrey then relayed the information to folks around the farm. Harper picked up her messages and headed to her office, thanking Pepper for clearing out everything from the buffet so efficiently.

"Wasn't just me," she said. "Everybody helped out."

She settled in to return calls and clear her desk. Again the question surfaced—where had Red been? Harper wondered if he knew about what she was now pretty convinced Moreno was up to—the guy seemed almost a caricature of a South American drug dealer. Maybe not. Maybe Red was in the dark, and Steve had been the front man, the only one Cooley had been in contact with.

She'd have to feel Red out about Moreno.

Harper put that off for another time. She had other things to focus on at the moment, the first one being John Henry's care once he was released from the hospital.

She called Surrey who recommended a nurse friend who'd retired a short time ago—the woman would be perfect. John Henry would hate being cared for. Harper smiled. He'd rather bed down in Grandpa's barn than have a full-time nurse in his apartment, but he'd just have to put up with it. She made a mental note to begin locating another spot to erect his new home.

Next she called the buffet guests who'd so selflessly helped out. They were all still in town; Keeneland's race meet was not yet over. Lucas had mentioned Walt, Blue, and Cassidy were all putting money into the California stallion. Harper was grateful for that as it would help with the note the bank was calling in. She thanked them for that, too, and sat back in her chair, thinking over the talk she and Cooley had at Mariel's, the one that likely was the catalyst for him setting the fire and shooting John Henry.

Cooley had admitted he'd been responsible for the stud's track losses. Knowing Marshall was shouldering way too much trying to train the runners, shore up Paris, and keep Eden Hill afloat, Cooley had taken advantage of him.

And just as Paris had likely discovered, the colts and fillies he'd targeted were trained poorly, entered in races they weren't bred for, and pushed too hard. Some of them had won due to

Cooley's drugs likely given on top of slight injuries, and two had died because of it.

Again, though Harper had seen how crushed and sorrow-filled he was, she was also furious. A vet—their vet—harming their horses in that way. It was unthinkable.

Money. Wave enough of it in front of your eyes and it blinded as surely as if it was acid.

And if Paris had discovered what Cooley was doing, it could well have gotten her killed. Harper's conversation with Cynthia came to mind. Maybe Paris had confronted Steve and that's what he was so upset about. And maybe he'd told Cooley or maybe Moreno and it had gotten her sister killed.

And again, Harper considered whether or not drugging their horses began and ended with Cooley, or if others were involved before him. Like Red and her father.

She thought about Rafe, wondering if she'd ever know the truth about her father. To think that he'd hidden the truth from everyone seemed impossible to her. But she considered that perhaps she was wrong. And if she was wrong about that, she also wondered how she could trust her reading of anyone. JD, for instance.

She'd been closer to him than to anyone other than Paris, and yet they'd drifted apart. Whether she could rely on her reading of him when he got back was an open question.

She drummed her fingers on the desk, wishing the detective would call. She needed to know where Cooley was when Paris was killed. Unlike the musings about Rafe, Moreno, and JD, this was a small question, easily answered. It made perfect sense that if Cooley discovered Paris had been close to figuring out what he was up to, he'd get rid of her as easily as he'd nearly done away with John Henry.

Harper put her head in her hands. Her head had resumed the throbbing she'd felt off and on over the past two weeks. Maybe coffee would help. Her stomach muscles had stopped paining her, though. She was thankful for that.

She sighed. Calls to return . . . best get to it.

Working through the list, she was surprised to find Murray Rickels' name. Harper's mother, who rarely had a bad word to say about anyone, had hurled a few choice ones in Murray's direction. He'd cheated her father a few times, but not more than a few. He had a terrible reputation; Harper was surprised he was still operating in the racing industry. Well, she corrected herself, all she had was a call. Maybe, like many others, he wanted to express his condolences.

She doubted it, but you never know.

Pepper brought in a cup of coffee and a corned beef sandwich. *She is psychic, I swear.* Harper gratefully picked it up and took a few bites before carrying on.

She called Murray back, expecting to hear some words of kindness—best to give everyone the benefit of the doubt—but no such luck. All Murray wanted to know was how many horses they'd lost, whether there were particular mares for sale, and whether the barn was seriously damaged. He'd heard the farm was coming up for sale soon. And he'd chuckled when referring to the mares, which Harper thought was in very bad taste; everyone had heard about the thefts.

Horse racing has a higher number of jerks than other industries, and Murray's type headed the list. He conveniently couldn't recall where he'd heard of the sale. Harper disabused him of his error, spent the shortest possible amount of time on the phone with him, and rang off.

Then it hit her. Didn't Murray have a three-horse trailer? Just like the one Marshall had seen streaming past the stud farm that awful night Steve had been murdered and their mares taken? She wondered if Rickels was involved—he certainly fit the character profile.

She hauled out the paper and CD sent up to Steve Hamilton from Argentina. M.R. were the first initials on the list. Murray Rickels. So maybe he was involved in a lot more than stealing her horses—if it actually had been him. The CD caught her eye, so she popped it in Paris' computer.

It was a comprehensive list, much the same as the printout, but including the previous year up through September. Same sorts of notations, but different quantities and dates. Harper felt certain it referred to shipments of heroin. With all the other evidence she'd gained, there seemed simply no other explanation. And if her calculations were correct, an enormous amount of heroin had been distributed through Eden Hill last year.

She put the CD and printout in the bottom drawer and locked it. It was the tangible proof she needed for motive, but without something equally as tangible to explain the dates, weights, and initials, she still effectively had nothing.

Pepper buzzed to say Surrey was on the line. Harper picked up and she said she'd be over to fix dinner at six, after she fed Marshall. Harper said that wasn't necessary but Surrey, mother that she was, reminded her that she needed to eat. Harper thanked her, grateful for her thoughtfulness. Between Pepper and Surrey, she clearly would not go hungry.

She sat back, thinking over her recent find, trying to figure out how to prove Emilio Moreno was the real culprit, always lurking behind the scene. She'd bet money he was involved in the drugs Cooley had gotten from Steve and sold, but she still had to prove it.

She sorted through the calls she needed to return and punched up Jen's cell phone. Not surprisingly, she was concerned about the stallions. Only after that did she ask about John Henry and was totally shocked to hear about Cooley.

"Mariel's here, hang on," Jen said before Harper could protest. Then her partner picked up the phone. Harper didn't have a lot of time to explain everything to Mariel, but she would later. Mariel, more than anyone, would understand.

"My darling," Mariel began, "I am so sorry to hear of the fire. Jen say the horses are okay? And John Henry?" She asked Harper to hold on then came back. "It was Cooley? This can't be true!" Mariel routinely used Cooley's vet services, too.

Harper assured her it was true. No sense in keeping it to herself, the news would be out soon enough. Cooley had worked a lot of breeding farms in the area over many years. Jen and Mariel's feelings would be echoed in many corners of the industry.

He'd brought it all on himself, she thought, regardless of how remorseful he was. She thanked Mariel for her concern, assured her that if she needed anything, she'd be sure to call, and hung up, shoving in another mouthful of corned beef.

Harper finished up the sandwich and the rest of her work then headed out. Before going home, she stopped by the stallion barn now housing Sugar, Deacon, and Nico. Her father had been wise to build several small structures rather than one big barn for the studs. This, their largest stallion barn, had three empty stalls; the rest of the horses Lucas had moved to the next closest barn.

Sugar and Deacon looked fine. But Harper knew that could be deceiving. It was smoke that could do the damage; fluid in their lungs might appear days after the incident.

They could still lose their two best colts and the stallions.

As she checked on Deacon's coat beneath his singed mane, Lucas came out of the feed room and headed toward Nico, wheeling the feed cart.

"How's John Henry?" he asked, thinking she'd been at the hospital. Pepper had updated her prior to leaving the office; last report, John Henry was sleeping.

Better that than no news at all. Or bad news.

"Good, I think. How are the boys?" Harper grabbed a feed scoop and helped Lucas feed. Creatures of habit, the stallions were all at attention, calling to Lucas to be fed first. Sugar, Deacon, and Nico joined in, she was happy to see. Maybe they'd get through this without any more damage.

"How's Sugar's leg?" she asked. She'd been so frantic to get them out of the barn and worried about John Henry, she had no idea if Sugar had damaged his leg or not.

"Tim was by first thing this morning. Says Sugar looks fine." He opened Deacon's feed window and poured in the feed. Nico voiced his disapproval as Deacon dug in. They moved to the next stall. "And the rest are good, too."

Harper inhaled the horse's earthy scent, the fresh hay and sweet feed, relaxing for the first time in it seemed like weeks. Paris had been right about Tim. With all that had happened the night of the fire, she hadn't thought to ask him to check in on the stallions; maybe Lucas or Marshall had the presence of mind to mention it. Or maybe Tim had just come over. He struck Harper as the type to do that.

"It'll be a while before we know for sure if these guys are in the clear," Lucas continued, working the feed scoop into the bucket and dumping grain in the next stall. "Me and Cheyenne are gonna keep a close eye out."

Harper nodded, noting Lucas had already given the stallions their hay. "Thanks, Lucas."

"Yeah, and Tim'll be by this afternoon. Said he'd stop by twice a day till we know for sure."

She checked on the other stallions in the next barn and relieved that, at least for now, things looked okay, headed for the house.

Chapter 18

The next morning, Detective Walker called to say Cooley's whereabouts during Paris' death were accounted for. He'd been by Emma's side at the hospital and had countless nurses and doctors who'd attested to it.

Harper put down her spoon, dumped the rest of the oatmeal down the disposal, and gulped her last swig of orange juice.

Great, she thought. So, it couldn't have been Cooley.

That left . . . perhaps Steve? Or Emilio Moreno.

Detective Walker pressed Harper on why she was suspicious about Paris' death. He wanted details. She didn't have many. He said that after their conversation he'd looked again at the report on Paris' death and concluded that accidental death might have been a hasty finding. He could see where murder might be as plausible an explanation for her death as an accident.

He was blunt about his frustrations with her. "We should be working as a team—I'm not your enemy. I'll be reopening the investigation into Paris' death and I'll need you to share any information you haven't given me."

When Harper didn't respond, he became firm. "You'll do that now. If you'd prefer, I can have a policeman escort you to the station." His message was clear—he wasn't taking no for an answer this time.

Harper relented. She explained the litany of reasons she thought Paris had been murdered, including her conversations with Dylan and Anna Cole, and including what she thought was the printout of drug shipments. She laid out her suspicions about what had been going on at Eden Hill, including Steve Hamilton's involvement and her suspicions about Moreno. Walker said he'd be in touch with Dylan and Anna. He wanted a copy of the CD and printout, too, saying he'd alert the DEA. He seemed to be taking her thoughts seriously, for which Harper was grateful.

She looked out the kitchen window, watching Cheyenne turn out Zydeco for a morning romp in the paddock.

She stared, unblinking, at the barn. Her Grandpa's barn. How many times they'd all looked down over Bucks Creek to that barn from this very spot in the kitchen, watching the horses sticking curious heads out of windows, or seeing the soft barn lights shining steadily at feeding time.

Harper missed her family. The sight of the barn was painful in a way, but also gave her a sense of peace and she didn't look away for the longest time.

Her conversation with Cooley again came back to her, as it had all night long. She hadn't gotten much sleep.

And Red, too, came to mind; she wondered if he knew about the heroin. Or maybe he was involved? But even if he was involved or knew or even had suspicions, he would gain nothing by killing Paris in terms of his pronounced interest in buying the stud. Harper would have to approve any sale, and Red must have known she'd be just as opposed to selling as would Paris. If that wasn't clear to him prior to Paris' death, she thought, it was certainly clear now.

Unless Paris had discovered that he knew about the drugs, Harper couldn't think of any plausible reason he'd kill her, and Red was nothing if not calculating. He'd always given himself the best odds. Killing Paris served no purpose.

She washed the few dishes she'd used and set them on the drain board then went upstairs intending to dress and head to the office.

Lucas called as she was getting ready to say they'd be installing the security system in three days. Harper called Tim who said the horses still looked okay—no fluid in the lungs. They'd keep their fingers crossed.

She headed to the office and made copies of the CD and printout herself; nothing was safe until the police had it locked up. Then she ransacked Paris'—*no, my office* she reminded herself—but didn't find anything resembling the proof she had so hoped Paris had discovered and secreted away. She called Detective Walker, sealed the copies in a mailer, and set it on the entranceway table; he'd pick them up over lunch. She stressed to Pepper that under no circumstances was anyone but Detective Walker to even touch the package. Pepper nodded, looking at Harper curiously. She declined to explain.

Pepper and Dave headed out to grab a bite to eat and asked if Harper wanted anything. She thanked them, but said she had other plans. She did some errands in town, stopped by Mariel's to see how the mare she and Cooley had treated was doing and around two o'clock, headed back to the house.

Things, she felt, had come to a standstill. She needed proof of whatever Paris had discovered that had gotten her killed. She trudged up the stairs, thinking these frustrating thoughts and found herself in Paris' bedroom.

Harper sat on the padded bench at the end of her bed, her hands in her lap. She glanced at the empty wall where her childhood bed had stood, remembering all the snippy conversations they'd had, all the times they laughed till their sides hurt. In her mind's eye she watched Paris fly through the door, elated, waving some ribbon she'd won wildly above her head. Harper saw her batting the comb aside, insisting Harper do her hair differently for prom. She smiled. Paris was as headstrong as Deacon.

It was difficult to be in Paris' room. Harper looked around, noticing everything—the colors they'd chosen for her walls, the quilt they'd found last summer at a flea market, Paris' reading chair.

Maybe Paris had proof and had hidden it somewhere in her room. Harper eyed the shelving circling the room high up by the ceiling, loaded with trophies and ribbons. She hauled the desk chair over and ran her hand behind everything. No luck.

She went through the pockets of all Paris' coats and jackets. Dried up carrot bits, some change, a small tube of Carmex, one soiled riding glove. Nothing of interest.

She turned over all her boots, but again nothing. On to the walk-in closet. Harper pulled out all the drawers in the center island . . . lingerie, socks, flannel pjs, scarves, some photo albums stuck in the bottom of a drawer. She searched the clothes, pushing them back, looking for a safe, a hiding place, something in the wall she hadn't known about. Again, no luck.

She searched the racks above the hanging clothes. Afghans, boxes of photos, more albums, extra pillows, blankets. Nothing.

Harper crossed the room to Paris' desk, turned on the green-glass shaded lamp. She picked everything out of her drawers and laid them on the worn wood top. There was a strip of photos taken of her and Dylan; clearly they were more than friends. Ticket stubs, matches from restaurants . . . stationery, a manila folder filled with old photos of their parents, JD, Red and Anna, and Paris.

Harper sat back, going through those photos. Everyone was so thin. And young. She sighed. It was a long time ago. She lingered on Paris' photo, and then momentarily on JD's, and then packed it all away.

The rest of the room yielded nothing but more difficult memories.

She left, closing the door gently behind her and changed into riding clothes. Might as well take Zydeco out. There wouldn't be too many more nice days.

She walked out on the porch, taking in the late October sky. Not much more daylight for a ride, so she hurried over the bridge to the barn. Zydeco was beginning to put on a tad more weight and was bright-eyed, which Harper was happy to see. She opened the window and plunked a few carrots in his feed bowl, which he gobbled up then turned back to his hay. She picked out the saucer-shaped plastic tray to clean it before their ride; it was grimy and she felt Zeke deserved a pristine stall befitting his sterling character. Harper smiled to herself, glancing down to disengage the bowl.

Underneath it, taped to the wall, were a tiny, plastic-encased cassette and a small thumb drive. She stood a moment staring at both of them, unable to move a muscle. Paris had to have put them there. Oddly, a flush of fear went through Harper, looking at her find. She glanced around nervously to make sure no one else was in the barn.

Her sister had quite likely died because of what was on that thumb drive. Part of Harper didn't want to touch it.

She chided herself. She should have known to check the horses in the barn first. Paris was more particular about Zydeco's stall than her office or bedroom and prided herself on taking care of everything associated with him. No one else would have dared to fool with his feed, or tack, or stall, not even John Henry, but Harper had to admit the feed bowl was an unlikely place to store evidence, even for Paris.

After staring at the finds a minute more, she plucked the cassette and drive from the wall and patted Zydeco, promising him a ride if there was enough light after she'd looked at what was on the drive. He nodded his head as she briefly scratched his neck, and then went contentedly back to his hay as she exited the stall and headed to her office, closing the door once she'd arrived.

She set her riding helmet beside the computer and hauled out the small portable cassette player Paris had used to record her thoughts while on the road. She'd check the thumb drive after listening to what Paris had recorded. Her sister loved her audio recorder and had carried it with her on every road trip. Harper inserted the small cassette and hit "play."

It was a conversation between Paris and Steve. When she realized that, Harper withdrew the cassette and checked the date, which turned out to be a week before Paris' death. She re-inserted the cassette.

Harper rewound it and began it again. Hearing her sister's voice caused a sudden wave of grief. She stopped the recording again and sank down in the desk chair, her hand over her mouth. Paris' voice jarred her emotions.

After a minute or two to regroup, she again hit "play." The recording wasn't long, but it did contain Paris' outraged confrontation of Steve. She accused him of doping their horses, and he denied it. He sounded pitiful, speaking merely above a whisper as he admitted skimming heroin from recent shipments and selling it, indicating there was an ongoing operation in place. Paris pressed him hard on that point, but he only implicated himself—there was no word about Cooley's involvement or Moreno's or anyone else's.

Harper realized she was listening to the conversation that had so upset Steve, the one Cynthia had mentioned. She popped the cassette out, squeezed it in her palm, and sent a sad, sweet thank you to her sister for having the foresight to tape the conversation.

If she was disappointed in the lack of clear proof that Moreno was involved, Harper was grateful to have solid proof of at least this much. Maybe the thumb drive would be more directly incriminating.

Now Steve's death, given his confession to Paris, made even less sense as a suicide and much more sense as a murder. If someone had learned of the conversation, getting rid of Steve because he was skimming was an easy decision. Getting rid of Paris was riskier—one death could be overlooked. But two were much more difficult to ignore.

Which meant that Paris had made it impossible to keep her alive . . . she'd done something to make the risk worth the reward.

For someone.

Harper palmed the cassette and stared at the thumb drive wondering what additional information it might contain while trying to ignore how difficult it had been to listen to Paris' voice— so alive, so angry. So determined.

She called Detective Walker again but got his voicemail. She left a message about the new evidence. He'd already picked up the mailer Harper had left for him, so she stressed he should find her and pick up the cassette and thumb drive as soon as possible. She'd keep them with her until then.

Harper wasn't going to let either of them out of her sight.

She sat at the desk, as emotion flooded through her. The sound of Paris' voice recalled her sister so vividly; it was as if for a moment she'd been present—alive, vibrant, forceful. And then silence. Here, and then just as suddenly, she was again gone, forever gone.

She put the cassette and thumb drive in her jodhpur pocket, zipped it, unable to deal with one more aspect of her death at the moment. She picked up her helmet and with a last look outside decided there was time for a short ride before evening. A ride she hoped would restore her emotional balance. She'd check the thumb drive after she put up Zydeco.

Elle and Oliver nickered at Harper as she saddled him up and headed out into the day's fading warmth.

They took it slow, walking toward the mares' barn. She tried to relax, let the sound of Paris' voice on the tape fade. Ahead, the pastures rolled out gently. Well over the next rise was the far pasture where Lucas had put Mariel's new rescues. They trotted up to the fence line. The horses all stood close to one another, munching contentedly at the remaining grass. Mostly bays, their group was punctuated by two pretty grays. A couple raised their heads to check out the new arrivals, ears pointed forward, then they went back to eating.

Harper brought Zeke to a halt and watched the horses quietly grazing. Like all horses, there was a stillness in them. She allowed her body to relax, taking in their serenity, remembering how restorative it had always been to her—a serenity that's as real to them as our chaotic world is to us, she thought.

She felt the world's quietness envelop her and gazed around slowly at how gently the evening was coming on, with its soft blues and pinks in the sky and the softening fall colors. She'd forgotten so much of this in the city. It had slipped from her memory without her noticing.

After a time, as the light faded, she turned Zeke, glad to see there was still some good pasture for the rescues. The horses would be fine. Every one of them looked filled out and healthy.

She again took in the wide landscape and open sky, allowing her emotions to finally settle back in place. She left the sanctuary of the silent pasture feeling somewhat renewed.

She let Zydeco out then, cantering along the rise, feeling the slight breeze with its taste of winter, trying her best to stay in the moment. She listened to Zydeco breathe, felt his relaxed, natural motion and let it inhabit her.

As he slowed to a trot then a walk, she felt able to consider what she'd recently learned. However horrendous, things did seem to be falling into place—the proof she needed to put things right was surfacing. Finally. Zydeco halted, shifted under her, cocking his back leg, content. Then for a brief moment, her universe was calm and quiet.

Harper felt almost at peace.

Back in the barn, she removed her helmet, put up Zydeco's tack, brushed him and turned him into his stall, forking in a bit more hay.

As she turned to leave a dark shadow appeared at the barn entrance. Behind her, Zydeco sent out an alarming snort and began circling his stall.

Red walked in, emerging out of the shadows.

"How you doing, girl?" he said, approaching Harper, glancing dismissively at Zydeco who was still obviously upset.

"Horse ain't got no sense," he said, moving past her and on to Peyton's stall further down the barn aisle. Zydeco ceased circling but remained in the back corner of his stall, his breath coming in nervous snorts.

Zeke's response put Harper on guard; she trusted his instincts. Like all horses, he had a sixth sense about things that seemed off.

Red stuffed his hands in his oversized coat pockets and stood there staring at Harper.

She didn't say anything.

"I come over to see how you're gettin' on," he said finally.

That again. The unspoken question was whether or not she'd decided to sell to him.

"I'm fine, Red," she said.

"Uh-huh," he said, looking at his work boots. "Well, we need to come to some terms here on the farm deal pretty soon." He looked up, his eyes narrowing.

Not thinking about the implied threat, she replied just as strongly: "Red, if you're asking about me selling the farm again, that's not going to happen." She'd already told him that, but maybe best to be crystal clear so they could both move on.

He was not pleased. "Naw, now, I think you're gonna reconsider that," he said, stuffing his hands further into his pockets. He smiled.

The smile was unnerving and suddenly Harper was aware that she was alone with Red. Cheyenne would be around to feed in half an hour or so but until then, no one knew where she was.

Peyton's head hung out her window to Red's left. He pushed her back in the stall as she shook her head angrily. Harper didn't like the way he handled her at all.

"I've thought about it a lot," she said. "I'm not selling, but I hope you'll stay in our partnership."

He stooped down and slit open a square hay bale in the aisle.

He straightened and gave Harper that eerie smile again. "Some might say you didn't think on it at all." He paused. "Some might think you're trying to put one over on ole Red."

Not only Peyton could tell his presence was ominous. Around them, in the gathering darkness, all the horses sensed something was not right; Harper could hear them pacing.

Red shook his head. "We're gonna come to them terms," he said, staring at her. "Right here. Right now." He snapped shut his knife and put it back in his pocket.

Harper realized he'd cut the bale to show her the knife.

He caught her arm as she turned to leave, shoving her down onto the bale. Menace definitely showed in his eyes. Anger, too.

A disorienting panic shot through Harper. The bale gave way and she sprawled on the floor, looking up at him hovering over her.

"No time like the present, girly," he said, and spat to the side.

In a rush, Harper realized maybe she'd been wrong. Maybe it wasn't Moreno orchestrating all this, but Red. Behind the menace in his eyes was a burning hatred that startled her.

She struggled on the ground, her back wedged against the stall.

Zydeco stuck his neck out of his stall window and rolled his head, the white of his eye showing. He pawed at the wood, snorting, his ears flat back in anger.

"Why, Red?" Harper choked out and he understood what she meant.

He chuckled. "Why, whut?" He hauled an overturned feed bucket close and sat on it, right in front of her, waving a dismissive hand at Zydeco's high-pitched, angry squeal.

Harper sat up against the stall. No use trying to run. He had a knife and was a strong bull of a man.

"Why all of it?" She stared at him, hoping he'd unburden himself, much as Cooley had done.

But Red was not Cooley. His acts weren't born of desperation; he was as calculating as they come.

"Tell me what happened to Paris," Harper said clearly. Whatever happened to her, she was determined to get the truth out of him about Paris.

"Aw, that Paris girl," he said, looking up at the barn's rafters. "She was a piece a work." He looked back at Harper, hunched over on the bucket, his big coat billowed around him. "Wouldn't hear nothin' about selling." He put his head down, kicked at the barn aisle, his skull showing through sparse hair. "Wouldn't hear nothin' of it."

"Why would you hurt her? You've known us all our lives." Maybe tapping into their long history together would open some vein of sympathy in him. Then again Anna's word for him came back to Harper—evil. No room for sympathy in evil.

Red snickered. "That is true, little girl. That is definitely true."

Harper sat up straighter, shot a look out the door of the barn, measuring the distance; it was too far a run—she knew she'd never make it. She turned back to Red.

"How long have you been running drugs through here?"

Virginia Slachman

Red sat back and raised his palms, a look of mock surprise on his face. "So, you figured that out all by your lonesome? My, my, ain't you the smart one." He laughed. "Shoulda figured, you were always the brains of the bunch."

"Paris figured it out, that's why you killed her."

Again, Red showed surprise. "I ain't kilt nobody." He laughed, mockingly protesting his innocence.

The stalled horses sent out intermittent snorts, feeling tension fill the air.

"Is JD involved or are the drugs coming from Moreno?"

Red's eyes narrowed. "JD? He ain't got nothing to do with this. Never has." Red pulled his knife out and opened it up. From the same pocket, he pulled out a piece of wood and began to whittle. "Naw, JD's just like his momma. Too soft to make the real money."

At least her intuition was right on that account.

"So, you and Moreno. You two put this together." Harper was scared of Red, but also, she oddly felt a sense of relief. At last she was going to get to the truth. "You're bringing drugs up from Argentina."

He scowled at the beautiful stalls her Grandpa had crafted— arching wrought iron bars above stained wood and spat again in derision. "Yeah, ole Paris, she did figure it out, too." He smiled at her. "Long before you did, little girl . . . Couldn't have that, now could we?"

Red smiled, rested his hands on his thighs. "Let me clear up a bit of whut's botherin' you, girl." He spat again. "I been running drugs since my Texas days riding bulls. Learned my trade good down on the border."

207

"Then I come up here and behold whut a business was to be had." He grinned. "I swear to the Lord, you ain't seen so many high rollers with an appetite for drugs as round them tracks."

He slapped the dust off one thigh. "Did a hell of a business . . . An your ole Steve there, he was useful as all hell." He'd gone back to his whittling, but at that comment looked at her. "Up to a point."

"He confessed to Paris."

"He did that." Red nodded. "And skimmed a tad, too, come to find out. Had to sic Emilio on him." Red snickered. He shook his head, amused. "I told him make it look kinda perplexing. And give them mares to a guy deserves them more than you." He sneered at Harper. "And that's whut he done."

So Red had Steve killed and set it up to look like a suicide. It was just like him to add in stealing the mares, just to confuse the point.

"So, did you drug our horses all along, even back when my father was alive?" she said, needing to know if her father had been involved in Red's deadly scheme. "You and your cartel buddies?"

Red snorted. "Cartel buddies? Whut would I need them idiots for? Honey girl, I been running drugs all by my lonesome all my life." He winked, causing Harper to flinch. Then he grinned and shook his head. "Drugging horses is for fools. I cain't tell you how happy it made me to see Cooley fiddling around with them runners. He was a gol durn gift." Red glanced up to the heavens as if in thanks for his stooge. He snorted and looked at Harper. "Ain't wasting my product on them brainless pieces a horseflesh. I got me plenty a folks want whut I got all for their stupid selves."

"So, you didn't drug the horses?" she said. "My father didn't? You two were not in this together?"

Red smiled. "Ignorant. That's all there is to that. Steve, Cooley, just stupid as the day is long. Sellin' my drugs to buy them fancy ones?" He shook his head, inspecting what appeared to be a little whittled horse. "Idiots. Them boys got no more brains than a ham sandwich." Red laughed at his joke. "An I'll just let you think a little about your ole pappy," he continued, looking up at Harper and poking his knife in her direction. "You're so smart, let's see whut you can come up with on that one." He leered at Harper, then waved a dismissive hand like she was some two-year-old toddler, not worth expending any further breath on.

She was not going to get a straight answer out of him about her father.

Zydeco kicked hard against the back of his stall. She sent him a mental "Peace, be still." Didn't want him splintering the wood and injuring himself. He moved to the stall window again, checking on Harper, tossed his head angrily.

She turned back to Red. "Those people who were murdered and dumped on my property," she said, the seven skeletons coming to mind. She wondered if they'd been involved in his drug running and had to be disposed of as had Steve Hamilton. "A nun, for God sakes. Did you do that, too, Red?"

Red's phone rang. He unzipped his big coat and pulled the phone out of his breast pocket, checking the call.

"Whuddya know," he said, ignoring Harper's question and turning the phone to her. "It's ole Marshall." He answered the phone, nodding and talking calmly and pleasantly with the trainer. He said he'd be over to see Nico soon. He was just taking care of something out in a pasture.

He winked at Harper.

She opened her mouth to scream, but Red leaned over and put his little knife up to her eye, all the while talking amicably with Marshall.

"Yeah, I think I got me a good idea," he said after ringing off and sitting back, flipping that little knife over his fingers.

Harper looked around. The light was nearly gone as the day descended into darkness. Detective Walker was due at the farm after work to pick up the audiotape and thumb drive. The ones still in her pocket. If she wasn't around, maybe he'd look into where exactly she was—clearly, she wouldn't blow off the only hard evidence she had about drug trafficking and why Paris had been murdered.

Harper returned to their conversation. "Were we all just stooges for you? Steve, Cooley, . . . Paris, me? Marshall?"

Red chuckled. "Ya'll just think you got everything all figured out all the time. Ya'll are foolin' yerselves. I just made the most of it, is all."

Harper was furious, her pulse pounding. Scared, yes, but she also saw how right Anna had been—Red had been taken over by something dark, something evil.

He chuckled. "Yeah, ole Paris, she had that same look on her ever time we talked."

He examined his knife and drew it against the piece of wood he'd been working on. He flicked off short, expert slips of wood as his little horse continued to take shape.

Red watched Harper out of the corner of his eye. "Ye like them flowers I sent?" he said, his voice friendly. He laughed. "'Red' roses. Get it?"

Red roses . . . so it was Red who'd sent the flower arrangement after the deaths at the track. She looked at Red and shuddered.

"And my tire?" she said. "Did you manage that, too?"

"Aw, you weren't hurt but a bit," he said amicably. "No harm done, that's whut I heard."

Red stood up and took a lead rope from the hook at the stall door, wrapped it around her wrists and tied her roughly to the stall bars. He went to the office and got a cup and filled it with water at the spigot. Placing his hand at the back of Harper's neck, he brought the water to her lips. She shook her head so hard water sloshed over the cup rim.

"You got to hydrate, darlin'" he said, forcing the liquid into her mouth. She swallowed. "There you go." He seemed pleased with himself and sat back down.

His mock kindness further horrified Harper—one minute a threatening presence, the next a concerned host.

"So, we got some things to get to."

Harper sat up as best she could, facing him. He wasn't going to loom over her again if she could help it. Her wrists chafed with each move.

"Now I'm gonna let ye loose here, if you'll be a good girl and promise there won't be no funny bidness." He brandished his sharp little knife at her.

She nodded, and he undid the ropes on her wrists. At least she was free. Red was a big, strong man, but at least now she had a chance. He was a fool, she thought, to release her.

"Now, sweetie girl, I can see them wheels a turnin' and it ain't gonna do you no good." He flicked the knife over the wood. "Ain't gonna be around long enough to do nothin'." He smiled at Harper.

"You don't have to do this," she said. "Put an end to this, Red." She looked down at her chafed wrists. "You've been like family to me," she said softly.

Red thought that was funny. "Yep. One big ole happy one."

She tried another approach. "You must have known Paris wouldn't sell you the farm. None of us would. You knew my Grandpa. You knew we'd never sell out."

"You think I care about this here farm?" He looked around, gestured derisively down the barn aisle.

Several of the horses had retreated into the depths of their stalls; Harper could hear them anxiously stomping and churning the bedding.

Now that truly made no sense. Why would he pressure Paris, then her, to sell to him if he didn't really want the farm?

But his mind had wandered off again: evidently, a different topic held more interest.

"Your daddy," he said. "Now there was a man could charm a snake right outta his rattler."

What did her father have to do with this? "My father was a good man," she said hotly.

"Oh, yeah he was," said Red, piercing the wood with his little knife, twisting it there. "Yeah, he was that most certainly." He peered over at Harper. "My Anna sure thought so." He nodded, smiling horribly. "She surely did."

Harper stiffened. Anna? Why bring her up? Her parents couldn't have been closer to Anna and Red.

"What are you getting at, Red?" she said. "What does any of that have to do with Paris? Or me?"

He stabbed the knife suddenly at her, venom in his voice. "Your daddy, he was so dang high-falutin' my Anna couldn't see nothin' but stars ever time she was around him."

Her head jerked back as if she'd been hit. Her father. Anna. Is that what this was all about?

He sneered. "Saw how she done herself up?" He snorted. "An how she done up that son a mine? Stole JD right out from under me." He went back to whittling. "That was your daddy," he mumbled.

He looked at Harper and smiled. "And no one suspecting him ever now and then dabbling with the needle."

There it was again, the drugs. The entire situation shifted in Harper's thought. No, not just the situation. Her whole world shifted. Her father and Anna . . . All those times they'd conferred so closely, so familiarly. Harper had thought nothing of it. Her father was helping Anna learn the business, just as he'd helped countless people get into the racing game. And her mother . . . had there been an affair? Had she known, and done nothing?

And the drugs. Avalon's vet report had forced Harper to consider whether her father had been doping their horses and now Red was implying that was true. She had no idea what to believe.

All those family outings with the Coles. The cookouts, the birthdays, the Christmas dinners, the horse shows and sales . . . it had all been laced with lies.

She looked at Red, whittling away so calmly she wouldn't have been surprised had he hummed a tune. It dawned on her then. None of this had to do with protecting Red's drug trade or annexing her farm. Or gaining control of their colts. This had nothing at all to do with business. Harper stared at Red, chilled to the bone.

This wasn't about business. This was about revenge.

"Yeah," Red continued, focusing on the final few knife strokes, "my Anna she had herself a lil baby girl." Red's face flushed, as he looked up at Harper. "An guess whut."

She knew already. The conversation had been headed in this direction all along. She saw that, finally.

"I told Paris, she was a bit perplexed by it all," said Red, smoothing his fingers over his handiwork.

So that's why Paris had talked with Anna about her pregnancy. It made perfect sense now.

"You're saying Anna's baby was my father's?"

"Yes, ma'am, that's exactly whut happened." He rested his elbows on his knees, looking at the dirt aisle. "Everbody said I beat that woman. I didn't beat her. She left on her own carrying that lil girl baby." His voice lowered. "An I was sorry as hell she did."

Harper had seen that in her kitchen the day Anna dropped by. Red's eyes followed Anna with a hunger and longing she couldn't understand at the time. Now it was clear that he was still in love with her.

Why hadn't she seen that?

And, she suddenly realized, she had a sister somewhere out there in the world.

"Yeah, I thought on taking that farm of yours . . ." He paused and stared off into the gloom. "Durn near ten year, it's been." His hands hung limply in front of him. "Was gonna give it to Anna, she always hankered after it. An your daddy, a course."

He shook his head. "Paris, she was a hard-hearted woman, when you get right down to it."

Harper inched her way toward the edge of the split square bale. Her plan was to bowl Red over and race for the barn door. Red seemed caught in his own demented, twisted world.

"You seen how that JD turned out?" He looked up and Harper froze. Red didn't seem to notice she'd moved. "All dandied up like his momma? An your daddy, the Thoroughbred saint?" He spat again. "Your daddy's gonna pay, like I told Paris. Pay like I paid."

"My father's dead," Harper said softly.

She willed herself to be silent. Let Red get lost in that world.

"Don't matter a lick," said Red in a reasonable voice. "Didn't matter a hill a beans to Anna when I told her I would get your daddy's farm for her." He stared at her, but Harper didn't think he really saw her. "It was your daddy or nothin'."

He barely glanced over at Harper. "So, I kilt ole Paris an I'm gonna kill you, too, little girl."

The hatred in his voice made her whole body go cold. She shivered.

"Then I'm gonna get your farm for peanuts an' sell it off piece by piece . . . Gonna kill everthing in sight, while I'm at it."

He stood, placed his little wooden horse in his pocket and studied her.

"I been thinking on how to do you," he said. "Ole Paris, she was easy to figure. Rode that durn horse out ever morning. Wasn't difficult at all."

Harper winced, thinking of Paris happily riding Zydeco that last morning, without any thought that someone lay in wait for her.

"Can't do it here." He looked around, thinking. Then he smiled, hitting on a plan. "Could be you'll take a leap a faith off that cliff over Bucks Creek you and Paris liked so well." He looked at Harper and laughed. "Seems fitting, don't you think?"

With that, Red hustled her out of the barn into the gathering darkness, shoving her into his truck, pushing her to the floor on the passenger side. She hugged her knees to her chest, wedged on the floor between the console and dashboard.

She gazed up at his profile. Even if he threw her off the cliff, she thought horribly, that still didn't mean she'd die. Unless Red had something else in mind.

"I don't know," said Red, his face a twisted mask in the dashboard lights, "I could maybe keep that big black colt a yours. Run him into the ground." He stared down at Harper. "Ruin him. Like y'all ruined me."

"We didn't ruin you, Red," she spat, her back beginning to spasm. "You did that all by yourself."

He reached over and hit Harper hard in the face, pushing her into the dashboard. "Don't sass me, girl."

Her cheek stung, likely from the blow and her anger. She struggled to right herself.

The rancid smell of spoiled grain rose from the back seat, nauseating her.

Red pulled out his knife and waved it in her face. "I could cut you up good, girl. Just stay put."

He sped on past the other barns, heading out toward the big pond and the cliffs beyond.

"You don't have to do this," she said. Her legs were cramping, though Red had moved the seat all the way back.

"Hell, of course I do," he said happily. "Y'all gonna get a taste a your own medicine."

"There's none of us left," said Harper.

He smiled down at her. "Pretty soon that'll be right as rain."

He pulled up and stopped the truck, clicking off the lights and turning the engine off. The rising moon cast an eerie, unsettling silver light over everything.

Red tried to haul Harper out of the truck. Getting roughed up by him was getting to feel like a habit.

Not this time.

She fought him off with her clenched fists, punching his chest and reaching for his face. She got in a couple of good jabs to his jaw, but Red just laughed. He fended off her flailing as a minor irritant, rather than the threat she'd hoped it to be.

Harper felt ridiculous as well as terrified.

Then he gave her a good wallop in the eye with a closed right fist; it sent her reeling into the dashboard again, rendering her dazed. If she got out of this one, she'd have a black eye big as Rhode Island.

Red grabbed her collar and yanked her out of the truck. Harper landed on the ground, sprawled and helpless. He loomed over her. In moonlight, he was even more horrifying. His face was shadowed, but she did see a cut on his jaw; she'd landed something.

"Get up, bitch," he said. So much for Mr. Congeniality. He grabbed Harper under the arms, lifting her like a limp doll.

The clean scent of pines rose on a soft breeze, shifting over Harper. Its familiar, comforting scent strengthened her. She gathered herself and looked toward the trees, calculating how far it was to the woods.

Red watched her eyes and turned, peering into the woods, then pushed her down hard.

She struggled up and sat facing him "You can't possibly think you'll get away with this."

"I will, little girl. I thought this out for years and years." He smiled condescendingly at her. "You forget, I cut my teeth on drug running. Used to getting away with whutever I choose to. This'll be no different from the rest of it."

Maybe . . . But maybe not. "You can't possibly think Anna won't figure this out," she said, recalling their last conversation.

He seemed to ponder that. He looked up at the sky and down to the ground, bent, picked up a stone and tossed it. Picked up another and threw it up in the air, catching it as it fell.

Red squatted down and looked into Harper's face, searching it for something. If it was fear, she determined not to show it to him.

"I know you can't forget about her," she said, staring him in the eyes. "She knows you better than anyone. Do you think for one moment she'll rest when she finds out I'm dead? She knows you're a spiteful, evil man. She'd never stop until she proves you did this."

It hit home.

"Evil?" he roared. "You think I'm evil? After what your daddy and her done to me?" Red was livid. "She couldn't care less about you. Believe me. She'd not run off on me like she done if she'd cared a lick about anyone but herself." He spat hard on the ground.

She stared into Red's eyes. They were hard little marbles swimming in a sea of silver light. There was nothing but madness there. Glee, maybe, mad glee. Nothing else.

"I think it's time, little missy. You're just too damn full of yourself."

Red's rough hands pulled her up, shoved her toward the shale cliff. She strained against him, but Red was much stronger than her.

He pushed Harper forward with his leg, buckling her knees.

"You're through sassing me, little girl," he said angrily. "I only wish you'd be around to see what I'll do to your daddy's stud farm." He wrapped his arms around her waist. The foul stench of his body made Harper's stomach turn.

Red hoisted her up, chuckling a little. "Yeah, I'd like to see it break your heart," he whispered in her ear.

Once on her feet, she finally had her chance. She kicked Red hard in the stomach, surprising him. He bent forward, and in that instant, Harper raced away from the cliff. Dashing for the woods, she stumbled over the small stones, keeping her eyes on the big pines, seeking safety in the darkness within them.

Red was catlike for a big man. He lunged at her, howling like an angry animal. Then he was up and running fast. He said nothing as he pounded behind her. She glanced back, saw he was gaining, and tripped over a branch. He caught her, threw her to the ground amid the moldering leaf rot. He kicked her hard in the ribs, then turned her over with the tip of his boot. She writhed in his grip as he hauled her back to the cliff's edge.

She gazed out onto Bucks Creek. This was the highest point on the farm; it was a long, rocky way down to the water.

How many times had she and Paris come here as kids? And then later, she and JD . . . so many memories. So soon, she thought, turned to dust.

Still, the least she could do was make it hard for him and put up a fight.

Harper's eye was quickly swelling shut, her leg throbbed, and her ribs hurt with every breath she took. She glanced around with her one good eye, then stared into Red's wild, little pig eyes.

Deacon flitted to mind for some reason and the thought of Red harming him filled Harper with rage.

When he shoved her to the very edge of the cliff, she pivoted, pushing him off-balance. He stumbled away, his arms flailing, grabbing at her as he went down on one knee, his face white in the moonlight, his eyes wide with surprise and hatred.

They paused only a moment and in it, Harper sensed the last chance she had was to lure him closer to the edge. When he grabbed for her, still on one knee, she moved perilously close to the drop-off. He paused and glared at her. She tried not to move a muscle, willing him closer. Seconds ticked by. A stand-off. His eyes flickered between her and the cliff's edge and she knew he considered his options, his chance for success.

Slowly, he rose to both feet, still staring at Harper, then peered down to the drop-off. He understood the risk. He nodded, his mad grin sending a chill up her spine. Then with sudden fury, he lunged and as he did, Harper gingerly took a step to the side.

He grasped only air, his heavy body carrying him over the edge, somersaulting, roaring his outrage, as he tumbled into one rocky outcrop after another until he lay at the bottom, silent and broken and still.

Chapter 19

Harper sat on the cliff for the longest time, waiting to see if he stirred. He finally did, which had terrified her.

She couldn't make herself go down there. She couldn't make herself help Red. It was miraculous he'd not been killed in the fall, and she had no way of knowing how badly injured he was.

Other than anger, Harper felt nothing. Not relief, not release, not anything. And so, she finally rose and, holding her side and squinting out of one eye, she hobbled, painfully and slowly toward the house.

Once home, she called Marshall. She couldn't help Red herself, but she couldn't let him die, either. After her brief explanation, during which Marshall interrupted her countless times—he was horrified—he said he'd call an ambulance and Detective Walker. He did what he always did, and told Harper he'd go to Bucks Creek himself and see what he could do for Red.

He told her sternly to stay put, and he'd send Surrey right over.

But Harper said no. No Surrey. She couldn't face anyone. She leaned heavily on the cool granite counter in the kitchen, pressing a cold pack to her swollen eye. Then finally, in darkness, she headed upstairs.

She awoke some time later, unsure of why she was in her bed. She sat up, a startled cry of pain erupting as her ribs protested, and saw Surrey rising beside her in the dimness.

At Harper's cry, she gently put her arm at her back as support.

Harper smiled weakly then collapsed back, the pain nearly making her pass out.

She'd survived.

When she woke in the morning, she could hardly move—every single muscle in her body hurt, and her eye was swollen shut. Surrey helped her downstairs, wrapped Harper in her grandmother's afghan, made a fire, made tea, and got another ice bag for her eye.

"You need to get to the hospital," she said, checking her out in the light. She sat down gently beside Harper on the couch and switched out the ice pack.

"Ow," said Harper, wincing. The ice hurt, but every time she pulled it away, Surrey gently pressed it back. "Keep that on, sweetheart," she said.

"I'm not going to the hospital," she said, looking at Surrey with her one good eye.

Harper knew she was probably concussed, among other things, but at that moment she wasn't moving from her home.

Surrey nodded quietly, as was her way. Harper knew she was biding her time until Harper came to her senses.

Her whole body felt limp as well as painful. The first memory to return was Red hurtling down to the creek bed; she didn't realize all the tension she'd been carrying until it left her as she replayed how she'd outwitted him, and then watched him fall.

Harper felt more drained than she had in her life. But, finally, she felt safe.

She was due at the police station later that morning. After a difficult shower, Surrey taped her ribs at her insistence, then Harper dressed and took stock of herself. Her eye was getting more vividly purple by the minute and her face was bruised and cut. Though Surrey had given her some over-the-counter-pain meds, moving still resulted in enormous pain, especially up one side of her body, likely where Red had kicked her so hard. Another memory.

But no, she said again to Surrey, she was not going to the hospital. Maybe the doctor could come to her, but later. Harper felt she had to see things through at the police station.

She'd survived Red. She needed to finish this.

With effort, she brushed and dried her hair. No use applying any make-up, so she struggled into some jeans and a sweater and off they went.

Detective Walker took her statement, meager as it was, wincing every time he looked at Harper's face. Evidently Red had Type 1 compound fractures of both legs, a concussion, and had badly bruised some internal organs. But he was alive. And he'd recover. It would take nearly two months for the fractures, but they weren't life threatening and he'd be able to be interviewed, charged, and moved sooner than Harper had thought possible.

She was glad of that. He'd finally pay for what he did to Paris. And Steve.

As to the drug trafficking, Detective Walker said all they had was a lot of dates with weights and initials that couldn't be tied to Red or Cooley, with Steve dead. No hard proof. At least none pertaining to Red. He asked Harper about the audiocassette and thumb drive. She'd forgotten all about both of them, but said she'd find them. Hopefully, she'd recall where she'd put them soon; the thumb drive could well contain something useful to the DEA.

Detective Walker said Red would be transferred into a secured hospital as soon as he was stable. Murder charges, based on what Harper could piece together of his confession to her, would be drawn up following her statement. It was circumstantial but seeing that she had no reason to provoke Red, and given her injuries, it would have to do for now.

The next two weeks were spent mending, both mind and body. Harper recalled nearly all of the events leading up to her struggle with Red at the cliff, and that was also returning, piece by piece. But she still didn't know where she'd hidden the cassette and thumb drive, try as she might to recall that. She'd finally gotten the medical attention she needed, and her ribs and eye were healing. No riding, of course, but she could see to the stud farm's business, if at first from her bed.

Since she couldn't remember where she'd put them, Harper had searched for the thumb drive and audiocassette in all of the likely places, including her clothes hamper. But Surrey had been thorough. She'd washed everything and put it away, including the clothes from that night. She hadn't found anything in her pockets and Harper had no idea what she'd done with possibly the two most valuable pieces of evidence.

She knew she must have put them somewhere "safe" the night she'd stumbled home from the cliff, but her mind had erased everything related to that. There were still large gaps in those harrowing hours.

Red's headlong dive onto Bucks Creek's rocky bank, though, kept playing and replaying in her mind, mostly at night. Everything leading up to that awful moment, too, seemed to haunt the dead, dark hours when she'd wake sweating, again seeing Red's leering face over her. She refused pills, hoping that somehow the whole experience would descend on her all at once if she just endured the worst memories.

She had to remember it all, if for no other reason than the cassette contained the last recording she had of Paris' voice.

Anna stopped by one afternoon to say JD was due home the next week. She'd let him know all that had transpired. Harper wasn't surprised he hadn't contacted her. They'd been lovers for years, but neither of them had made an effort to keep in touch after the breakup. She wondered if JD had gotten over the hurt of her leaving him. She felt both frightened and anxious to see him.

Marshall was happy with Tim's vet work and that confirmed Harper's commitment to him. He'd come on formally right after Cooley was charged. Sugarland's fracture was healing nicely and Deacon, Nico, and the other stallions were all well and happy.

The world seemed to be finally righting itself.

Except for the unresolved question about the seven skeletons found on the property. There was still no word on the Mexicans.

But most importantly, Harper constantly wracked her brain to recall what she'd done with thumb drive and cassette, but still had no idea. It was nearly more than she could bear because her sister had died for what was on them and she'd effectively lost them both.

Harper couldn't do anything about the skeletons, but she vowed she would somehow bring Red and Moreno to justice for her sister's death. She felt frustratingly close to setting things right for Paris, as well as for Steve.

At mid-morning two weeks after that horrid night, she sat on the couch quietly, waiting for the light to dawn. She wasn't going to budge until her memory returned and she recalled what she'd done with the evidence.

Never a patient person, the enforced mental silence made her squirm. She stiffened her back, tried to be calm, and waited on. She would never make it as a yogi.

After a time, up from the depths again came the image of Red lunging at her and tumbling over the cliff. She gasped as instantly she was transported back to the horror of all that had gone on that night. Usually such visits were reserved for the middle of the night, but Harper forced herself to stay with it, to relive every excruciating detail of the night Red had tried so hard to kill her.

And then she saw it. Harper closed her eyes and saw herself in the darkness, hunched over, holding the ribs along her right side with her left hand, dragging her left leg behind. Inch by inch she watched herself hobble through the fields, up the gravel road to the house, mount the steps, go in the front door, pick up the kitchen phone, wince at the ice pack, crawl on all fours up the steps to her bedroom.

No, Paris' bedroom. She'd gone into Paris' bedroom.

Excited, her eyes flew open. Harper shut them tightly, again picturing her painful efforts. After a few more moments, she knew where she'd hidden the evidence. She smiled sadly. The secret place seemed fitting.

Harper walked slowly upstairs into Paris' bedroom and pulled her desk chair over to the far wall, climbed on it, and plucked down the blue ribbon she'd won last summer jumping Zydeco. Behind it, lying innocently on the walnut shelf that ran the whole wall and held trophy after trophy, was the little thumb drive and tiny audio cassette.

Harper kissed the ribbon, weeping, and gently replaced it, climbing down carefully and holding the precious evidence tightly in her damp palm.

Across the hall, her computer sat open on the bed. Stifling sobs, she inserted the thumb drive while punching Detective Walker's phone number in on her cell phone.

She inhaled to steady her voice and left word when he didn't pick up.

The thumb drive was a copy of the dates listed on the CD, the one she'd already sent to the detective, but these dates extended the length of the whole year—drug shipments, Harper suspected, complete with their distributor's initials, just as in the earlier version she'd seen. The dates ran regularly from the first of the year through December. She ran her finger down the months, arriving at October.

Sobered by her finding, she collected herself and checked the next few delivery dates. There was still time to catch Emilio Moreno if he'd extended his stay longer than the Keeneland race meet.

Harper would bet he had. With Red indisposed, she was sure he'd want to see to the delivery himself. Surely the DEA could use the list, follow Moreno, and find the shipment location. She called the detective again, and this time he picked up. He agreed it might be just the break the DEA needed. He'd pick up the drive that afternoon.

Harper went back downstairs, made some Lapsang Souchong and sat on the couch letting the smoky tea and fire warm her. She allowed herself a moment of gratitude and satisfaction; after weeks of trying so hard to remember, after enduring night after night of wide-awake nightmares, she'd remembered. Maybe now she could let those memories finally fade.

Harper held the warm cup in both hands, giving thanks.

She was more relaxed than she'd been in weeks, but there was still some distance to go before things were completely resolved. She wondered if she'd ever feel completely free of sorrow.

They were in the early days of November. It amazed Harper how little time had passed, yet so much had transpired. The Breeder's Cup was nearly upon them, one of the biggest meets of the yearly schedule.

Marshall wanted to run Deacon in the mile and sixteenth juvenile. At two million dollars, it's the richest purse for two-year-old colts and the perfect set-up for the Triple Crown year. He'd won enough and had been entered, but with recent events, Harper wasn't sure it was the best idea. She literally couldn't bear another calamity.

And with Evan's death, she didn't know who could ride Deacon. Marshall had contacted jockeys' agents and had been trying out a few in the colt's workouts but hadn't found one so far. They'd have to wait and see.

Frequently, her thoughts went back to Red. He'd also been on the mend. Detective Walker had been nice enough to continue keeping Harper in the loop. Red was now in custody, soon to be released from the hospital and moved to answer Walker's questions. He was finally well enough to give account of himself on the murder charges.

Harper wanted to be there, hear what he had to say. But no matter how many strings she pulled, that wasn't happening.

As she'd hoped, with healing and recovering the evidence, the horror of that night faded a bit. She looked at Red with a bit more objectivity. With him out of commission, the drug trafficking would come to a halt—at least through him as a channel. If the DEA nabbed Moreno, the conduit might just be completely sealed.

Harper resolved to be satisfied with Red's murder charges, and not anguish about all the deaths he'd inadvertently caused by drugs.

And there was still the possibility that if the DEA did arrest Moreno, he might implicate Red. They'd have to wait to see on that one.

She realized, too, that for Red, losing Anna to someone else would have been bad enough. But to her father? And a child on top of that. Harper could see where it would break a man as prideful as Red. In some ways, at least relative to Anna, he was as much a victim as any of them.

Except for Paris. She paid a price she shouldn't have. A price that had nothing to do with her.

Harper felt continuing anguish over that, and her part in it. Had she only been home when Paris needed her . . . Her sister had worked so hard to build a good life for herself and keep Eden Hill going. She and Dylan could have made a go of it. Harper would have doubted that until recently, seeing him mature right before her eyes.

She vowed he'd always have a place with them at the stud. If it wasn't too painful for him. She'd leave the ball completely in his court.

And the baby. Paris' child. Harper had mourned the loss of her sister. Now she would mourn the loss of her child.

But there was another child out there somewhere. JD and her half-sister, as it turned out. Harper should have been angry with Anna; after all, she'd irrevocably damaged her parent's marriage, and done much harm to her mother. Harper saw that now. But she'd also seen what anger, resentment, and bitter hatred had done to Red and she wanted nothing to do with that. Things were as they were. She couldn't change the past and wouldn't judge relationships she really knew little about. Harper settled into the couch, pulling her grandmother's afghan close around her.

She would ask Anna about her sister: She'd lost one and was determined to find the other.

Harper knew there'd be time, too, to think about her father's role in all this. Anna had seen the evil in JD's father. Harper hadn't seen the duplicity in her own. She'd been blinded by family and the ties of love.

Well, she sighed, turning her thoughts back to farm business, there was plenty of time to sort all that out.

Virginia Slachman

Chapter 20

She had an appointment at the end of the next week at the police station, and so bright and early Friday morning, she drove herself over. Her eye was now a faded lavender laced with a putrid yellow and green, but her mind was clear.

Detective Walker greeted Harper with a raised eyebrow; he seemed fond of that gesture, and said he was glad to see how much she'd improved. He smiled, likely recalling what she'd looked like the last time he'd seen her.

He said the DEA had called just that morning, noting they had two possible locations for the drug shipments and were staking out both of them. A bust, they felt, was imminent.

At the mention of drug shipments, something niggled at Harper's thought. She couldn't put her finger on it, but there was something tugging at her about the drug trafficking. She asked to be informed about any progress and Al, as he'd asked her to call him, said he'd let her know as soon as he had word. He gently escorted Harper to his office.

It hit her as she sat down. She requested to see the printout of the drug shipment dates, if the detective had kept a copy. He rustled around in his desk, pulled out a file, flipped it open, and handed Harper a sheet of paper.

She didn't concern herself with the dates; her focus was on the initials. M.R., C.T., S.D., and A.D. M.R. might be Murray Rickels. Harper mentioned that to Al. It could be good to have the DEA speak with him, though knowing Murray, she doubted much would come of it.

She had no idea about S.D. or C.T., but did wonder if A.D. might be Abel Desormeaux, the Creole man who once worked for Eden Hill and had been recently arrested in possession of heroin. She pointed to the initials and explained what she was thinking.

"Yeah," Al said, after hearing her out. "Seems worth it to have a little chat with him. We don't have leverage with Rickels, but Desormeaux's in custody and facing a long stint." He took the paper back and smiled. "Nice work. I'll put in a call once we're done here."

He replaced the file, glanced up, rose, and excused himself. Harper turned to see him walking through the rows of desks toward a man entering the far doors.

Oh good Lord. It was JD. And not in uniform.

She stood, dumbfounded, and stared as JD and Al Walker made their way toward her. They were in conversation. JD nodded, his shaggy auburn hair falling in his face. He pushed it back as he responded to the detective, then looked ahead and saw Harper. He stopped briefly and smiled slowly, his piercing green eyes taking in everything as they always had. Especially, it seemed to Harper, her.

She'd thought about this moment over and over since returning but had not intended to look like she'd been in a bar fight when it happened. As he moved in front of her, Harper smiled up into his face, feeling the force of his presence, just as when they'd been together. She felt her face flush and looked away, embarrassed, feeling like a deer caught in the headlights— excited, surprised, a little scared, and rooted to the spot.

God, it had been a long time.

He gently turned her face back to him, still smiling, evidently as happy as she was about the chance meeting. She reached up and put her hand over his, feeling the warmth of it on her cheek. They stayed that way, searching each other's face, for what seemed a long time. Neither of them seemed interested in breaking the moment.

Her smile widened, the air charged between them.

"Harper, my God, I'm . . .," and he moved to her, gathering her to him in a warm embrace. She closed her eyes, inhaling his long-familiar, clean, masculine scent.

They lingered that way, his body softening as he held Harper gently. She felt the tears well up, her body remembering how safe, how right, they'd always felt together. How could she have forgotten that?

He pulled back to again take stock of her.

She did the same, trying her best to control her emotions.

He'd always been a big, lanky, loose-boned kid, but she saw he'd grown into a man. His body was now filled out, fit and hard.

They stared at each other, smiling and silent, as some long quiescent connection rose again between them.

Taking a look at her eye, he said "Nice shiner you got there, lady." He grinned mischievously at Harper.

Harper grinned back. "Lady." That was a new one. And effortlessly, the mood was broken. They were back on familiar ground. Harper took a deep breath. They needed to get to the business at hand.

As JD turned to the detective, Harper stole a last look at him. He'd grown up, and—if their embrace was any indication— evidently forgiven her. The atmosphere still felt electric between them as Harper took in his high cheekbones and the firm set of

233

his jaw. His blue-striped oxford shirt was rolled on his forearms and he looked as he always had, easy in his body but with those alert, hawk-like eyes that held intelligence and, behind that, a patient power. He'd matured in the service, that was evident.

She sighed. A lot of time had passed. She had to be realistic. He was someone she knew and, taking account of him now . . . didn't know.

As if sensing her stare, JD reached out and took her hand, not taking his eyes off Walker.

Yes, thought Harper, he'd grown up. But had he finally seen the truth about his father? Her mood sobered.

Detective Walker cleared his throat, bringing them back to why they were there. She smiled again at JD and took a seat. They'd have time to themselves later.

JD sat next to Harper as the detective went around to his own seat behind his desk. Two new photos of his family stood in a frame on his desk— a sweet-looking wife and two small boys whose blond hair stood on end, the image of their father.

"I appreciate you coming down again," the detective said to Harper. "And I apologize for not taking your concerns about your sister more seriously . . . earlier."

Part of that was her fault, she knew. She'd kept a lot to herself, divulging what she suspected only when he'd pressed her.

He'd charged Red with murder quite a while ago. Harper glanced at JD as the detective mentioned it, but his face suggested he'd known that for some time. She reminded Al of Paris' baby; she assumed charges would be added.

"Before we deal with that," said Detective Walker, "there's another little problem." He looked at JD. "It's why I requested you be here."

That didn't sound good.

"Mr. Cole is being rather intractable, I'm afraid." The corner of the detective's mouth turned down as if he'd eaten something sour. "He says he's innocent. Has no idea who murdered your sister." He turned in Harper's direction. "Says he heard it was an accident. Your word against his."

"He tried to kill Harper," JD interjected. Evidently Anna had filled JD in on all the particulars.

"Yeah. He says that's not true, either," said the detective.

JD and Harper exchanged looks.

The detective jumped in. "I know, JD," he said, putting up a hand. Then to Harper, "I believe you. I mean, look at your injuries . . . But whether I believe you or not isn't the problem. As it stands, it's just your word against his. Even with your injuries, it's all circumstantial. I want to nail this guy and I'd like more than what we've got so far."

Walker looked at JD apologetically, evidently regretting his comment; after all, Red was JD's father.

Same old refrain, thought Harper. Couldn't catch Red on drug trafficking and now this.

"I'd like to see him." JD had always stepped up, so she wasn't surprised at the request.

She gazed at JD and saw nothing but steely, emotionless resolve.

The detective looked at JD appraisingly, picked up his keys and began flipping them in his hand. A habit, Harper assumed, as he considered JD's request. Round and round his finger the keys went while they waited for his response. Al Walker looked over at Harper.

"Is something wrong?" she asked.

More flipping with the keys.

"I guess I could arrange you seeing your father," he said to JD, finally. "I'll need to be there."

JD nodded. The detective left, asking them to wait in his office. Harper hoped JD could make some headway with his father. Red's audacity was astounding.

As Al Walker left, JD and Harper looked at each other. She felt no need for words.

He took her hand and his eyes softened. His presence strengthened her, and a wave of sadness about Paris' death washed over her. Harper blinked back tears and took in JD's gaze, feeling safe there, seeing sadness in his eyes, and perhaps a bit of promise, too.

She took a slow, deep breath to regain some emotional balance.

JD had faced more difficult situations than this in the service, she told herself. But this was his father. Anna's comment about Red being evil came back to her.

Who could have seen this coming?

The detective returned and motioned for JD.

"I'll be back," he said to Harper, his face suddenly unreadable. He rose and followed the detective down the hall to the right of the doors.

Red protesting his innocence made her sick to her stomach. Suddenly Red's looming face was again over her—a nauseating presence.

The two were gone a long time. Harper kept looking at her watch. Forty-five minutes had passed. She left for the bathroom, getting a cup of disgusting coffee on her way back.

Anna Cole stood at the door, peering in the detective's office. Harper startled her.

"Harper!" she said, surprised. "What are you doing here?"

"What brings you here?" she countered, sipping the awful coffee. Why couldn't institutions get a decent coffee maker and a good sack of beans, for goodness sakes? Not rocket science.

Anna seemed flustered, her eyes flitting to the detective's desk, the floor, then back to Harper. "Detective Walker called this morning, said he had some follow up questions." She faltered. "From my statement. Seems Red's thrown a wrench in the works."

She noticed Harper's eye. "Looks a lot better," she said, smiling softly. "What are you doing here?"

Harper filled her in on the details as well as JD's presence as they both entered the office; she sank, unsettled, in the chair recently vacated by her son.

"Harper, oh my God," she said when she'd finished, her face blanched. They sat, and she gingerly touched Harper's cheek just below her swollen eye. Harper flinched.

"The detective said Red was being a problem, but I had no idea. The man is completely corrupt." Evidently Al Walker hadn't filled her in on the specifics of Red's "wrench." She wrapped her arms around herself as if she'd had a sudden chill. "And JD is here?" It seemed hard for her to grasp both things at once.

Harper nodded. Her thought turned to Anna's child. She could understand now why she'd given her up. Harper wouldn't want Red anywhere near a child, let alone under the circumstances Anna had experienced.

Harper longed to ask her about her father, about the two of them, about what had happened to her half-sister, but it wasn't a good time. They had to make sure Red paid for what he'd done. Only then could they sort out the rest of their lives.

Surrey called to make sure Harper was okay. Marshall had asked her to check in. Harper glanced at Anna who sat still as a statue, likely thinking the same dark thoughts Harper had been having since the news of Red's self-proclaimed innocence.

She filled Surrey in then rang off, assuring her she'd let her know how everything turned out at the station.

JD and Detective Walker appeared at the door, chatting like old friends. When they entered, though, Harper saw JD's expression and knew he was putting on a good front for the detective. He had to be devastated.

Oddly, JD's anguish made her happy. At least it confirmed her feeling that he couldn't be involved in any of Red's hateful plans. She looked at Anna. JD's mother saw the same thing Harper had.

Detective Walker noticed Anna. "Mrs. Cole, thank you for coming." She nodded as he jerked a thumb at JD. "This is some kinda guy you got here." Then, noting Anna's expression, he stopped.

JD watched his mother and Harper saw emotion momentarily flicker over his face—was it longing or distaste?—then disappear just as rapidly.

JD turned to Harper, a sympathetic warmth in his eyes. "He confessed. Said Paris was killed . . ." He looked at her with concern. She nodded for him to continue. "Said he killed her easily. Seemed almost proud of it." He sank down next to her. "You don't have to hear this, Harper."

After so much absence, it was strange how his presence calmed her just as it always had. "No, I do," she said, looking deeply into his eyes. She had to know what happened to her sister.

How had he made Red confess?

Detective Walker and Anna were silent. Respectfully silent.

JD remained quiet.

"Just tell me, JD."

It seemed that nothing had marred the trust they'd forged all those years ago.

"He waited for her ride out on Zydeco. Waylaid her. He hit her on the head with a rock, made it look like she'd been thrown. Had it all planned." He spoke rapidly, getting it all out at once.

Harper closed her eyes, but was instantly overcome by dizziness. No, definitely, that was not a good idea. She felt JD's hand on her arm and opened them. She smiled at him, which hurt her eye; funny she hadn't noticed the pain before.

It's okay, her smile tried to say. It's not your fault.

Anna moved to JD's side and put her hand on his shoulder as he knelt by Harper's chair. He didn't move.

Detective Walker cleared his throat. "We have the one murder charge, but if you can find any evidence that your sister was pregnant, we can up that." He spoke to Harper, but she couldn't take her eyes off JD. He was her island of safety.

"I'll find it," she said flatly.

Anna moved to her side and took her arm.

"Let's get her home, JD," she said, and Harper rose from the chair, looking toward the detective.

"No problem," he said. "You all go on. JD, stay a minute."

Anna put her arm around Harper's shoulder and they both walked toward the door. As they made their way out, Harper heard Detective Walker say "We could use a man like you in the department. If you'd consider it . . ." The rest faded out as she and Anna passed the first bullpen desk and headed toward the double doors. JD soon joined them.

They found their cars and drove off, a trio of cars in a close line all the way home.

Once in the house, Anna and Harper sat on the couch while JD got busy making a fire.

"How'd you do it?" she asked softly. "What did you say that made him tell the truth?"

Harper looked out the window toward the bald cypresses and the pond. The colors of the world were so familiar, yet as she gazed out, everything looked foreign to her.

"I didn't really say much," he said, stacking kindling and striking a match. He spoke only to her. He wouldn't look at Anna.

Harper stole a glance at her. Her head was bowed as if she couldn't bear to be ignored by her son.

"Just tried to make him see I knew what he'd done. All of it." JD ran a hand through his auburn hair. It was an old gesture, one he'd had since high school. Though his hair wasn't long, he must have been out of the service some amount of time for it to get that shaggy. JD turned back to the fire, stacking on a couple of quartered logs. She surmised he'd learned some lessons in the service about keeping emotions at arm's length. Yet, this had to be painful. To see the man who'd raised him for what he was—a monster.

Even monsters feel sorrow. Betrayal and sorrow.

"He said if that was true, then he'd lost everything in his life," JD continued, sitting down on the hearth, his voice emotionless. "I reminded him that he had confessed to you. Said we'd exhume Paris' body if need be." He looked at Harper. She knew he'd do anything to avoid telling her all this. "I told him in my experience, she'd likely have some evidence, some DNA, on her body. It's hard to pull off a pristine murder. I let him think about that a while."

There was a pause. "He pretty much broke down after that."

Harper suspected Red knew more about JD's Afghanistan service than Dylan had let on; he probably trusted JD knew what he was talking about. Still, only facing his son could have broken Red. He didn't care about anyone else in the world except Anna and JD. Harper would always be grateful to JD for putting himself through it to get Red to confess. She didn't know whether or not she could have actually exhumed Paris' body.

"Did he say anything about the skeletons?" Detective Walker—Al—had filled JD in on everything before they'd gone in to see Red.

"Yeah," said JD, stealing a look at her. "You want to hear this now?"

She nodded. She had a special feeling about the woman who had tried so hard to protect that child, just as Harper had watched over Paris all their lives.

JD said what they'd unearthed was the evidence of Red's shift from importing drugs from Mexico to getting them from Argentina. The remains were the result of a power struggle, and the nun, whose name was Hortensia, had been caught in the middle.

Red's drug mule from Mexico had smuggled up his sister, Hortensia, and her small charge along with some people from their church. They'd wanted a new life in America, a better life, and had run headlong into the Argentinian crew determined to take over exclusive control. At Red's behest, JD reminded them.

The mule had been murdered, along with the rest, to send a message to the Mexicans. Now it made sense why Harper and Paris had felt uneasy around some of the tobacco workers hired by Red and her father.

The Argentine assassin, out of respect, had buried them as he'd thought religious tradition dictated—with their clothes and belongings to help them on their way in the afterlife.

Respect. Harper shook her head. Murdering innocents and then being concerned about religious rites. It was a world she'd lived in without knowing anything at all about it. That poor woman and child. And the others. Victims of Red's greed. Red's and a whole host of others on this and the other side of the border.

She still hoped for justice for them, somehow. Maybe if Moreno was caught . . . but no. She couldn't fathom what might amount to justice for people who only wanted a safe, quiet life for themselves and had ended up slaughtered.

The three of them sat there in silence for a while. Harper excused herself finally, going upstairs to shower and change. She sent a prayer of peace to the seven, hoping they'd somehow sense that at least their story had been told, their bodies lain to rest properly.

Her thoughts then turned to Anna. Even with her involvement in her family's painful past, Harper's heart went out to her and she wanted to give her and JD time to connect if they could. She hoped she'd be able to reach him. They likely needed each other more than they realized.

Harper came downstairs a while later, her hair wrapped in a towel. JD and Anna stood in the kitchen with cups of coffee in serious conversation. Harper grabbed a water from the refrigerator and hoofed it back upstairs.

No one tried to stop her.

She dried her hair, then checked in with Pepper, Lucas, and Marshall. The farm seemed to be running like clockwork. Marshall asked her about how things ultimately went at the police station and she filled him in. She told Lucas she'd get to the barn to check on the stallions a bit later. First, she wanted to find any evidence that Paris had been pregnant. She had Anna's word, of course, but Detective Walker said he needed proof. If it was in the house, Harper intended to find it.

She went through Paris' room again and searched her drawers, her jewelry box, running her hand under every surface for anything taped there. She took the mattress off the bed, searched under it. As before, she found nothing.

JD called from downstairs, then Harper heard him on the stairs.

"Come on down," he said, as she appeared at the top of the landing. He held out his hand to her, his face relaxed. Harper assumed his talk with Anna had gone well.

She took his hand and they headed to the kitchen where Anna was cooking up a storm. Harper didn't feel like eating, but just the sight of someone puttering around her kitchen made her feel a semblance of comfort and normalcy. She excused herself as JD went around the island to help his mother, and headed for the study. She needed to be alone with her family. Their ghosts inhabited that room.

Harper shut the door behind her and took in all the history surrounding her on the walls. The leather and brass, the photos, mementos . . . she didn't know how, but she wasn't selling the stud farm. They'd make a go of it somehow.

Did that mean she was ready to give up her life in Manhattan, a life she'd worked hard to make successful? She thought about JD and what had passed between them. She'd been pretending she'd put their past behind her. How could she have forgotten how deeply connected they were?

She gazed from photo to photo along the wall, her thoughts going to her family and the stud farm, their breeding and racing successes. JD had always been a part of that, even when they were kids. Now they could all go on freely without Red's malevolent interference. Would JD still be a part of that?

She considered her choice—life in the fast lane or life in the Bluegrass. Two such different worlds, yet she cherished them both. But she knew she couldn't go through another heartbreaking separation from JD. She wouldn't put either of them through that again.

She couldn't decide which path to take.

Thankfully, she thought, I don't have to just yet. She put the issue aside. At the moment, Paris' pregnancy took precedence. Since she'd found nothing in her sister's room, that left the study.

Harper moved to the desk, pulling out every drawer, searching for anything Paris might have hidden away that documented her pregnancy. If she knew her sister at all, she'd bet her life Paris had kept something tangible about one of the most important events in her life.

If she wasn't forced to exhume Paris' body to prove Red's guilt, she didn't intend to in order to prove her pregnancy. The proof was there, somewhere.

She pulled out the family's worn leather studbook and opened its pages, again running her fingers over the evidence of her grandfather, her father, and Paris in their hand-written notations. She went through the book, looking for anything she might have overlooked when she'd been so taken with the pedigree investigation. It would be just like Paris to hide something important away with her beloved horses.

Harper found it stuck in the back flap. A tiny corner of white peeked out of the leather pocket. She pulled it out slowly, realizing as it inched upward that it held the results from Paris' last pregnancy checkup; her doctor's name and contact information were listed at the top, and the results of all her previous visits were noted.

Harper held it in her hands as if it was as fragile as her newborn child would have been, grateful for the intuition or divine providence's presence that had so gently guided her hand to it.

Red would pay for what he'd done.

No, she corrected herself. There could never be enough payment for what he'd done.

JD's soft knock at the door startled Harper. She traced her finger across Paris' name then placed the document in the desk drawer. Time enough to get it to Al Walker.

She opened the door and JD walked in, closing it gently behind him. Neither of them spoke as JD moved to Harper, taking her in his arms, and gently, lightly, kissing her.

Harper raised her arms to his face then wrapped them around his neck as their kiss deepened.

Abruptly she pulled back, staring into JD's eyes as she had so many times before. She couldn't give in completely, not yet.

245

Blood in the Bluegrass

There was too much at stake for both of them. Besides, thought Harper, all that faced them was not done yet. Red must pay. The drugs must stop.

Yet she found it impossible to look away. The familiar depth and intelligence in JDs gaze were there and a deep calmness. And love. She felt that wash over her and closed her eyes, allowing his arms to pull her to him. She rested against his chest, hearing his heart beat its rhythmic assurance. If she was being honest, she'd always known their reunion would be exactly like this.

"Take all the time you need," he whispered, bending to her, kissing the top of her head and inhaling the scent of her hair.

Anna knocked softly at the door. "The food's getting cold," she said quietly. "Come eat."

They separated then, reluctantly, and holding hands, walked slowly into the kitchen smiling.

Anna had set the small booth at the edge of the kitchen with silverware. JD and Harper scooted in. Their lives seemed to revolve around meals. Well, that's fitting, thought Harper, for family. She looked from Anna to JD, wondering what the future held for all of them.

Harper didn't feel hungry, but sensed it was important that Anna feel useful, so she smiled at the *huevos rancheros* set before them, huge amounts of hot sauce ladled over the dishes.

Anna sat across from her son, and as they chatted, the tension eased between them. Harper forked in hot-sauced eggs, alternating with huge gulps of water. Anna and JD laughed at her. She grinned back, falling into their growing family bond.

Anna's little girl kept coming to mind. Harper wanted to ask her about her sister. She looked at JD. *Their* sister.

246

Anna dabbed the corner of her mouth with the paper napkin, slid it back into place on her lap. She turned serious, suddenly, her smile gone.

"There's so much I want to say to you both," she began, looking from JD to Harper. "I have so much to apologize for." She sipped her coffee, setting the cup down delicately in the saucer. "If I'd been more responsible, I'd have helped Paris." She studied Harper. "I knew what Red was capable of and I didn't act . . . I didn't do what I should have."

Harper felt her sadness powerfully. She understood completely. "Anna, no. I feel the same way. If I'd known what Paris was facing. If I'd just known . . . or been interested enough to ask." Harper looked down at her plate, unseeing.

JD sat back in the wood booth. "Both of you need to let that go. You both loved Paris. She knew that." He glanced at Harper. His voice was firm, but she knew he had a hard time saying these things to them. He'd known Paris all her life. "Paris made her own decisions, always did. You can't blame yourselves for things she either didn't tell you," and here he looked at Harper, "or felt she could handle on her own," and here he looked at Anna. "You both have got to stop blaming yourselves for things out of your control."

He was right. Harper knew that. Well, her mind understood that. Her emotions would need a lot of time to catch up.

"And I'm sorry, Harper," Anna continued, "so sorry for all the sadness I must have caused your mother." Tears welled in her eyes. "We just couldn't seem to help ourselves, and I was so . . ." She sighed. "Red was such a hard man . . ."

Harper reached her hand across the table and took Anna's. She'd been an adult long enough to know that the intricacies of people's relationships were complex. She'd had enough of

247

assigning blame. As far as Harper was concerned, circumstances were as they were and no use would come from resentment or anger. "No need to apologize," she said gently, and Anna smiled through her sadness.

But Harper did wonder about her father. She asked JD if Red had implicated him in the drug trade or in doping their horses, as he had in his conversation with her.

"He said he was in charge. Said Rafe knew nothing about what he was doing. Seemed pretty swelled up about it." Then JD shrugged. "But you never know with Red."

Anna nodded, looking at Harper. "He might simply have said that to confuse you, cause you more anguish. It would be like him."

She understood. Red had said her father had been involved in doping their horses then told JD the opposite. She wondered again what to believe. Who to believe in.

Red had duped a lot of people for a lot of years. Perhaps her father was among them. Sometimes you just have to trust in the better angels of our nature, she thought, and go on. She'd try her best to live up to that.

Anna turned to JD "And I'm so very sorry I didn't tell you why I left." She and her son locked eyes. "I should have. It was cruel what I did to you." Anna sent a fleeting, sad look to Harper then turned back to JD. "I didn't mean to hurt you. Either of you. That's the last thing I wanted."

JD didn't say anything. Harper imagined, like herself, it would take some time for his feelings to catch up to his desire to forgive.

But, she thought, looking at them both, they were well on their way to that.

"Anna, do you know who adopted your little girl?" Harper said. She craved any information she could get about her half-sister.

Anna seemed surprised. "Adopted?" She smiled softly. "She wasn't adopted by anyone. I raised her on my own. To make sure Red didn't find her, I legally changed her last name then I put her in boarding school when I moved back here. I fly out to see her every chance I get."

Anna must have seen Harper's growing excitement because she smiled broadly, happy it seemed, that her news had pleased Harper. "I spend all her school breaks with her," she finished, reaching her hand across the table and taking Harper's.

JD and Harper exchanged looks. Anna had kept the child.

"I couldn't bring her here," she said, more seriously. "And I couldn't tell anyone about her, not even your dad, Harper. Red would've traced her through anyone here in Kentucky."

Of course not. That made perfect sense, given Red's hatred. Suddenly Harper saw how horrendous Anna's life must have been these last years—leaving one child to reclaim another. JD understood that, too, Harper could tell by his expression.

"But I will now," she said softly, pulling her hand back. "Riley can come home now."

JD smiled, thinking, Harper was sure, how oddly their lives had turned out. They had all finally reconnected. And now they had a sister to share, as well.

Harper looked from Anna to JD, and sensing they needed some time to themselves, she quietly exited the booth and went to the kitchen to wash up.

She paused a moment over the sink, looking out the window toward her Grandpa's barn. She smiled as behind her Anna and JD murmured together, catching up she hoped, on all the time they'd lost.

As Harper gazed at the barn, she thought about the stud, about all that her family had worked so hard to build. She wasn't sure how to preserve that, now that responsibility for it was solely hers.

She glanced back at JD and his mom. She supposed it didn't mean she'd have to stay on the stud farm; she could have Marshall run things if she went back to New York and her family's legacy would be a part of her wherever she went. But she wondered about JD . . . she'd left once, and he hadn't followed.

No, keeping the stud didn't mean she'd have to stay. But it didn't mean she had to leave, either.

Harper turned back toward the two. Whether she stayed or didn't wasn't important at the moment. They'd all had enough death to last a lifetime. She returned to the table and resumed her place next to JD. Time now for living.

Epilogue

The next day Harper walked to Paris' gravesite alone, and sat there in the warmth of the sun, trying to feel whole again. Trying to let her grief go, finally.

She wasn't successful.

She would always miss Paris. There were times in the past several weeks when she didn't think she could actually go on without her. Losing Paris was like losing half of herself. But she would go on, she knew that. Not for any sentimental reason, but simply because that was all there was to do.

Harper sat there a long time, glancing at her parents' graves, her sister's, then into the dense woods beyond. In the boughs of the slim oak tree at the woods' edge, a mourning dove sat quietly watching her.

The dove was respectfully quiet, and Harper felt grateful for that, not wanting to hear her sad song. In a moment, she gently lifted into the air, circled the little tree, and flew off into the woods out of sight.

Harper watched her go, watched until she couldn't see her any longer, until she disappeared into the darkness deep in the pines.

She resolved to think about Paris in the same way. Paris wasn't gone, really, any more than the little dove winging its way forward on its own private journey—she was just out of sight for a time. Likely, Harper thought with a lighter heart, she was wreaking some havoc up there in the heavens, tormenting one or another of all the people that had gone before her, their mother and father especially. They were probably rolling their eyes as she raced the heavens on one of her beloved horses.

The thought made Harper smile, finally. She'd think of her that way from now on—impish and irresistible, just as she'd always been. Until it was time to see her again. That surely would be a happy day.

Coming next from Virginia Slachman

Vanished in The Bluegrass

When Anna Cole is called to Australia to oversee the breeding program of a major stud farm, newlyweds JD Cole and Harper take in their half-sister, Riley. Harper is instantly reminded of Paris, her murdered sister, as Riley steps off the plane—she is the spitting image of Paris. She acts like her, too, full of spunk and stubbornness. As Harper and JD get used to this willowy firebrand, Harper is alternately committed to her welfare and thrown back into remembering her own childhood with her beloved sister. When Riley goes missing, Harper is panic-stricken—she couldn't prevent the loss of one sister, but she is determined not to lose her only remaining blood relative. Is the abduction tied to something in Anna's work overseas or something closer to home? Newly appointed Detective JD Cole is put in charge of the investigation, and together the couple races against time to find the whereabouts of the missing child and bring the culprit to justice.

Introducing two new characters to the series—Riley Cole and Memphis, Harper's super-sensitive ex-racehorse whose "6th sense" helps the amateur detective solve the frightening mystery surrounding her half-sister's disappearance.

Also by Virginia Slachman

The Lost Ode
https://www.amazon.com/Lost-Ode-Virginia-Slachman/dp/069225529X/ref=sr_1_3?keywords=Virginia+Slachman&qid=1565042568&s=gateway&sr=8-3

When the owner of Brookfield Stud, Gray Burke, is arrested for homicide, amateur sleuth Julia is left to solve the murder and prove his innocence while following the trail to a lost fortune. Solving the murder may lead to love and treasure, but has Julia backed the wrong horse by believing in Gray Burke's innocence?

Many Brave Hearts
https://www.amazon.com/Many-Brave-Hearts-Virginia-Slachman-ebook/dp/B00AHZRFD8/ref=sr_1_1?keywords=Virginia+Slachman&qid=1565042606&s=gateway&sr=8-1

Many Brave Hearts is an unblinking, eloquent, deeply felt memoir of how war can shatter emotional lives and undermine our deepest bonds, redeemed--in the only way possible--with love.

--Kurt Brown

World of Mortal Light
https://www.amazon.com/World-Mortal-Light-Virginia-Slachman/dp/1937793141/ref=sr_1_7?keywords=Virginia+Slachman&qid=1565042606&s=gateway&sr=8-7

Slachman moves with remarkable skill in long, musical lines creating a richly textured poetry that vividly paints the "real world."

--Allison Funk

Inside Such Darkness
https://www.amazon.com/Inside-Such-Darkness-Virginia-Slachman/dp/0981675239/ref=sr_1_5?keywords=Virginia+Slachman&qid=1565042606&s=gateway&sr=8-5

A poetic collection that fiercely engages the reality of loss in poems whose brilliance cuts through the darkness.

--Don Bogen

About the Author

Virginia Slachman is a devoted advocate for retired racehorses as well as for outlawing drugs and inhumane treatment in racing. In addition to continuing her writing and university teaching career, Slachman has worked for years with ex-racehorses in one way or another—caring for them, rehabilitating or retraining them for new careers, and writing about them. Her work in rescue lead to her adoption of Corredor dela Isla, her own ex-racehorse who continues to be her loved companion. You can read about their journey here (www.d-and-me.com). She's a certified EAL practitioner, the author of three collections of poetry and her memoir, as well as a first novel set in the Thoroughbred racing world. . . www.virginiaslachman.com

Made in the USA
Columbia, SC
15 December 2020